Nancy Drew

Read all the titles in the Nancy Drew Mystery series

Carolyn Keene

Mystery of Crocodile Island

The Secret of Red Gate Farm

This edition published in 1996 for
Parragon Book Service Limited
Units 13–17 Avonbridge Industrial Estate
Atlantic Road
Avonmouth, Bristol BS11 9QD
by Diamond Books
77–85 Fulham Palace Road
Hammersmith, London W6 8JB

First edition published 1992 for Parragon
Book Service Limited

Printed and bound by Caledonian International
Book Manufacturing Ltd, Glasgow

Contents

Mystery of Crocodile Island

First published in a single volume in hardback in 1979 by
William Collins Sons & Co Ltd.
First published in paperback in Armada

·1·

A Risky Adventure

NANCY DREW and her friend Bess Marvin were seated in the Drew living-room, eagerly awaiting the arrival of Nancy's father.

"I wish your dad would hurry and get here," Bess said impatiently. "Nancy, have you any idea what the trip he wants us to take is all about?"

The attractive eighteen-year-old strawberry blonde shook her head. "I know the place, but not the mystery we're to solve."

"Where is the place?" Bess asked.

"Florida. Dad didn't tell me what part, though."

Bess giggled. "Any part will be all right with me, as long as there's warm weather and swimming."

Nancy smiled. "Probably all of us will be glad to swim. At this time of year it can get pretty hot down there."

A ring at the front door interrupted her. Nancy hurried to answer it. The visitor was Bess's cousin George Fayne. George was a vivacious dark-haired girl with a winning smile and a great appetite for adventure. She and Bess had helped Nancy with many mysteries.

"Hi, George!" Nancy said. "Come in."

9

When the two walked into the living-room, Bess pointed to a shoe box George carried. "What's in there?" she inquired.

George's eyes twinkled. She took off the lid, which had several small holes punched in it. "You can see," she said, "but don't touch."

In the box lay a twelve inch baby crocodile. Since it did not move, the girls assumed it was asleep. George held up the box and tapped the underside. At once the crocodile began to wiggle! It opened its jaws wide and swished its tail.

Bess screamed. "Put the lid on and get that thing out of here!" she demanded.

George laughed. "It's not real! Nancy, your dad asked me to stop at the River Heights Trick Shop and buy a rubber crocodile. He didn't explain why."

She replaced the lid and set the box on the table. "The clerk in the store said if you tickle the trick crocodile, it will wiggle. It's meant to scare people, but it can't possibly hurt you."

Bess looked doubtful, and George went on, "If this reptile were real, the government would take it and fine me twenty thousand dollars."

"What!" Bess cried out. "That's incredible."

"Or I could spend five years in jail for possessing it without government permission."

"But why?" Bess asked.

"Because crocodiles are a vanishing species," Nancy put in. "There used to be plenty of them in this country, but now there are only a few left in Florida."

Bess's eyes opened wide. "Do you think your father will send us where there are crocodiles?"

Nancy was looking out the window. "We'll soon know," she replied. "He's driving in now."

Carson Drew, a leading attorney in River Heights, parked his car in the garage, then came into the house by way of the kitchen. When he reached the living-room, he kissed Nancy and greeted the other two girls.

"Don't keep us in suspense any longer," Nancy pleaded. "Are we going to crocodile land?"

Her tall, handsome father sat down on the couch. "In a way, yes. This is the story. An old college friend of mine named Roger Gonzales lives in Key Biscayne outside of Miami. Biscayne Bay is full of small islands, which are called keys. Most of them are inhabited, but some of the smaller ones are like jungles and nobody lives on them. Some twenty miles from Key Biscayne there's a key that has been nick-named Crocodile Island. A group of men operate a crocodile farm on it. They breed these reptiles to sell to zoos or other places where sightseers can view them."

As Mr Drew paused, Bess spoke, with fright in her voice. "And you're going to ask us to go to this alligator farm?"

Mr Drew smiled. "Crocodile farm, Bess. There's a difference."

"There is?"

"Yes. The American alligator has a much broader snout than the crocodile, and is less vicious and active. The two reptiles are about equal in size and can grow up to twelve feet in length, but the croc weighs about a third less than the 'gator."

Bess shivered. "I don't want to meet either one."

George laughed. To tease Bess, she said, "Mr Drew, tell us some more scary things about crocodiles."

Bess groaned.

"They like to live in large bodies of shallow salty water," Mr Drew continued, "preferably in sluggish rivers, open swamps, and marshes that are brackish. They raise their heads when you go near them and—"

"Oh, stop!" Bess begged.

Mr Drew grinned. "But I'm not finished. In this country crocs were formerly found around the southernmost tip of Florida, but because so many people went to live on Key Biscayne, the crocs moved into the Everglades. They have webbed feet and can walk on soft ground."

"How fast can they run?" George asked.

"Very fast. Like horses!"

"Forget it!" Bess declared. "I'm staying home. Who wants to be eaten?"

"American crocodiles occasionally do attack animals and people," Mr Drew admitted. "A croc can twist a large animal to pieces by seizing one part of it, then turning rapidly in the water."

George grimaced. "I think I agree with Bess!"

"Don't worry," Mr Drew said. "You probably won't meet any wild crocs. What I'm talking about is a farm where they're bred in captivity. There's a mystery connected with the place that I hope you girls can solve."

"What kind of mystery?" George asked.

"I'll tell you in a minute." Mr Drew looked at the shoe-box. "I see you did the errand, George. Thank you very much. I thought you girls might want to study a rubber crocodile to get acquainted with its looks."

He rose and walked over to the table and removed the lid. George suggested that he lift the box and tap the bottom. He did, and once more the baby crocodile wiggled its tail and opened and closed its jaws.

"This is certainly a good imitation," Mr Drew remarked. He sat down again and went on with his story. "Mr Gonzales has stock in the crocodile farm, which is called Crocodile Ecology Company. He doesn't live or work there, however. He's a silent partner, so to speak.

"Recently he has become suspicious that the business arrangements on the island are not what they should be, and that his partners are up to something dishonest."

Nancy asked, "And this Mr Gonzales has requested that we investigate Crocodile Island?"

"That's right," her father replied. "However, he doesn't want his partners to know it, so you girls are not to visit his home or his office, or even phone him. Roger Gonzales is afraid his partners are spying on him, and in some way may find out he's starting an investigation."

Mr Drew told the girls they should pretend to be just tourists. "I'd even suggest that while you're there you act like silly young girls, so that the Crocodile Ecology people won't catch on. The last thing you want them to know is that you all have high detective IQ's."

Bess laughed. "That'll be easy enough for me. I

can act silly any time, but Nancy will really have to play the part."

Mr Drew asked to be excused. "I must get back to my office for another case."

After he had gone, the telephone rang and Nancy hurried to answer it in the hall.

"Is this the Drew home?" a man's voice asked.

"Yes. Who is this?"

"The River Heights Trick Shop. I want to speak to the girl who bought the crocodile."

Nancy motioned to George and handed her the receiver.

"Hello?" George said.

"Are you the girl who bought the crocodile?"

"Yes. Why?"

"You're in great danger!" the man told her. "The boy who was working here gave you a live one by mistake."

"What!" George cried out.

"Bring it back right away," the man ordered. "If you don't, the police will arrest you!"

Nancy, who had overheard the conversation, looked towards the box on the table. Her father had not bothered to put the lid on after examining the crocodile. Now the reptile was climbing out of the container!

It opened its jaws wide. Though the crocodile was only a baby, there was no doubt about its viciousness. It could easily snap off someone's finger!

Just then the other girls in the room noticed that the crocodile had escaped from its container. As Nancy dashed towards it, George froze and Bess screamed in fear!

·2·

New Names

Mrs Hannah Gruen, the Drews' housekeeper, heard the commotion and rushed in from the kitchen. By now the baby crocodile lay at the edge of the table, making low hissing sounds.

Hannah backed away in alarm, even though she usually had plenty of courage when confronted with a crisis. A middle-aged woman, she had brought Nancy up after Mrs Drew's death, when Nancy was three years old. Since then kindly Mrs Gruen had fostered the girl's natural instinct to face danger without flinching.

"Wh—what on earth is going on here?" Hannah asked.

Before anyone could answer, Nancy's bull terrier, Togo, slipped into the room behind the housekeeper. As soon as he spied the little reptile, he began to bark wildly. He jumped up in the air, trying to reach the crocodile with his paws.

"Don't hurt it!" Nancy exclaimed. She grabbed Togo by his collar and tried to keep him from nipping the little creature.

"I'll take Togo," Hannah offered.

Nancy walked up to the table and turned the

15

shoe-box on its end. Then, with the lid, she gently pushed the crocodile back towards it. Apparently the dog's barking and yapping had frightened it, and the little reptile willingly crawled into the box.

"Thank goodness!" Hannah Gruen said with a sigh of relief as Nancy put the lid back on.

"I'm glad that's over!" Bess added. "If one little baby can scare us like that, what'll we do when we get to a farm full of great big crocs?"

Mrs Gruen laughed. "No doubt the reptiles are kept in pits and can't get out," she said. "Don't worry, Bess."

Togo continued to bark and jump, so Nancy led him outside and put him in his run. The dog had helped her many times in her detective work, which had started with *The Secret of Shadow Ranch*. Recently she had unravelled *The Strange Message in the Parchment*.

Meanwhile, Hannah had found a sturdy cord to secure the shoe-box. When Nancy returned to the living-room, she suggested that the three girls go downtown and deliver the crocodile to its owner.

"I second the motion," Bess said. "The sooner we get this creature out of here, the better I'll like it!"

When they reached the store, Bess stayed in the car, while Nancy and George went inside the shop. The owner, Noly Reareck, greeted the girls with a look of relief.

"You have no idea what a load you've taken off my mind," he said. "You see, I have a licence to keep Crocky as a pet and have agreed to keep it in suitable surroundings and never to abuse it, kill it, or sell its hide."

Mr Reareck explained that it was unfortunate the little reptile had been sold to George. "I had to go to the post office," he said, "and asked a neighbourhood boy to watch the shop for a few minutes. He decided to play a joke on me. Instead of selling you a rubber crocodile that can be made to wiggle and open its mouth, he gave you my pet. It's a good thing you told him it was for Carson Drew, or I wouldn't have been able to trace it. I'm mighty relieved that Crocky didn't bite anyone."

Bess, who was waiting in the car, wondered why the girls did not come back and walked into the shop. George explained about the switching of the crocodiles, then Nancy asked Mr Reareck where the young reptile had come from.

"Crocodile Island in Florida," he said.

The girls looked at one another in amazement.

"Crocodile Island?" Bess blurted out. "Why, that's where—"

She stopped suddenly because George stepped on her toes. Nancy was relieved. If Mr Reareck had any connection with Crocodile Island, she did not want him to know about the girls' mission.

The three thanked the shop owner and left. Nancy dropped Bess and George off at their homes, then returned to her own house. With Hannah Gruen looking on and offering advice from time to time, Nancy chose a wardrobe to take on the trip. Among her summer clothes were two bathing suits, a terry-towel beach robe, and a jump suit.

After she finished packing, Nancy learned from Hannah that her father had come home. She went into his room, where he was reading.

"Dad," she said, "Mr Reareck told us that he got his pet from Crocodile Island. It would be a good idea if you could find out if he has any connection with the Crocodile Ecology Company other than just having bought Crocky."

Her father promised to do so. "I'm glad you told me."

The next day Nancy and her friends climbed into a plane bound for New York, where they would change for a non-stop flight to Miami. After they landed in New York, the girls hurried into the huge airport building to arrange for seats on their jet to Florida.

The clerk smiled at Nancy and said, "You are Miss Nancy Drew?"

"Yes, I am."

"We received a message that you are to get in touch with your father at once. It's possible your trip will be cancelled."

Puzzled, Nancy hurried to a phone and was soon talking to Mr Drew. "Is something wrong, Dad?" she asked, worried.

The lawyer replied that his friend Roger Gonzales had called him to say that his suspicions about the Crocodile Ecology Company had been unfounded. "He told me there is no need for legal or protective action," Mr Drew explained, "and he has cancelled your motel reservations."

Nancy was stunned by the news, but before she could express her dismay, Mr Drew went on, "I'm afraid that Roger was forced to make that call, and needs help. That's why you should go ahead with your trip. But don't get in touch with him until you hear from me.

"I have arranged for you to stay at the home of friends of mine, named Mr and Mrs Henry Cosgrove in Key Biscayne. They have a sixteen-year-old son, Danny, who's an excellent sailor and familiar with the keys. He can take you around in their motorboat. I'm sure he'll be of great help to you in your sleuthing."

"Oh, good," Nancy said. "I'm glad we don't have to give up the trip."

Mr Drew urged his daughter and her friends to be very careful.

"We will," Nancy promised, then asked, "Have you had a chance to speak to Mr Reareck?"

"Yes. He saw an ad in the paper about the Crocodile Ecology Farm and wrote to them, ordering the pet. He doesn't know the partners or anything about them. Well, goodbye, dear, and have a great time."

When Nancy joined Bess and George, they were worried about the turn of events.

"Do you suppose," Bess asked, "that somehow the people on Crocodile Island found out that we were coming, and that you're an amateur detective, Nancy?"

"That's possible," Nancy replied. "Anyway, since Dad wants us to go ahead, let's get our seat numbers."

The girls did, then went to the lounge and settled on three seats away from other waiting passengers to discuss what they would do when they reached Key Biscayne.

George said, "Perhaps we should disguise ourselves with wigs and quick-tanning lotions. Bess could become a brunette, I could be a blonde, and Nancy a grey-haired old lady."

"Thanks." Nancy laughed. "It would be fun, but the suspects on Crocodile Island have never seen us before. What good would a disguise be?"

After a few moments' thought, Bess spoke up. "You're right, they haven't seen us. But they evidently know who we are. Do you think it would be safer if we changed out names? We could use pseudonyms when necessary."

"What names do you suggest?" George asked.

Nancy smiled. "Suppose I call myself Anne, and Bess can be Elizabeth, and George—"

Quickly George interrupted her. "Not Georgia!" she exclaimed.

Bess laughed. Georgia was her cousin's real name, but she would never allow anyone to call her by it.

"I'll be Jackie," George declared.

The girls discussed a last name and finally decided on Boonton, which was Mrs Marvin's maiden name.

Nancy looked at her watch. "I'll have time to phone Dad and tell him our new names. He can inform Mr Gonzales."

When she returned, George said, "Okay, Anne. Our section of seats has been called to board. Let's go!"

Bess grinned. "Oh, Jackie, dear," she said. "You have such brilliant ideas!"

The girls entered the giant airliner in a happy mood, and sat down side by side. During the flight they teased one another, using their assumed names. They passed part of the time reading magazines and eating a delicious lunch.

In the middle of the afternoon they arrived in Miami and went to the baggage-claim area. As they retrieved their suitcases, a young man walked up to them.

"Pardon me," he said, "but are you the girls who are visiting the Cosgroves?"

"That's right," George said. "And you?"

"My name is Steven. They sent me to drive you to their house. We'll get a porter and have him bring your bags."

Steven led them to a beautiful gold-coloured car.

"Does this belong to the Cosgroves?" Nancy asked.

"No, it's mine," he said and opened the doors for them.

"It's yummy," Bess remarked and plopped into the cream-coloured, velvety back seat. George climbed in next to her, while Nancy rode in front with Steven.

On the way the girls admired the sprawling, large homes and the glistening bay. Steven, who was not very talkative, answered their questions merely with a yes or no, so after a while they gave up including him in their conversation. .

He drove over the causeway and through Key Biscayne. At last they came to an area of beautiful homes that occupied large pieces of property. Steven turned into a long driveway and approached an elegant mansion. He stopped at the front door and offered to carry the bags up to the girls' rooms.

Nancy rang the bell. The door was opened by a middle-aged couple.

"You must be Nancy Drew," the woman said. She was cordial but did not smile. "And these are your friends, Bess and George."

Nancy nodded and asked, "And you are Mr and Mrs Cosgrove?"

"Yes," the man replied. He did not smile either, and the girls felt uncomfortable at the cool welcome.

The couple silently escorted them upstairs and showed each visitor to a large and expensively furnished bedroom. Steven followed with their luggage.

Nancy walked to the picture window at the far end of her room to gaze down into the beautiful garden. Bess and George also looked out their windows. None of them had noticed that their hosts had silently closed the doors to the hall.

When the three friends tried to get together before joining the Cosgroves downstairs, they found that they had been locked in!

·3·

Escape

ALTHOUGH Nancy felt a tight knot of alarm in the pit of her stomach, her mind was racing. Obviously she and her friends had been kidnapped, and what made it worse was that the three girls were locked in separate rooms! No chance to plan an escape!

Before the young sleuth could decide what to do, she heard Bess cry out, "Anne, Jackie, where are you?"

"Locked in, just like you," George's voice came faintly.

"This is awful!" Bess wailed. "What'll we do?"

"Don't panic," Nancy advised. "That won't get us anywhere."

The girls realized that if they tried to discuss a plan of action through the walls, their captors would hear them and foil any attempted escape. Each one had to fend for herself!

While Bess and George began a minute examination of their prisons, Nancy looked through the keyhole. The key was gone, but she was sure the lock on this bedroom was a common type.

"That's a break," she thought and opened her purse.

23

She took out a hair-pin and a nail file. First she inserted the file into the keyhole and held it tight. Next she pushed in the hair-pin. By manipulating first one, then the other, she finally managed to get the door open.

Silently Nancy stepped into the hallway and listened. She heard the front door slam, and tiptoed to a window just in time to see the sham Cosgroves get into a green sedan and roar out of the driveway.

Obviously Steven had left too, because his fancy gold-coloured car was nowhere in sight. All was quiet, and Nancy was inclined to think they were alone in the house. But she could not be sure.

Quickly she went to Bess's door and started to work with her makeshift tools. Bess heard the noise. "Nancy? George?" she called.

"Shhh!" Nancy whispered. "I'm trying to get you out."

Within minutes she had released the lock and entered the room.

"You're a doll, Nancy Drew," Bess cried out, hugging her friend in relief. "Have you any idea where we are? This is a pretty grand-looking place. I can't imagine that the kind of people who live here would imprison us in their own house!"

"I can't either," Nancy replied. "I have a strong hunch that our captors borrowed this place. By the way, I saw those people leave. But they could come back any minute. Let's work on George's door!"

The girls quickly went to their friend's room and again Nancy inserted her nail file into the lock. There was no sound from inside the room. Had something happened to George? Finally the bolt snapped and

Bess pushed the door open. The room was empty!

"George!" Nancy called out softly. There was no reply.

"Oh, dear," Bess said. "Maybe those people took her out of here!"

"I doubt it," Nancy reasoned. "We would have heard the commotion. Besides, we spoke to her just a few minutes ago." She walked to the window, and a big grin spread over her face.

"Bess, come here!" she said, pointing to a large maple tree directly in front of her. A long branch extended almost to the window. Climbing down the last two feet of the trunk was George!

"Hi!" Nancy called softly.

George looked up and chuckled. "I'm an escapee!"

Nancy smiled as Bess reached her side and heaved a sigh of relief. George continued her descent. "Bess, do you want to come down the way I did? Or use the stairs? And how did you two get loose?" she queried.

Bess made a face, then smiled. "Nancy is a great lock picker."

"Shh!" Nancy warned. "We don't know for sure that everyone's gone. Somebody could have been left to guard us!"

"So what do we do next?" Bess asked.

"I think you and I can risk tiptoeing through the house," Nancy replied. "Quick! Grab your bag. I'll get George's and mine. We'll meet her outside."

She motioned to the girl below to wait for them and the two quickly got their luggage. They hurried down the stairs, trying to move as noiselessly as possible. They opened the front door and slipped outside. George was waiting for them.

"I don't think we should take the road," Nancy said. "The kidnappers could come back. Let's walk through the backyard and see if we can get help at one of those houses in the distance."

The girls had not gone far when they realized that the ground beyond the garden was marshy. The mud ruined their shoes and spattered their dresses, but the three friends hurried on until they were out of range of the house.

Bess stopped and put down her bag. "My arm is killing me," she said. "Can't we rest a minute?"

Nancy looked back. The house behind them seemed deserted. "I guess we're safe enough," she decided, so she and George dropped their heavy suitcases.

"Boy, what an experience!" George said. "Our kidnappers must have overheard Mr Gonzales's call to your father, Nancy, when he asked for help."

Nancy nodded. "And the second call, when Mr Gonzales cancelled our reservations, must have been made from another phone," she said thoughtfully, "otherwise they wouldn't have sent Steven to the airport to get us."

"Who do you think our kidnappers are?" Bess asked.

"They must be connected with the Crocodile Ecology Company," Nancy replied.

"I wonder if they own that house." George said.

"I doubt it. They wouldn't be foolish enough to imprison us in their own home. If we got away, it would be too easy to trace them."

Bess giggled. "They were foolish to leave us alone."

"I think we should hurry on," George said. "If they come back and find we're gone, they're bound to look for us."

The girls picked up their bags and trudged through the swamp until they reached the house they had seen ahead of them. As they went up to the front porch, Bess looked down at her dress and shoes. "We're absolute sights," she said. "What will the people think when they see us?"

"That we're swamp ducks," George quipped.

The girls rang the bell. There was no answer. Nancy knocked, but no one seemed to be home.

"What are we going to do?" Bess asked, worried. "We can't go on like this! And there's not another house in sight!"

They left their suitcases on the porch and walked around to the back. Luckily, there was a wall telephone on a rear patio. Nancy called the operator and asked to speak to the police department. When a sergeant answered, she explained the girls' predicament and asked if someone could come and help them.

"Right away, miss," he replied, and within ten minutes a squad car pulled up with two officers in it.

One jumped out and walked up to them. "You say you were kidnapped and escaped?" he said.

"That's right," Nancy told him and explained exactly what had happened. "We're on our way to visit Mr and Mrs Henry Cosgrove, but we don't know how to find the place."

"I'll order a cab for you," the officer said, and asked his companion to make the call. "I know the Cosgroves," he continued. "It's a long way away."

He took a notebook from his pocket and wrote down the circumstances of the kidnapping. First he requested the names and addresses of the girls. This time Nancy gave him the correct ones. She described Steven, the young man who had met them at the airport, as well as the couple who had locked them into the bedrooms.

"We'll get to work on the case at once," the officer promised.

He walked to the squad car and picked up his radio phone. First he asked that a taxi be sent out, then gave a full report on the case. When he returned to the girls, he said, "A cab will be here in a few minutes. Is this your first visit to Key Biscayne?"

When the three nodded yes, he shook his head. "I'm sorry your introduction to our town was so disastrous. Believe me, you'll find that Key Biscayne is a mighty nice area. Well, I hope you'll have an enjoyable time while you're here."

In a few minutes a taxi pulled up in front of the house. The driver looked at the girls curiously.

Bess explained they had walked through the swamp after coming from the wrong direction to the Cosgroves' home. She gave the correct address and they set off.

Unlike the couple who tried to kidnap them, Helen and Henry Cosgrove were delightful. Nancy quickly explained why they were so unkempt.

"What a dreadful experience!" Mrs Cosgrove exclaimed. "We must report it to the police at once!"

"I've already done that," Nancy said, and told the whole story.

Mr Cosgrove said, "I got to the airport late

because our car wouldn't start. When I arrived, you had already gone. I thought you might have taken a taxi and come back home. We started to worry when you didn't arrive. I even called your home in River Heights, but no one was there."

"Good," Nancy said with a chuckle. "Dad and Hannah didn't have a chance to become alarmed."

At this point a sixteen-year-old boy with red hair and twinkling eyes walked in and was introduced to the girls as Danny Cosgrove. He looked at their dirty shoes and clothes and said, "I guess you got here the hard way. What happened?"

Nancy told him and he responded, "Your dad said you would be here to solve a mystery and there might be some danger connected with it. You sure made a good start!"

The girls laughed, then asked to be excused to change their clothes. Mrs Cosgrove led them to two bedrooms. "Who wants to share the big one?" she asked.

Bess and George said they would, so Nancy took the smaller room.

During dinner Nancy explained more about the mystery, but asked the Cosgroves to keep it a secret. "We decided to use fake names to avoid detection by any suspects," Nancy said. "But now I'm not so sure it's worth it."

Mrs Cosgrove spoke. "I'd try it if I were you. Even if part of this group you're about to investigate knows who you are, not everyone connected with the Crocodile Ecology Company has seen you. By using fictitious names, you can probably fool them."

"What are your new names?" Danny asked.

"I'm Anne," said Nancy.

"And I'm Elizabeth," Bess replied.

George grinned. "I'm Jackie."

Nancy's first bit of detective work was to call the police early next morning. She inquired about the house where they had been imprisoned and was told that the owners were away on vacation.

The girls' kidnappers had broken in and "borrowed" the premises for their scheme. The police managed to track down Steven, who told them the couple had approached him in a supermarket and asked him if he would like to earn some money. They needed someone to pick up three visitors from the airport and bring them to their house.

"Steven agreed and assured us he knew nothing about a kidnapping," the officer concluded. "We're inclined to believe his story, but we'll keep an eye on him."

After Nancy had put down the phone, Mr Cosgrove asked the girls if they would like Danny to take them to Crocodile Island in the family's flat-bottomed swamp boat.

"It's high tide now and a good time to go," he said. "I wish you luck in your sleuthing," he added.

"Thank you very much," Nancy said. "Do you think we'll have a chance to go on the island?"

"Sometimes they do allow visitors," Mr Cosgrove explained. "On certain days of the week, but I don't know about today. You'll have to see."

The four walked to the marina where the boat was kept.

"How do you like the name I gave it?" Danny asked.

The girls laughed when they saw what was painted on the side of the boat.

"*Pirate!*" George exclaimed. "Even if you hadn't told me, I'd have known a boy picked it."

"Do you go after all the treasure that's supposed to be buried on these islands?" Bess asked him.

"I sure do," Danny replied. "The trouble is, some of the small keys floated away in hurricanes and any treasure on them is lost forever."

"What a shame!" George teased. "And here we came all the way to Florida, thinking we could dig up a million doubloons!"

The young people laughed, then stepped aboard the boat. Four swivel chairs were bolted to the deck, and Danny explained that this made it easy for fishermen to turn in all directions. Then he pointed to the large outboard motor in the rear of the craft. "It weighs two hundred and fifty pounds and is raised and lowered hydraulically."

"Why do you have to raise it?" Bess asked.

"When you get caught in low tide, you literally have to jump along over the sand dunes at a very fast clip. If you don't, you're apt to get stuck."

Danny settled himself behind the wheel and started the boat. As they rode along, he pointed out the shoreline of Key Biscayne with its highrise flats and hotels. But soon they left the area and one little island after another came into view.

"All of these were built up by coral formations and mangrove trees," Danny explained. "I'll show you some trees along the edge. The way they grow is fascinating."

He pulled up to a small key and stopped the boat.

The narrow mangrove trunks rose some fifteen feet into the air, then started to bend over. Their branches were heavy with leaves, which in turn hung down into the water. Being thick and close together, they were a natural catch for whatever floated by, and together they formed a solid shoreline.

"Over there," said Danny, pointing, "is a place where the water is a little deeper. We can glide in between two of the wide-spreading trees and you can get a better look."

He raised the outboard motor somewhat, moved the skiff forward, then headed among the mangroves. It was a strange sight. Roots twisted and turned. Among them and beyond the shoreline lay fragments of weathered coral rock.

Suddenly there was a grinding sound under the boat, which stopped so abruptly it almost threw the girls into the water!

·4·

Crocodile Farm

"WHAT did we hit?" Bess cried out. "Oh, I hope it didn't ram a hole in the boat!"

"I doubt it," Danny replied. From the deck he picked up a long pole with a pronged hook on the end. Leaning over the side, he poked around under the boat and raised an enormous pile of matted mangrove roots and leaves. With a chuckle, he swung it into the boat.

"Ugh!" Bess cried out. "What are all those crawly things in there?"

"Crocodile food," Danny said and handed her a tin-can. "Pick them up and drop them in this."

George laughed. "You asked the wrong person, Danny. Bess hates that kind of thing."

"You bet I do," Bess said, pulling her knees up to her chin.

Nancy took the tin and she and George scooped up the small marine creatures. Some of them were no longer than half an inch.

Nancy remarked, "A crocodile would have to eat a million of these to get even half a meal."

"That would do for a snack," Danny agreed. Then he made sure the outboard motor was not clogged.

Fortunately the green mass had come up in one big lump, and he was able to back the boat away from the key. George threw the leaves and roots far out and once more the boat headed for Crocodile Island. The water was very shallow, and sand dunes stuck up here and there. Once in a while the boat ran through an area where the water was dark green in colour.

"These channels run quite deep," Danny explained. "Larger craft can travel only in these, whereas a flat-bottomed boat like ours can go anywhere on the bay."

A few minutes later he pointed to their left, where series of tall, stout poles protruded from the water. Many had small cottages on top.

"I've never seen anything like this before," Bess stated. "Are they summer homes?"

Danny nodded. "Right. They're weekend retreats. The owners like to get away from the city. Out here there are a lot of interesting things to see, and many birds. But no noise except from the motors of all the boats."

"What about the poles with nothing on top?" George asked.

"The houses they supported were blown away in hurricanes," Danny explained.

Bess shivered. "I'd run at the first sign of a breeze if I lived in one of them."

Danny laughed. "I'm sure people don't stay and wait for the storm."

An hour later he reached another key. It was surrounded by a line of mangroves. As they drew closer, the girls saw stakes driven into the water, forming a fence. It stretched as far as they could see. Here and there warning signs were posted:

CROCODILE FARM
NO TRESPASSING UNDER PENALTY OF THE LAW

"So this is Crocodile Island," George remarked.

Just then Nancy noticed two bright spots in the water behind the fence. "What are those?" she asked.

"Crocodile eyes," Danny told her. "You see, these reptiles can stay completely underwater except for their eyes, which are raised high in their heads. Watch!" He picked up the tin of little marine creatures and tossed them towards the crocodile. Its great jaws rose and took in the food. Then the reptile swam away lazily.

Bess, who had drawn her feet back on deck, said, "I see now why the owners put up this fence. They left enough water between it and the island so the crocodiles can enjoy themselves."

Danny told her that this was the first time he had ever seen one of the creatures in this spot. "Usually they're kept in pits and guarded carefully," he added.

"Where's the entrance to the island?" Nancy questioned.

"On the far side of the key. You girls are lucky. Today is a visiting day."

There were several boats with tourists waiting to see Crocodile Island. A boardwalk ran from a small dock up through mangrove trees to a partially open area. Here, among the mangrove trees, were shallow pits fenced in with five-foot thick concrete walls.

Fresh sea water flowed into them through pipes.

There was an elevated area in each pit so the reptiles could stay either in or out of the water.

A small Irish terrier ran around, barking loudly at the visitors.

"His name is E-fee," Danny explained. "I know because I've been here before."

"E-fee?" Bess asked. "That's a strange name."

"It's Seminole for 'dog'," Danny said. "He has six toes on one front paw and likes to be the centre of attention. He's always around on visiting days." The boy petted the little animal.

A guide asked the group to follow him, and told them about the crocodiles. "The youngest ones have a greenish cast with black markings," he said. "The half-grown ones are olive green, and the senior citizens are all grey."

They came to an enclosure with a fifteen-foot-long giant in it. "This old fellow has to stay by himself," the guide said. "He doesn't seem to get along with the others. Does anyone have any questions?"

Danny spoke up. "I've heard that crocodiles can drown. Is that true?"

"It sure is," the guide replied. "Both alligators and crocodiles can stay underwater until the oxygen in their lungs is used up—alligators longer than crocodiles. But finally they both have to surface."

"How often do they have to come up?" George asked.

"Oh, I'd say the crocs come up about once every hour. It depends on the water temperature. The warmer the water, the more often they have to breathe. In cold water they can stay below a lot longer."

"Do they have to surface to eat?" a man inquired.

"Yes. They can seize their prey underwater, because they have valves in the backs of their throats that close when they open their mouths and the water can't flow into their lungs. But they have to stick their heads out to swallow."

The group walked on, and Nancy asked the guide, "What do you do with all these crocodiles?"

"The Ecology Company sells them to various zoos and parks and even to the government," he replied.

"The government?" George repeated. "What would Uncle Sam do with a lot of crocodiles?"

The guide told her they were distributed to certain areas. "You have probably heard that the crocodile is a vanishing species. We are trying to do our part in seeing that American crocodiles do not become extinct."

At this remark Bess heaved a great sigh. "Would America really be badly off if it didn't have any?"

The guide looked at her with contempt in his eyes. "Young lady, if you knew anything about ecology, you would realize how useful they are!"

Bess had no chance to reply because a loud bell rang.

"This is an alarm!" the guide exclaimed. "I must ask you all to get back to the dock as quickly as possible and leave the island!"

"Why?" Nancy asked, disappointed. "Does it mean a crocodile is loose?"

"It could be," the guide replied. "Now please, ladies and gentlemen, return to your boats without delay!"

The tourists ran. Bess was one of the first, and the

others, for once, had trouble keeping up with her. Just before they reached their boat, a guard at the dock asked them if they had registered when they came in.

"No, we forgot," Danny said. "I'll do it now." He hurried into a small office building and signed his name. Then he entered the girls' names as Anne, Elizabeth, and Jackie Boonton.

When he came out again, they had already climbed into the boat. A man in overalls approached the *Pirate*, pulled out a camera, and snapped their pictures, then hurried away and disappeared among the mangrove trees.

Danny jumped into the boat and pushed off. "Why was that guy taking your pictures?" he asked.

Nancy looked concerned. "I have no idea. He did it so fast we didn't have time to turn our backs or refuse."

"He didn't photograph any of the other visitors," George stated. "He singled us out— for a reason!"

Nancy nodded. "I'm sure the top men here realize who we are. Perhaps they wanted our picture to distribute to the members of the gang who haven't seen us yet!"

George frowned. "This could mean we'll be harassed by all kinds of people, wherever we go. I'm worried."

"So am I," Bess added. "I think we should return to River Heights and get out of this whole dangerous mess!"

"You don't mean that!" Nancy exclaimed.

"Yes. I do!"

Nancy and George looked at the frightened girl.

Finally Nancy said, "If that's what you want to do, Bess, go ahead. As for me, I'm staying right here and seeing this mystery through!"

"So am I," George added.

There was silence for several minutes, then Bess gave in. "You know perfectly well that I wouldn't run out on my friends. But I warn you to be careful. I know I'm not as brave as you are. I hate to get hurt!"

·5·

A Threat

DANNY and the girls moved away from Crocodile Island. All of them watched anxiously to see if they were being followed.

Other tourists were leaving in their motorboats. Nancy wondered if one of them might contain a spy from the Ecology Company, sent out to pursue the *Pirate*.

"I hope not," the girl detective thought.

Nancy observed through binoculars what directions the various craft took. One seemed to stalk the *Pirate*, and Nancy had an uneasy feeling about it.

"Do you see anything?" Bess wanted to know.

"There's a fast motorboat called *The Whisper*," Nancy replied. "It seems to be tailing us."

"Is that unusual?" George asked. "After all, other people might be heading for Key Biscayne."

"Of course," Nancy answered. "It's just that most of the boats have scattered. This one stays right in the wake of our boat."

"Oh, oh," Danny murmured. "Maybe they want to find out where we're headed. On the other hand, they wouldn't really have to bother. Anyone can check the local boat registry to see who owns the

Pirate and where we live."

"That's great," George said. "They already know who we are, and now they can find out where we're staying!"

Bess became alarmed. "Let's head for home!" she begged.

Danny looked at Nancy. "What do you say?"

"I'm not ready to leave Crocodile Island just yet. Let's go around it and see what's on the other side. We might pick up a clue."

Danny followed the shoreline of the key. *The Whisper* stayed right behind them, and soon there was no doubt in the girls' minds that the boat was pursuing them. The fast craft finally pulled alongside the *Pirate*.

With some apprehension the young people watched the two men on *The Whisper's* deck. Both had swarthy complexions and unpleasant faces. One of them shouted, "Get away from this island!"

"Why?" Danny asked innocently.

"Because it's private property!"

"The water isn't!" George pointed out. "Besides, we're not doing any harm!"

"We don't want you here," the man insisted, and shook his fist. "Now get lost!"

"Who are you?" Danny asked. "And why should we listen to you?"

"It's none of your business who we are. And if you don't listen, you'll be in trouble!"

Danny paid no attention to the warning. Instead, he revved up his engine and pulled away from the other craft. Obviously the two men did not know what to do next, so they followed the young people all the way around the island.

Bess had scanned the shoreline through binoculars as unobtrusively as possible. She focused on a metal tube sticking out of the water. It seemed to give off bursts of light, as if it were studded with prisms and mirrors reflecting the rays of the sun.

"Hey, see that thing over there? I wonder what it is!" she said, excited.

The others looked and George gasped. "It could be the periscope of a submarine!"

"What!" Danny exclaimed. For a moment he forgot to keep his engine racing.

Nancy took the binoculars from Bess and trained them on the strange object. "Is the water deep enough for a submarine to get in?"

"Yes," Danny replied. "Notice that the thing is sticking out of one of the channels where the water is green. That means it's deep enough for a small sub. As a matter of fact, during World War II enemy subs got in here this way. The government had mined all the larger, more important channels to keep them out, but small enemy craft slipped in anyway."

"Danny, can you go into the channel?" Nancy asked. "I'd like to see if that really is a periscope."

"Sure," Danny said and changed course.

But they soon realized that the men on *The Whisper* had no intention of letting them go through with their plan.

"They're coming closer," George said tensely. "Obviously they don't want us to check that thing out there."

"Which proves that they have something to do with it," Bess added.

Again the other boat pulled alongside the *Pirate*. "You kids think I'm fooling!" the skipper shouted. "I'm not. If you don't turn around instantly, your boat is gonna get rammed. And it'll cost you a pretty penny to have it repaired!"

"But we're leaving the island," Danny pointed out. "Just as you told us to!"

"You're going in the wrong direction. Turn back!"

Danny hesitated. He realized that this time their pursuers meant business. Before he had a chance to pull the wheel around, *The Whisper* came so close to their boat that it scraped the bow.

"All right! All right!" Danny cried out. "We're leaving. You don't have to damage us."

The skipper chuckled evilly. "And don't ever come back. You hear!"

Bess had turned white and sat frozen in her chair, her hands clamped tightly round its edge. Nancy and George realized that the situation was critical and did not object to Danny's pulling away in the direction the men had indicated.

The Whisper followed them for a while, then turned off. Obviously the men were satisfied that they had chased the intruders away.

"Wow!" Bess said finally. "I don't want to see those people ever again!"

Nancy grinned. "I do. They're up to no good, and I'm planning to find out what it is."

As the *Pirate* headed towards Key Biscayne, George said, "I wonder who those guys are. Let's stop at the Coast Guard office and see in whose name *The Whisper* is registered."

"We don't have to do that," Danny said. "My dad

has a book containing all the information. Unless it's a brand-new entry, it should be in there."

"I wish we could be sure that we saw a periscope," Nancy said, still pondering their strange experience.

"How do periscopes work?" Bess asked.

"Oh, I know that because we just had it in school," Danny volunteered. "You see, the periscope is the eye of the underwater craft. A submarine builder by the name of Simon Lake invented the first good periscope, which was way ahead of the technology and science of his time. He bought a lot of lenses and began to experiment."

"Not too complicated!" George said.

"Maybe not, but one day he hit upon a lucky combination. He could look down the street and see people walking and wagons rolling through the harbour. He called it an omniscope. It offered enough magnification and clearness of optics even for night vision, so it was a big success."

"How long ago was that?" George asked.

"Nineteen hundred and two," Danny told her. "Before that they just had makeshift equipment."

As soon as they arrived at the Cosgrove house, Danny went to get the boat register. It was large and heavy. He put it on the dining-room table. The girls peered over his shoulder as he checked "W" for *Whisper*.

"Ah. Here it is," he said triumphantly. "It belongs to two men, Matt Carmen and Breck Tobin. They live in Bridgeport, Connecticut."

"Do you know who they are?" Nancy asked.

"No. Never heard of them. I wonder what they're doing down here. They're a long way from home."

"I'm sure they're in league with the men who run the Crocodile Ecology Company," Nancy said.

"Maybe they're supposed to guard the place," George spoke up. "They got rid of us in a hurry!"

"I hope they don't check up on who owns the *Pirate* and then come here and bother us!" Bess said, worried.

Danny insisted upon being cheerful about the whole affair. "We may be boxed in, but we're not going to let those guys get the better of us!" he vowed.

Nancy smiled. "That's the spirit! The question is, what are we going to do next?"

When Mr Cosgrove returned home, the young people told him what had happened and asked his opinion on the case. He thought for a few moments, then said, "Frankly, I'm puzzled. We now have a list of suspicious people, but we still have no idea of what they're up to."

"Or how the periscope fits in," Nancy added.

Mr Cosgrove smiled. "Are you sure you weren't looking at a marker for a buoy?"

"I don't think so," Nancy replied. "But the only way to find out for sure will be to go back and look again."

"Maybe we shouldn't use the *Pirate*," Danny said. "Our enemies are familiar with it. Whenever they see us they'll come after us."

"What do you have in mind?" his father asked.

"Perhaps we could ask our friends the Piarullis if we can use their cabin cruiser." He turned to the girls. "They dock right next to us, and if they're not using the *Sampson*, I'm sure they'll let us have it. It's enclosed, too, which would help. Those men couldn't identify us."

"That's a good idea," Mr Cosgrove agreed. "I'll call them and ask."

He went to the telephone and returned a few minutes later. "Mr Piarulli said you can have his boat tomorrow. Unfortunately, their son and his wife are taking it up north the following day."

Danny grinned. "One day is better than none!"

"True," George agreed. "But what do we do after that?"

"Play it by ear," Danny said with a grin. "We'll take things as they come. Let's leave early in the morning. The tide should be just right."

"Do you think it's necessary for all of us to go?" Bess asked. "Mrs Cosgrove promised to show me how to make a lemon nut cake. I don't want to pass up the opportunity to enlarge my knowledge of recipes."

"If you'd rather cook than be a detective, you're welcome to stay home," George said.

Bess could not stand her cousin's condescending tone. "On second thought, I'll postpone my culinary education," she decided.

Bess was relieved, however, when the plans changed abruptly later that evening. The Cosgroves and their guests were seated in the living-room, discussing the mystery. The visitors were trying to figure out the connection between the men on Crocodile Island and the two from Connecticut when the telephone rang.

Mr Cosgrove answered, then said, "Nancy, there's a long-distance call for you!"

·6·

The Impostor

THE caller was Mr Drew.

"I've had a long conversation with Roger Gonzales," he told Nancy. "He's eager to see you and has asked that you meet him at twelve o'clock tomorrow at his golf club. Mr Cosgrove will give you directions. You're to tell the man at the desk that you're Miss Boonton."

Nancy did not reply immediately.

"Is something wrong?" her father asked.

"I don't know. Dad, have you any idea where Mr Gonzales called from?"

"No. His house, I suppose. Why?"

"Because I think his phone is being tapped."

"Why do you say that?"

"His enemies knew all about our arrival," Nancy said, and told her father about the kidnapping attempt.

"I don't like this!" he exclaimed. "The case is more dangerous than I expected."

"One thing is sure," Nancy said. "Our masquerade is known. When we visited Crocodile Island, someone took our pictures."

"Great!" her father murmured. "Perhaps you

should come home right away."

"Oh, no!" Nancy cried out. "Please, Dad, we'll manage. We have Danny to help us, and even though the crooks know who we are and why we're here, we'll figure out something to outsmart them. Besides, I have to keep my date with Mr Gonzales tomorrow, so I can warn him."

"True," her father agreed. "If the Crocodile Ecology people overheard my conversation with Roger today, they'll probably try to follow you and prevent you from reaching the club. Keep that in mind."

"I will," Nancy promised. "Don't worry. I'll think of something."

"All right. And good luck!"

When Nancy told the others about the new developments, they agreed that she should meet Mr Gonzales the following day.

"I suggest," Mrs Cosgrove said, "that when you leave here you go shopping. Then take a cab to the club from a store. This way you won't be followed."

"That's a good idea," Nancy agreed. The next day Mr Cosgrove drove her to a department store, where she made a few purchases, then went out a side door and took a taxi. When Nancy arrived at the club, she went to the desk and asked for Mr Gonzales. "I'm Miss Boonton," she added.

The clerk looked at her searchingly. "There must be some mistake," he said slowly. "Miss Boonton is already here."

"What!" Nancy was stunned by the announcement. So that's how her enemies had doublecrossed her!

She asked the man for a piece of paper and a pencil, and quickly scribbled a note to Mr Gonzales. Nancy explained the situation and asked if he would come to the lobby. Then she handed the note to the clerk.

"Would you please send this to Mr Gonzales," she requested.

The clerk summoned a boy and within a few minutes, Nancy saw a handsome, dark-haired man of about fifty, wearing a white suit, approach the desk. The clerk motioned to the girl.

"This is Mr Gonzales," he said.

Nancy nodded, then asked her father's friend to move a little distance away so they would not be overheard.

"I'm Nancy Drew," she whispered. "The Miss Boonton you're entertaining is an impostor."

Nancy opened her purse and showed Mr Gonzales her driver's licence. He looked at it, then at her, in amazement.

"How do you do," he said in a low voice. "I'm dreadfully sorry about this. Do you know who the other girl is?"

"No," Nancy replied. "Let's go inside and find out."

Quickly the two went to the dining-room, and Mr Gonzales led the way towards a table at the window. Suddenly he stopped short. "She's gone!" he exclaimed. "The other Miss Boonton is gone!"

Nancy was not surprised to hear it. She deduced that when Mr Gonzales had received the note and gone to the desk, the girl realized that her trick had been discovered and she decided to disappear at once!

"She had a good head start!" the girl detective thought.

Nancy suggested that they give an alarm to the man at the main desk so he could ask the clubhouse guard and various workers on the grounds and golf course to look for the impostor.

Mr Gonzales went to the headwaiter's desk and picked up the phone. Nancy heard him tell the story to the man in charge of the club and ask that a search be made for a tall, slender young woman with a lot of blonde hair.

"She was wearing a white skirt and blouse, with a red-and-white sleeveless pullover," he said.

The message was passed along at once. Nancy, impatient to find out where the girl had gone, told Mr Gonzales she wanted to do a little hunting on her own account. He offered to go with her.

"Where do you want to look first?" he asked.

"How about inspecting all the cars parked on the grounds? She might be hiding in one."

Mr Gonzales led the way to the far side of the dining-room and out a sliding glass door. A caddy came by, and Mr Gonzales asked him if he had seen the girl. The answer was no, and the search went on. They checked every car in the area. All they found inside them was a sleeping dog in one with an open window, and a large teddy bear in another.

"Of course there's a third possibility," Nancy said. "The phony Miss Boonton could have been brought to the club by a friend, who could have waited for her."

"True," Mr Gonzales agreed.

As they turned back to the clubhouse, Nancy

stopped a couple who were driving in. She asked if they had seen a girl dressed in white except for a red-and-white pullover. "We don't know whether she was on foot or in a car."

"No, we didn't," the man replied.

"Thank you," Nancy said, disappointed.

Moments later a sports car came from the opposite direction. Mr Gonzales asked the driver if he had noticed a girl on the road.

"A blonde wearing a red-and-white pullover?" the man asked.

"That's right," Nancy answered, excited. 'Where did you see her?"

"I passed her about a mile down the road. She was riding in a brown car with a man."

The information was sufficient for Nancy to conclude that the fraudulent Miss Boonton had made a quick getaway. "No use in looking for her any more," she told Mr Gonzales.

He nodded. "I owe you a lunch. You must be starved. Let's return to the dining-room."

After they had ordered salads and iced tea, Nancy and her host talked about the mystery.

"I don't understand how this could have happened," he said, puzzled.

"I do," Nancy said. "Your phone must be tapped. Do you remember where you were when you called my father on various occasions?"

Mr Gonzales frowned. "The first call I made from home. The second one too—no, wait a minute. I made that one from the club. Yesterday I phoned from home again."

Nancy nodded. "That proves my theory," she said

and told him about all that had happened, including the kidnapping attempt.

The man turned pale. "This means that not only am I in great danger, but you are, too!" he said. "I never would have asked you to come here if I had known!"

"Mr Gonzales,' Nancy said, "I think you have more to worry about than I do. I have two friends with me, and a boy is helping us. We'll be all right. But you would probably be better off if you left this club as little as possible while we're working on the case."

Mr Gonzales nodded. "I see your point, and I'll do as you say."

Nancy changed the subject. "You told my father that you were suspicious of your business partners. Who are they, and exactly what worries you?"

"There are three partners in the Crocodile Ecology Company," Mr Gonzales said. "Hal Gimler, George Sacco, and me. Recently, the two active partners were evasive when I asked them about certain matters. I had a feeling they were dodging my questions about what's going on. I found out they had made trips to Mexico numerous times, and I know we have no dealings with that country. I had the feeling that they were trying to deceive me."

"That's when you called Dad the first time?" Nancy asked.

"Right. When they realized I suspected them, they asked me to sell my interest in the company to them; and at one point I felt that would be the best thing to do. That was when I called your father the second time and cancelled your reservations."

"But then you changed your mind?"

"Yes, because it turned out that I was not getting any co-operation at all from my partners. I'm glad you're here, but I don't like the idea of exposing you to danger."

"We're used to that," Nancy said dryly. "Tell me, have you ever seen a submarine or a periscope near Crocodile Island?"

"No. Why do you ask?"

Nancy told him how she and her friends had spotted a periscope, and had been chased away before they could get a closer look.

Mr Gonzales frowned. "The company could be shipping out crocodiles and not listing the sales. A submarine would be a splendid way of concealing the transaction." He went on to say that some older reptiles had disappeared, and when he had inquired about them, his partners had merely said they had escaped.

"I don't see how they could have, with the fencing there is all round the island," Nancy commented.

"That's true," her companion agreed.

"How much of all this did you tell the other Miss Boonton?" Nancy asked.

"I mentioned that I was suspicious of Hal Gimler and George Sacco because I couldn't get straight answers out of them. Then you arrived and she took off."

"You didn't mention the phone calls to my father?"

"Only the first one."

By this time Mr Gonzales and Nancy had finished eating. They left the table and walked to the entrance.

The clerk at the desk called a taxi for Nancy. While waiting for it to arrive, she told Mr Gonzales how much she had enjoyed talking with him.

"Now I'll work harder to solve your mystery."

"You've made a very good start," he said, patting her on one shoulder. "From here on I'll make calls only from the club or a public phone booth."

Nancy rode off to the Cosgrove home. When she arrived, the couple was alone with Bess.

"George and Danny went out in the borrowed boat," Bess said. "I thought they'd be back by now."

"They may have hit low tide," Mr Cosgrove said. "Nancy, tell us how your luncheon date was. Did you get to the club all right?"

"I did, only someone else got there before me," Nancy said, and gave full details about the impostor.

"Incredible!" Mrs Cosgrove burst out. "Just think of the nerve of that young lady, pretending to be you!"

"I don't like the whole thing," Mr Cosgrove added. "These people are obviously very clever and don't shy away from anything underhanded."

"We'll be careful," Nancy said.

When Danny and George had not returned two hours later, she began to worry.

"Did they have another encounter with *The Whisper*?" she wondered.

·7·

Sea Detectives

MRS Cosgrove realized that Nancy was concerned, and tried to cheer her up. "Look, Danny is a very reliable boatman," she said. "They could have become stuck during low tide. Instead of sitting here and waiting, why don't we all go to see a friend of mine? She has a little private zoo, which I'm sure you would enjoy."

"That sounds great," Nancy said. "But before we leave, do you mind if I phone the Coast Guard and ask if they've had a report of an accident?"

"Of course not," Mrs Cosgrove said. "Go ahead."

Nancy learned that no trouble had been reported and felt better.

"I'll stay here and wait for George and Danny," Mr Cosgrove said. "You enjoy yourselves."

Mrs Cosgrove drove her guests along the waterfront until they came to a large estate. She pulled in, stopped at the front door, and rang the bell. To her disappointment she was told by the woman who answered that her friend, Mrs Easton, was away for the day, and so was the animal trainer.

"I'd like to show my visitors from the North your zoo," Mrs Cosgrove said. "Is it all right?"

"Yes, indeed," the woman replied. "Go ahead. You'll probably meet Eric, our gamekeeper. He'll show you around."

The man was not in sight. Mrs Cosgrove, who had been to the estate many times, drove on. She told the girls a bit about the birds, turtles, and snakes that were in large covered cages.

"That flamingo is gorgeous!" Bess exclaimed, watching the long-legged creature with the pink feathers and dignified-looking head walk daintily across a fenced-in lawn. In the centre was a pool.

Mrs Cosgrove pointed out an enormous turtle and remarked, "They live to a very old age. I've heard of some that had dates carved on their backs showing they were a hundred and twenty-five years old!"

In another wire-mesh enclosure were a variety of snakes.

"I'm not going to look at them!" Bess declared. "They give me the creeps."

Mrs Cosgrove laughed. "If you lived in Florida, you'd have to get used to snakes. We have all kinds and sizes. Some are beautiful, and all are very graceful."

"I'll take your word for it," Bess said and was glad when Mrs Cosgrove passed the snake pen and stopped the car some distance away. She and the girls got out and walked to a spot directly on the bay. Here there was a large enclosure, part of it extending into the bay.

"A pair of crocodiles," Mrs Cosgrove said, resting her elbows on the cement fencing.

As the onlookers watched, one of the reptiles got up and walked into the water. At the same time

Nancy spotted a canoe being paddled under the overhanging mangrove trees along the shore. In it were three boys. Without warning, one threw a large piece of coral rock at the reptile. Fortunately it missed.

The move annoyed the crocodile, however. He turned back to join his mate. The boys in the canoe paddled off quickly.

"I'm glad they're gone," Nancy said. "I'd hate to see the croc injured."

Mrs Cosgrove explained that the creature's hide was so thick that it was almost impossible to hurt its back. "But if something hits a crocodile in the eyes, it's very painful."

Bess asked, "Do these crocs have names?"

Mrs Cosgrove smiled. "Yes. They're Lord and Lady Charming."

Nancy and Bess laughed, and Bess remarked, "They don't look very charming to me."

As if he had heard her, the larger of the two crocodiles emitted a low growl, followed by a hiss. He opened his jaws wide.

Bess retreated in a hurry. "W-what's the matter with him?"

Suddenly several small fish, sucked up though a pipe running into the enclosure from the salt water, were sprayed into the pen. The crocodile forgot he was angry. With lightning speed he ran down into the water and grabbed several fish with his great jaws, then closed them with a resounding crack.

At this moment the canoe with the three boys returned. This time each of them was armed with large pieces of coral rock. They pitched them over the wall of the enclosure directly at the big reptiles. One of the rocks hit Lord Charming on one eye. It was obviously painful, for he began swishing madly in a circle, growling and hissing.

"Get away from here!" Nancy yelled at the boys. "Don't do that again!" The youngsters, looking scared, quickly paddled out of sight.

The crocodile swished his great tail back and forth so rapidly in the water that it sprayed into the air, soaking the onlookers.

"Eric!" Mrs Cosgrove called frantically. "Eric, come quickly!"

The gamekeeper, a tall man with a grey beard, ran towards the enclosure and looked at Lord Charming. "What's the matter?" he asked.

"His eye," Mrs Cosgrove answered.

"Poor old fellow!" Eric said. "He's in pain, all right. I hope he won't lose the sight of that eye. Let me get something to put on it."

He hurried off and returned with a tube of salve and a pole with a hook on the end of it. Fearlessly he jumped over the cement wall and talked soothingly to the crocodile. "Sorry, old boy," he said. "Come now, Lord Charming, let me help you."

Nancy and her friends watched in fascination as Eric flipped the reptile on to his back with the pole, and squirted some of the salve into his injured eye.

All this time Lady Charming had been watching from a distance. When her mate turned over on to his stomach, she hurried forward. Using the pole for support, Eric leaped high over the concrete fence.

The visitors clapped. "You're marvellous," Mrs Cosgrove said.

Eric grinned. "It's all in a day's work. Tell me how Lord Charming got hurt."

Nancy reported that three mean boys had come by in a canoe and hit the crocodile.

Eric scowled. "I can't stand people, big or little, who take advantage of a defenceless animal!"

"Where's the trainer today?" Mrs Cosgrove asked.

"It's his day off," Eric replied. "You must come back when he's here. I'm sure you girls would enjoy the various acts he puts on with the animals."

"We will," Mrs Cosgrove promised, then the visitors turned to leave.

When they reached home, George and Danny were back. They explained their delay, saying they had been caught in the low tide.

"Did you pick up any new clues?" Nancy asked.

"I think so," George replied. "We went all the way to Crocodile Island. There was no periscope in sight. But *The Whisper* was tied up at the dock. We got near enough to overhear voices. Apparently someone was talking on a radio telephone."

"What did he say?" Nancy asked eagerly.

"Tonight at eight," George replied.

"What do you think it meant?" Bess asked.

George said she and Danny had figured out that either someone was coming to the island or that *The Whisper* was taking off for a rendezvous with another boat.

Nancy was excited by the report. "I think you're right," she said. "Let's go out there this evening and see what happens."

Danny said that the tide would be perfect for the trip. "Okay with you, Mother?"

She smiled. "It sounds like a great adventure. Of course, you must be careful not to get caught. You've been warned to stay away from that place, so take it easy!"

She packed a picnic supper for the young people, and before six o'clock Danny and the girls set off.

They ate the food on the way, and arrived at Crocodile Island before sunset. *The Whisper* left sometime later, and Danny followed it.

Nancy remarked that she was glad they were in a covered boat. "This way our enemies won't suspect we're in it, even if they see the boat," she said.

Danny nodded. "And the *Sampson* is powerful enough so we won't lose them," he said.

The Whisper headed out into the green channel and travelled for miles and miles.

"It seems as if they're going round the world," Bess said after dusk had come on. "Do we have enough gas to follow them?"

"Our supply won't last forever," Danny said, "but we can follow for several miles and still have enough gas for the return trip."

More time passed, then suddenly the young people spotted the vague outline of a large freighter. It was too dark to see its name or country of origin.

"I wonder if *The Whisper* is going to rendezvous with that ship," Nancy said. She took the binoculars out of their case and scanned the area. "They're both running without lights. Danny, I think we'd better turn ours off, too."

Danny complied and said, "I wonder if *The Whisper* and the freighter are still in motion." He flicked on the *Sampson*'s sonar and detected the sound of *The*

Whisper's motor. "The freighter is standing still and *The Whisper* is idling alongside," he said.

"Can we go any closer without being detected?" George asked.

"I think so," he replied. "We'll advance slowly. I'll keep the engine as low as possible."

"It's getting very misty out here," George observed. "I hope we'll be able to see what's going on."

Danny chuckled. "At least they won't see *us!*"

He drew up to within a hundred yards of *The Whisper* and cut his motor again. The four young people strained their eyes and ears, eager to find out why the two craft had met. Suddenly a bright searchlight was turned on, revealing the deck of the freighter and illuminating the smaller boat alongside it.

Nancy and her friends were terrified that they might be seen. Would the beam penetrate the mist far enough so the *Sampson* could be spotted?

·8·

Indian Tricks

THE four watchers in the *Sampson* held their breath. Would they be kidnapped and taken aboard the freighter?

Although the brilliant searchlight showed up the *Sampson* clearly, the two men paid attention only to the freighter. The young people observed a large pine box being lowered from the freighter to *The Whisper*.

Bess gave a little low scream. "Let's go!" she urged. "Somebody's going to be buried at sea!"

The others disagreed. Nancy said, "If that box were a coffin, there would be no need for a secret transfer. The freighter could have lowered it into the sea."

"Then what is it carrying?" Bess asked.

Nancy said she wished she knew that and where *The Whisper* would take the box.

Suddenly the great searchlight was turned off. Then the regular lights on the freighter beamed again and its engines began to roar. Within seconds the large craft started to move northwards.

"Where do you suppose it's going?" Danny asked.

"My guess," Nancy replied, "is Bridgeport, Connecticut. Remember, that's where the owners of *The*

Whisper are supposed to be from."

"What do you think the freighter brought?" George asked.

Nancy shrugged. "Obviously something very secret. Maybe it'll be buried on one of the keys, like pirate treasure."

"I think the box contains something they need on Crocodile Island," George suggested.

"I doubt that they need corpses," Bess said dryly.

Danny laughed. "Let's follow *The Whisper*. I'm sure it'll go back to the island. Perhaps we can find out what's in the pine box."

The lights of *The Whisper* were still out, but they could hear its motor running. Danny listened carefully, then frowned. "It sounds as if they're going out to sea!" he declared.

"Can we follow it?" Nancy asked, excited.

"We don't have that much fuel. Also, with no lights it's almost impossible. It's so dark now we'd either lose *The Whisper* or run into it!"

"I have an idea," George said. "Why don't we return to Crocodile Island and wait? Perhaps *The Whisper* is only making a detour to throw off anyone who might follow it and will come back to the island later."

"Good suggestion," Nancy agreed. The young people turned round. After a while, Danny put the lights back on.

"I'm glad we're getting away from that coffin," Bess said. "I don't ever want to see it again."

When Danny saw the outline of the key, he shut down the engine and turned off his lights again. The young people settled down to wait for *The Whisper* to arrive, passing the time by telling Danny about various adventures they had had in the past. However, hours dragged by and nothing happened. Finally Danny suggested that they go home.

"My parents will be worried if we don't show up soon," he said. "And I really don't think *The Whisper* is coming back here tonight."

Everyone agreed, and Bess suggested that they report the incident to the police the following morning. Nancy reminded her that the authorities would not investigate without proof of their accusation.

"Right now we don't know if a crime has been committed. We're just assuming that something illegal is going on and we're angry at the skipper of *The Whisper*, because he chased us away from Crocodile Island. But that's not enough for the police."

When the young people reached home, the Cosgroves were relieved. "We were worried about you," Danny's mother said. "What happened?"

The girls reported the strange events, then Mrs Cosgrove said, "A man called here, asking for Anne Boonton. I didn't know whether it was Mr Gonzales or not, so I told him he had the wrong number."

"Good idea," Nancy said. "How did he react?"

"He just hung up and didn't call again."

For nearly an hour, Nancy, her friends, and the Cosgroves discussed what might have been in the box and where *The Whisper* had taken it.

Finally Mrs Cosgrove said, "If the people on Crocodile Island were shipping something out illegally, the box would have been hauled up to the freighter, not the other way around. It appears as if Gimler and Sacco were receiving something illegal. But then, why didn't *The Whisper* take it back to the island?"

"That's a good question," Nancy said and gave a frustrated sigh. "Anyway, I'd like to go back in the morning. Perhaps we can pick up a clue to the puzzle."

Danny offered to accompany her, but said they would have to wait until noon for the right tide.

Mrs Cosgrove spoke up. "In the meantime, why don't you girls visit Mrs Easton again? I spoke to her tonight and she invited you—said you can come any time tomorrow. Their Indian animal trainer will be there all day and will be glad to show you his tricks. He's a Seminole from the Miccosukee tribe and his name is Joe Hanze."

"That sounds great," Bess said. "I'd much rather go there than to Crocodile Island!"

The others laughed and the following morning Danny and the girls borrowed Mrs Cosgrove's car and set out for the zoo.

When they arrived, Nancy rang the front-door bell. Mrs Easton greeted them and talked for a while, then she said, "I'm sure you'll enjoy watching Joe with the animals. He's very entertaining and well informed. Just drive around to the back of the house. You'll see his cottage. Tell him I sent you."

The girls thanked the friendly woman and went to the Indian's place. Joe Hanze was a pleasant man who spoke English fluently. His bronzed face was handsome and his body muscular and lithe. Nancy guessed that he was about fifty years old.

Joe said he would be happy to show off his tricks. On the way to the turtle pen, he asked the girls if they knew anything about the background of the Seminoles.

"No," Nancy told him. "I'd love to hear some of their history."

Joe said that the original Seminoles had come from Canada. The reason why they trekked south was not known.

"Maybe it was the weather," he surmised. "In any case, some of them got as far as Florida and intermarried with other Indians who were already here. My great-grandfather came from Canada. He was a fine hunter and earned a good living on the way by trapping wild animals and selling their hides."

"Where do your people live?" Bess asked.

"Up in the Everglades. Life there is rather primitive, so I decided to come here when I was a young man and get some education. I liked it so much that I stayed. Whenever I want to see my folks, I just get in a car and drive to the Everglades."

The group had reached the wire enclosure where the giant turtle lived, and Joe went inside. The reptile poked its head out of the shell and looked at him.

The Indian pulled a little musical pipe from his pocket and played a tune. To the girls' surprise, the turtle began to dance. When Joe stopped the music, the amusing creature went up and down on its forefeet as if bowing.

"Wonderful!" Bess exclaimed.

The girls clapped and laughed, and Joe said he would have the flamingo put on an act next. When he spoke to the beautiful pink-legged bird, it went over to him and touched the Indian's lips.

"Thank you for my morning kiss," Joe said. "Now suppose you do your war dance."

The flamingo flapped its wings up and down furiously while running round the lawn. At one point the bird soared off and the girls were worried that it might not return. In a few moments it came back and strode about in a circle. Every few feet the bird jumped high into the air and landed neatly a few yards away. When the flamingo became tired of showing off, it walked back to Joe.

"That's great!" George exclaimed. "You must have a lot of patience to train these creatures."

The Indian said he loved animals and did not find it hard to work with any of them. "Now let's go over and call on Lord and Lady Charming," he added.

On the way Joe stopped at a large toolshed. He opened the door and the girls noticed a refrigerator inside. Joe took out a large chunk of meat that he wrapped in paper. He rejoined the girls and said to Nancy, "I want you to feed this to Lord Charming when I tell you."

"Is this breakfast or lunch?" George asked, grinning.

Joe smiled. "It's just a snack. Watch how fast it disappears!"

When they arrived at the concrete wall that surrounded the crocodile pen, he picked up a pole from the edge, then jumped over the fence and walked up to the reptile who was resting on the sand.

"Lady Charming," he said, "you'd better flip over and not give us any trouble."

He prodded her with the spiked pole until he was able to flip her over. Now she would take a few minutes to get back on her feet.

Lord Charming was lying in the water at one end of the pen, under the shade of the mangrove trees that hid the wall of the pen at this point. As Joe approached him, he said to the girls, "Notice his eye-teeth and see how they protrude below the gums? That's one way you can tell the difference between an alligator and a crocodile. The alligator's teeth are more even and do not show below the jaw when it's tightly closed."

He went on to say that Nancy was to throw the meat after he got the crocodile to open his jaws. She figured that from the angle where she stood, her aim would be poor, so she vaulted the fence and stood at the edge of the water.

Joe looked worried. "I wanted you to throw it over the fence!" he said. "But maybe Lord Charming will behave if you don't make a fuss."

He tossed a little stone, which hit the crocodile lightly on the snout. At once his jaws opened. Instantly Nancy threw the chunk of beef. Her aim was perfect and the meat disappeared within a second.

Nancy was so fascinated as she watched the reptile that she failed to retreat. Suddenly the crocodile moved its great tail. In a moment it would hit Nancy hard and injure her!

"Look out!" George shouted.

·9·

Hurricane Legend

WITH a leap Nancy cleared the top of the concrete wall surrounding the crocodile pen. She avoided the swishing tail by inches!

Joe shouted at the reptile in the Seminole language and prodded him with his heavy wooden pole. Finally the creature became quiet and the Indian hurried out of the pen.

Nancy jumped to the ground, still trembling slightly. She looked over the wall and said, "Lord Charming, your manners are pretty bad. That was no way to thank me for the meat."

Joe grinned. "Crocodiles aren't house pets, you know. I'm glad nothing happened."

Bess spoke up. "You almost gave me a heart attack, Nancy. I'm sure I would have been too terrified to jump over that wall."

George chuckled. "I'll bet you would have. But then, I doubt that you'd have gone into the pit in the first place."

Joe stood shaking his head. "You're some girl," he said to Nancy.

She smiled, then changed the subject. "Just before I threw that chunk of meat, I saw a man peering at me from among the trees. He didn't look one bit friendly."

"That's strange," Joe said. "The only other person who works here is Eric, and he's not around this morning."

"It wasn't Eric," Nancy said. "We met him the other day."

"What did this guy look like?" George asked.

"He had long black hair, small eyes, and looked like an Indian," Nancy whispered, not wishing to hurt Joe's feelings.

"I'll search for him," Danny offered and ran in the direction Nancy had indicated.

Joe joined in the hunt, but both of them returned a little while later without having seen the stranger.

"I noticed footprints along the shore," Danny reported. "They led towards the water. Whoever the man was, he wore a small-sized shoe with a rippled sole. When I reached the spot where the prints stopped, I saw a man in a small motorboat too far away to recognize. If he was the fellow who was watching us, Nancy, he's gone."

Joe promised to look out for the stranger in case he should return, then the young people thanked him for the tour of the zoo and went home. After a quick lunch, they set out in the boat for Crocodile Island.

"Do you think that man was spying on us this morning?" Bess asked while they were gliding along in the water.

"Maybe he was a sneak thief who was trying to make off with something from the estate," Danny suggested. "When he saw us, he ran."

"It's possible," Nancy agreed. "But it's more likely

that Bess is right. He could have followed us from your house to see what we were doing."

George looked behind them. "No one is following us now. Let's stop worrying about him."

The young people once again passed the stilts with cottages built on top of them, and it occurred to Nancy that they might pick up a clue to Crocodile Island from one of the inhabitants.

"After all, they live close to the place," she said. "Danny, do you think we might stop and call on the owners?"

"Why not?" he replied, and paused at each cottage. He received no answer to his "Hello? Anybody home?" Finally he laughed. "There aren't any boats tied up at the posts. Obviously no one is here."

As they passed a group of posts with nothing on them, Bess shivered. "Every time I think about a cottage being blown away in a hurricane, I worry about whether people were in it or not."

"I never heard of any," Danny said. "But did you know that crocodiles were blown here by hurricanes?"

The girls laughed and George said, "Don't kid us!"

"I'm not kidding," Danny replied. "The story comes from the Indians. They say that when the Seminoles arrived here many, many years ago, there were plenty of alligators, but no crocodiles. Then, after a terrific hurricane, crocodiles were seen along the shore of Key Biscayne."

Nancy, curious, asked, "Where did the crocodiles come from?

"Supposedly from Cuba," Danny answered. "But

they might even have travelled all the way from Africa."

"Oh, yes?" George said. "If I see that in a science book I'll believe it, but not from hearsay."

"Well, they got here somehow," Danny defended himself. "And certainly no one brought them. You figure it out."

He sent his boat past he houses on stilts. The *Pirate* had not gone far whe he pointed out an uninhabited key. "That's a good picnic spot," he said. "Friends of mine and I sometimes come here."

George asked if he could go closer. "I see a green bottle floating towards shore. Let's pick it up!"

Bess saw a good chance to tease her cousin. She rarely got the opportunity. "Are you collecting old bottles?" she asked. "From here that doesn't look very valuable."

"Possibly not," George retorted, "but it's corked. Maybe there's something valuable inside."

When Danny reached the spot, George got down from her chair, leaned over the gunwale, and grabbed the bottle out of the water. It was dark green and had no markings. She tried to uncork it, but at first the stopper would not budge.

"I guess we'll have to take the bottle home and work on it with a corkscrew," Bess said.

"Maybe not," George replied. She wiggled the cork from left to right, being careful not to break it. The cork loosened little by little. With one final yank, George pulled it out.

She turned the bottle upside down. Nothing fell out. Then she held it up to her nose.

"What does it smell like?" Bess asked. "Perfume?"

"Nothing," George said, disappointed.

"You might as well throw it back into the water," Danny advised.

"I guess you're right," George said. "The whole thing was— wait a minute!" She had given the bottle a hard shake and looked into it. "I see something inside!" she said, excited. "It might be a note!"

Everyone watched breathlessly as George held the bottle upside down and continued to shake it. Finally a rolled paper appeared in the long, thin neck. She reached in with one finger and gently eased the piece out.

"What is it?" Nancy asked.

George carefully unrolled the yellowed, crinkled paper. "It's a message!" she cried out. "Dated twenty years ago!"

"What does it say?" Danny asked impatiently.

"Captain Wayne," George read, *"USS Venerable sank in hurricane off Argentina. Twelve took to life boat. God's blessings."*

There was complete silence for several seconds, then Nancy asked to see the paper.

"I believe it's authentic," she said after examining it carefully. "The paper is well preserved and the cork was in tight. And down in the corner is a date. This was written twenty years ago!"

"Why don't we take the whole thing to the Naval Station at Key West?" Danny suggested. "They have all kinds of records there of old ships that went down in hurricanes."

"Good idea," George said. She was about to roll the note and put it back in the bottle, when Bess stopped her.

"Don't do that," her cousin advised. "It was hard enough to get it out the first time. Shoving it back in the bottle won't make it any more authentic, you know."

George laughed and slipped the message in her pocket, then replaced the cork in the bottle. "My dear cousin, you're right for a change."

"I'm right more often than you want to admit," Bess said haughtily.

Danny grinned and started the *Pirate*'s engine. Soon they approached Crocodile Island. The girls used the binoculars to search for the periscope in the deep, green channel, but did not see it. They circled the island from a distance and noticed a sign at the landing platform: NO VISITORS TODAY.

"They're keeping everyone out," Danny said. "No activity at all. I wonder for how long."

Nancy shrugged. "Let's just keep going round the island. Maybe we'll see something sooner or later."

They had almost completed the second circle when they heard an agonizing cry from somewhere on the island!

·10·

The Runaway's Clues

BESS turned pale. "Wh-what was that?"

Before anyone could guess, there were more blood-curdling screams from the island.

"Maybe a crocodile got one of the workers!" George cried out in alarm.

Just then a young bearded man raced from behind the mangrove trees into the water. He splashed through the shallow area, and when he reached the green channel began to swim.

Seeing the nearby boat, he cried out, "Save me! Save me!"

Danny guided the boat alongside the frantic swimmer, and the girls pulled him aboard. His eyes were bulging with terror, and his legs were bleeding profusely.

Danny quickly got a first-aid kit from a locker and handed it to the girls. They carefully washed the stranger's wounds and applied a soothing salve.

"What happened to you?" Nancy asked him.

"Just—just don't take me back to the island, please!" the young man pleaded.

"Of course not. Did a crocodile bite you?"

"No, no! I was beaten with one of the sharp

hooked poles they use on the reptiles."

"How dreadful!" Bess said. "Why would anyone do that to you?"

"Because I didn't clean the pits to suit the boss. Oh, he has a terrible temper!"

Nancy wound a bandage around the man's left leg, while George attended to the right one.

Danny looked back to see if they were being followed, then asked, "Where do you want to go?"

"To Key Biscayne," the fugitive replied.

The young people heard the sound of an engine and noticed a fast motorboat coming up in the deep channel towards the island.

Just then a man appeared at the shore, yelling at the top of his lungs. "Colombo! Colombo, where are you? You can't run away! Where are you, Colombo?"

The runaway lay down in the bottom of the boat, well protected by the three girls. He trembled with fright.

Danny put on extra power, and the *Pirate* skipped speedily across the bay. The man on shore continued to yell for Colombo, but suddenly he addressed the skipper of a passing motorboat.

"Follow the *Pirate*!" he ordered, pointing.

"The water's not deep enough," the skipper replied, much to the relief of Danny and his passengers.

The fugitive sighed, and Nancy asked him who he was and what had happened on Crocodile Island.

"My name is Colombo Banks. I'm from New Orleans, but I came here to get a job. I was hired to work on Crocodile Island. At first I liked it, but then the bosses became very cruel."

"In what way?" Nancy asked.

Colombo said that although he had requested permission to make a trip into Biscayne Bay on his free days, he had always been refused.

"I began to wonder why, and finally decided that the members of the Crocodile Ecology Company were doing something underhanded. Perhaps they didn't want me to leave and tell people what I had seen or heard."

"What did you see and hear?" George spoke up.

Colombo told them that a speedboat called *The Whisper* came and went mysteriously.

"Mysteriously? How?" Nancy asked.

"Often it docks or leaves in the middle of the night, and I was never allowed to watch what was going on. The bosses made me sleep on the far side of the island with one other man named Sol. He's black and a great guy. We were friends, but four other fellows who work there stay in the main house with the bosses."

"How mean!" Bess exclaimed.

Colombo went on, "I decided to find out what was going on. At night I would sneak out of my cabin and go to the main part of the island. Many times I saw Mr Sacco and Mr Gimler at the landing dock, but usually they whispered and I couldn't overhear anything.

"Once, however, Gimler spoke loud enough to a man I'd never seen. 'They want five hundred,' the boss said. 'Can you carry that many?' Unfortunately I couldn't make out the answer."

"Who was he talking to?" George inquired.

"The skipper of *The Whisper*."

"Do you think they were referring to crocodiles?" Danny asked.

"I don't know."

"Do they ever transport crocs in *The Whisper*?"

"No," Colombo replied, then added, "I was scolded a good deal, mostly for no reason. It seemed as if the bosses had a grudge against me. I think they figured I knew more than I really do."

"That's possible," Nancy said thoughtfully.

"I wanted to leave the job," Colombo went on, "but they would never let me. A few times I tried to sneak up to the visitors and ask for a ride. But one of the workmen who lived with the bosses always chased me away."

"Did Sacco and Gimler ever have anything delivered to the island, or did they do the shopping themselves?" Nancy asked.

Colombo said that as far as he knew all supplies were brought in by *The Whisper*, and whenever any of the men left, they used that boat.

"You mean," Nancy asked, "that they do not use any other means of transportation?"

"Not as far as I know. But then, I wasn't around to see everything. I just worked and ate and slept."

The young people felt sorry for the man, and his story made them more suspicious then ever of the partners in the Crocodile Ecology Company. By now they had reached Key Biscayne. Danny pulled into a public dock to let Colombo off, and asked him if they could be of any further help.

Colombo shook his head. "You've all been mighty kind, and I'll never forget it. If I can ever do you a favour, just let me know."

Nancy asked him where he would stay.

"At the YMCA," he said. "I have relatives here, but Mr Gimler knows about them. If I go there, he'll track me down and try to force me to return to Crocodile Island by threats, and make up some story."

"That's true," Nancy said. "Well, I hope your legs will heal properly. Perhaps you should see a doctor."

Colombo smiled. "I think you ladies did a fine job. I'll be well in no time." He stepped on to the dock with Danny's help, then turned around. "I don't even know your names," he said.

Nancy hesitated, but Danny spoke up quickly. "I'm Danny Cosgrove, and these are the Boonton girls, Anne, Elizabeth, and Jackie."

"Thank you," Colombo said. "I really appreciate your help."

Danny pushed off. "I hope you girls don't mind what I told him," he said. "But he can find out from anyone around here who owns the *Pirate*."

"That was perfectly all right," Nancy said. "Besides, I think we can trust him."

On the way home the young people discussed what the phrase "they want five hundred" could have meant.

"If not crocodiles, what else?" George asked.

"The thing that bothers me most," Bess said, "is that Mr Gimler might have known Colombo was on the boat. If so, he may make trouble. We'd better not go back to Crocodile Island."

"We've got to, Bess," said Nancy. "We're just beginning to get some good clues!"

When they reached the Cosgrove home, Danny's

mother was waiting for them. After greeting each one, she said, "I have a message for you, Nancy."

"Yes? What is it?"

"Mr Gonzales called. He has some valuable information to give you."

"Did he give any hint as to what it was?" Nancy asked.

Mrs Cosgrove shook her head. "He said that you would receive a letter in the morning."

Nancy wanted to phone Mr Gonzales at once, but realized that she should not let her curiosity get the better of her and possibly embarrass him.

Later in the evening, the group settled down to watch television, but the young detective had trouble concentrating on the show. Instead, her thoughts focused on what Colombo had told them about Crocodile Island.

Presently the phone rang. Mrs Cosgrove answered, then handed the receiver to Nancy. "It's for you."

"Hello?" Nancy said.

"You're not Anne Boonton!" a man said gruffly. "You're Nancy Drew. We know all about you. If you and your friends don't leave Florida at once, you'll *never* get home again!"

·11·
An Identification

"WHO are you?" Nancy asked the man on the phone.

There was no reply, only a click in her ear.

Nancy's friends looked at her questioningly. "Who was it?" George asked.

"One of our enemies, I'm afraid. He told us to leave Florida, or we might never see our homes again!"

"Oh, dear!" Bess wailed. "Now they know where we're staying."

"So what?" George said. "This isn't the first time Nancy has been threatened over the phone by her adversaries!"

Danny tried to break the tension. "Bess, will you stop worrying? After all, you have me to protect you!"

Bess laughed, and after a while the mysterious call was forgotten.

Next morning Nancy watched eagerly for the mailman. When he came up the street, she ran from the house to meet him. He smiled at her and asked, "Is a Miss Anne Boonton staying here?"

"Yes," Nancy replied. "Do you have a letter for her?"

"Indeed I do," the man replied. "And a lot of others. You want to take them?"

"I'll be glad to," Nancy said, and he handed her the bundle.

She thanked him, then hurried into the house and quickly scanned the stack. The one addressed to Anne Boonton was near the bottom. Nancy opened the envelope. The letter read:

> Dear Anne:
>
> I had a phone call from Hal Gimler today. He told me that one of our employees, Colombo Banks, has run away. He suspects that the workman escaped in a boat with three girls and a boy in it.
>
> Gimler thinks that Colombo may cause trouble and asked me to locate him. I was wondering, was your group responsible for his rescue, and do you know where he is? Gimler threatens to have him arrested for stealing.
>
> If you have any information about Colombo, meet me at my club for lunch tomorrow.
>
> G.

"That's today," Nancy said to herself.

By this time Bess, George, and the Cosgroves had joined her and wanted to know what the letter said. She read it to them.

When she finished, Mr Cosgrove said, "You'd better go to the club and talk to Mr Gonzales."

"There's only one problem," George said. "Nancy might be followed. Now that the Ecology people know where we're staying, they may have this place staked out."

"Well," Mr Cosgrove said, "we belong to the same club as Mr Gonzales, and we know many other members. Perhaps you could meet one of them and get a ride."

"That's a good plan," Nancy said. "Now we just have to figure out how I get from here to wherever I'll meet this person."

Bess had a suggestion. "Danny and Nancy are about the same size. Couldn't she wear his clothes and cover her hair with a golf hat?"

Nancy laughed. "I wouldn't want to have lunch with Mr Gonzales in dungarees and a T-shirt!"

"True," Mrs Cosgrove agreed. Then her face lit up. "I have it!" she said. "The delivery boy from Drummond's Market is due here at about eleven. He drives a van. I'll tell him to back up to our attached garage so you can slip into the van unseen. Then he can drop you off downtown."

"That sounds great," Nancy agreed.

"Okay. I'll call my friend Mrs Grote and see if she's playing golf today. If so, she can meet you at a drugstore on the main street. She has to pass it on the way to the club. What shall I tell her you'll be wearing?"

"If I put on my dark-blue trouser suit, I might still be taken for a boy from a distance, provided I cover my hair," Nancy replied.

Mr Cosgrove said he had a hat he used on the golf course, and offered to lend it to Nancy. "Come with me and see if it fits," he said.

While Nancy was gone, Mrs Cosgrove called her friend, who agreed to pick up Nancy at the drugstore.

Ten minutes later the girl detective appeared again, dressed in a blue trouser suit with white collar and cuffs, and the white golf hat.

"Oh, you look cute!" Bess exclaimed. "Not quite like Danny, but close!"

Just then Danny walked into the room and overheard Bess's remark. "You've got to be kidding!" he protested. "I don't own a fancy get-up like that, and if I did, I'd give it away quick!"

Everyone laughed, and Nancy said, "All that counts is that from a distance I don't look like me!"

"Nancy," Mrs Cosgrove said, "Mrs Grote will meet you at the drugstore. She'll be wearing a white dress with a multi-coloured embroidered belt."

Soon the delivery boy arrived at the back door in a van. Mrs Cosgrove gave him the necessary instructions, and Nancy slipped into the rear. After he had left the street she climbed into the seat next to him. He looked at her and gave a low whistle. "You're a doll," he said appreciatively. "Are you on a secret date?"

Nancy smiled. "Suppose you guess?"

"I'm sure you are," the young man said as he pulled round a corner, "so I won't interfere. But I'd like to take you out myself some time."

"That's very kind of you," Nancy replied. "Right now, however, I have to go on an important errand."

When they reached the drugstore, she thanked the boy, quickly hopped out, and went inside. She saw a rack of books and walked over to examine the titles. Just then an attractive woman walked into the store. She was dressed in white except for an embroidered, many-coloured belt.

"She must be Mrs Grote," Nancy concluded. The woman spotted her at the same moment, and walked towards the girl, holding out her hand. "Anne, I'm Mrs Grote. I'll be very happy to drive you to the club."

They left the store by the rear entrance, where Mrs Grote had parked her car. Nancy was relieved. If anyone had followed the van and was waiting for her in front, he would be fooled!

"Are you enjoying your visit here?" Mrs Grote asked as she drove off.

"Oh, yes," Nancy replied. "It has been very exciting."

"In what way?" Mrs Grote asked.

Nancy did not want to give any details concerning the mystery, so she merely talked about their interesting boat rides, their trip to the Easton estate, and the show the Indian had put on.

Soon Mrs Grote drove into the club grounds, so it was not necessary for Nancy to explain any further. She thanked the woman for picking her up and wished her a good score in her golf game.

Mr Gonzales was seated in the lobby. "I'm so glad you came," he said, and led her to the dining-room.

While they were eating, Nancy told him about Colombo and what he had said regarding the officers of the Crocodile Ecology Company.

"I'm not surprised," Mr Gonzales commented.

Nancy mentioned the phrase: *They want five hundred. Can you carry that many?* "Mr Gonzales, have you any idea what that could have meant?"

The man furrowed his brow. "No, I haven't. Surely they couldn't have been talking about crocodiles. There wouldn't be enough to fill such a big order."

"Do you raise anything else on the island that they could have referred to?" Nancy asked.

"No, nothing. I could ask my partners, but if I do

they will know that I received word from Colombo. Then they are likely to go after the poor man and harm him."

"You're right," Nancy agreed. "Would you like to speak to Colombo personally?"

"Indeed I would. Do you know how to reach him?"

"I'll try. Colombo said he would be staying at the YMCA."

Nancy stood up and went to a phone booth in the lobby. Luckily the receptionist at the Y confirmed that Mr Banks was registered and offered to get him. Soon he was on the line.

"Hello?" he said hurriedly. His voice sounded frightened.

"Hello, Colombo," Nancy replied. "It's Anne Boonton. Could you meet me at this club?" She gave the address. "A friend of mine wants to speak to you about Crocodile Island. Take a taxi. I'll pay for it."

"All right," he said. "I'm glad it's you and not one of my former bosses. I'll be there as soon as I can."

Half an hour later the man arrived. Nancy hurried outside to pay the taxi driver, then took Colombo to the tropical garden to meet Mr Gonzales. When the young man heard that he was one of the partners in the Crocodile Ecology Company, he looked at Nancy apprehensively.

"Don't worry," she said. "Mr Gonzales is not like the other men. He wants to find out what's going on at Crocodile Island and if his partners are dishonest."

This reassured Colombo and he talked freely about the hardship he had suffered and the things he had observed.

"I'm in real trouble," he finished. "I've been trying to find a job but haven't been successful. I'm running out of money, but I'm afraid to contact my relatives for fear of being tracked down by Gimler."

"Perhaps I can help," Mr Gonzales offered. "I heard the other day that one of the men in the club kitchen is quitting. Wait here, and I'll see what I can find out."

He went to the lobby to talk to the manager, and returned a few minutes later with a smile on his face.

"You're in luck, Colombo," he said. "Do you know how to prepare seafood?"

Colombo grinned. "I did that in New Orleans. But I never cut up a crocodile!"

Nancy laughed, and Mr Gonzales asked Colombo to come along with him to see the head chef in the kitchen.

"We won't be long," he told Nancy.

Within ten minutes the two were back with a third man, who proved to be the pastry chef. Mr Gonzales said that this man had finished his work and was about to drive home. He would take Colombo with him.

The cook went to get his car. Meanwhile, Nancy was told that Colombo had been given the job and was to report for work the next morning.

Colombo said, "I certainly appreciate what you've done for me."

Mr Gonzales patted him on the back. "We're glad to help, and thank you for some good clues. If you think of anything else about the Crocodile Ecology Company, leave a note for me at the desk."

"I will," Colombo promised, then hurried outside,

where the pastry chef was waiting for him.

When Nancy returned to the Cosgroves' home, no one was there. She knew where a key was hidden and went to get it. As she entered the hall, Nancy saw a note from George lying on the table. It said that Danny and the girls had gone to the small local Naval Station with the bottle George had found in the water. "Maybe we can find out about it without going to Key West," George had written.

At this moment, George was telling her story to a friendly young captain named Smith. He agreed that the old note appeared to be authentic and said he would try to verify its contents.

He stood up and went to a shelf containing books and registries. George meanwhile walked round his small office and glanced at photographs on the wall. Suddenly she stopped in front of a group picture of sailors. One of the faces looked familiar!

"Bess," George said, excited, "come here a moment. Doesn't this man remind you of someone?"

"Matt Carmen or Breck Tobin!" Bess answered. "Only the sailor's a lot younger."

As Captain Smith turned around, George asked who the sailor was.

·12·
Child in Danger

CAPTAIN Smith turned over the picture George had pointed out. He read the names on the back and said, "This fellow is Giuseppe Matthews. I'll look up his record."

After a search in several volumes, he came across the item. "Matthews went AWOL," Captain Smith explained, "and was never heard from again. Why did you ask about him?"

George replied. "We've met a man who looks very much like the one in this picture. He's older, but there's a strong resemblance."

"Where did you see him?" Captain Smith asked.

"Out in the bay, near Crocodile Island. If he's the same person, he's using a different name now."

"What is it?" Smith inquired.

"Matt Carmen or Breck Tobin," George answered. "We were never introduced so we don't know which name goes with whom."

"You realize, of course, that we're still looking for Matthews," Captain Smith said. "And that we'll have to arrest him when we find him. Can you tell me where these men live?"

For a moment George hesitated. "What if one of

them is the wrong person?" she asked. "I wouldn't want to get anyone in trouble."

"If they're not Giuseppe Matthews, they won't get into trouble," the captain pointed out.

"We saw a boat called *The Whisper*," Danny said. "We checked in a register of ships and learned that it belongs to two men from Bridgeport, Connecticut. One of them is Matt Carmen, the other Breck Tobin."

Captain Smith wrote the information on a pad, and said he would follow up the lead. Then he checked another set of records for proof that the note in the bottle was authentic. Finally he smiled.

"Here it is," he said. "This is really amazing. A ship named *Venerable* was last heard from in Argentina. Her captain was George Wayne. This is the first message received since then."

"No one reported that she was wrecked?" Bess asked.

"No. And this note must have travelled at least ten thousand miles. I presume it would be considered part of the *Venerable*'s records, so I'd like to keep it if you don't mind."

"Of course not," George said.

"Perhaps we can locate relatives of the captain and the crew, who would like to see it," Captain Smith added. He thanked the girls for bringing him their find and remarked, "The government may give you a citation for this."

George grinned. "That would be fun. I've never had one."

The girls said goodbye to the captain and returned home. There was plenty of exciting conversation as they exchanged stories with Nancy. Mr and Mrs Cosgrove listened and were thunderstruck at all that had been learned.

"Each day you prove more and more what good detectives you are," their host complimented them.

"But we haven't solved anything yet," Nancy reminded him. She turned to George. "Did you ask Captain Smith about the periscope?"

"Oh dear, I didn't even think of that," George said. "But we can go back another time and inquire if he's ever heard of a sub around here."

Nancy wanted to go out in the boat the following day, but Mr Cosgrove said that he had had the craft out in the morning and found that it had been tampered with.

"It was lucky I discovered the damage before you used the *Pirate* again. You might have had a bad accident."

Nancy exclaimed, "You say it has been sabotaged? I'm afraid our enemies have been at work!"

The others agreed. Mrs Cosgrove was worried. "This could mean that we're all being watched by spies. I think you should stay away from Crocodile Island for a while."

George grimaced. "At least until the *Pirate* is repaired."

"Meanwhile, why don't you visit Cape Florida?" their hostess suggested. "It's a lovely place. Beautiful trees and a nice beach. People go there for picnics. The main attraction is an old lighthouse. A guide will show you around and tell you about its history."

"That sounds great," Bess said. "I could use a change of pace."

The girls got directions and set off early the next morning in one of the Cosgrove cars. Nancy, at the wheel, drove across the bridge leading to Cape Florida, and turned into the park entrance.

"Look at those gorgeous trees!" Bess exclaimed as they rode down an avenue of tall Australian pines.

"I've read in a magazine that these aren't native to Florida," Nancy said. "They were imported."

The road twisted and turned; then they came to a shaded picnic area with a large sandy beach.

"This is a heavenly spot," Bess remarked. "No wonder it's so popular."

Many people were seated on the beach, while others had settled at picnic tables set up in a grove of trees. Nancy parked and the girls strolled towards the water.

To their right was a natural coral breakwater, which had been built up by polyps. It was very rough and Nancy realized at once that anyone slammed into it by waves could be badly cut. She noticed that bathers seemed to be avoiding it.

"What a lot of seaweed there is!" George remarked.

She picked up handfuls of it and rolled the soggy masses into a ball. "Let's play catch," she suggested.

The girls formed a triangle and threw the seaweed ball back and forth to one another. Whoever dropped it was eliminated from the game. After about ten minutes of play George was declared the winner.

To tease her, Bess picked up the ball and threw it hard at her cousin. Unfortunately it missed and sailed across the sand. The soggy mass landed *plunk*! on a bald-headed bather who was stretched out on the beach, sleeping soundly.

"Oh!" Bess cried in dismay and went over to the man.

He blinked at her and looked annoyed, but after she apologized and he saw the look of concern on her face, he sat up and smiled. "Hi!" he said. "My, you're pretty!"

Bess backed away. "He's old and fat and bald-headed," she told herself. "I hope he won't try to get too friendly!"

Her fears were confirmed when the man stood up and took her hand. "I believe you threw that sea-weed on purpose to wake me up. Well, here I am, at your service!"

"I—I—it was an accident," Bess stammered. Then she turned away and ran off as fast as she could. When she reached Nancy and George, they laughed.

"That'll teach you to aim straight when you throw something," George remarked.

Nancy, who had been watching various bathers in the water, now spotted a little girl who had not noticed that the tide was pulling her towards the coral breakwater. She realized that at any moment the child would be thrown against its jagged side and severely injured!

Nancy rushed down to the water's edge, slipped off her sandals, and waded in. The water was shallow for adults, but the little girl could have drowned in it. Nancy swam with powerful crawl strokes towards her. By now the child was only a few feet from the breakwater!

"Come here!" Nancy called out and grabbed the child's hand. Together they struggled to the beach, where they were met by a frantic woman.

"Tessie!" she scolded. "You were told not to wade over there!"

The little girl cried. "I didn't mean to, but all of a sudden I couldn't keep from going that way," she sobbed.

"Are you her mother?" Nancy inquired.

"No. I'm Mrs Turnbull. I'm in charge of a group of children who attend my day camp. I brought them here to swim, but it's hard to watch all of them at once."

"I understand," Nancy said.

"Thank you for going in after Tessie," Mrs Turnbull continued. "When I saw her, it was too late for me to help."

Now the other children ran to them. The woman opened her purse and offered Nancy money as a reward for saving Tessie's life.

"Thank you," Nancy said, "but I couldn't possibly accept any money."

Tessie had stopped crying. She took Mrs Turnbull by the hand, and said, "I know how we can reward her. Give her the map."

Mrs Turnbull smiled. "Tessie, we have no right to give the map away. We should turn it over to the authorities. But I will show it to this young lady. By the way, what is your name?"

Nancy introduced herself and her friends, who had joined the group, by their Boonton name, not wishing to be identified. The woman fished in her handbag and brought out a faded piece of paper. She unfolded it.

"I don't know whether this is authentic or not,"

she said. "We found it back in the woods. Somebody must have dropped it yesterday or today."

Nancy, Bess, and George studied the map. Not only was the paper old, but the printing on it was quite faded. Mrs Turnbull explained that she and the children suspected that someone had been hunting for a treasure, perhaps buried long ago by pirates.

"The person must have lost it. The map does seem to indicate a buried treasure," she said. "Perhaps it's here on Florida Key."

The girls were intrigued by the story, and Nancy looked closely at the map. On it were directional lines pointing north, east, south, and west. There were also a number of intersecting lines converging at one spot.

"This must be the place where the treasure was hidden," Nancy remarked.

"True," Mrs Turnbull said. "But how would one go about trying to figure out where it is?"

"We have to find a point of reference," Nancy said. "But what?" she puckered her brows and tried to figure out the strange map. Suddenly the girl detective had an idea.

"You see this line running directly into the water? It could be the coral breakwater!"

"You're right!" Mrs Turnbull agreed. "Let's draw a continuing line from it through the sand and then bisect it just as it was on the map."

Tessie jumped up and down in excitement. "Let's hurry up and dig!" she exclaimed. "I brought my sand shovel. I'll get it."

She ran off and soon returned with a toy shovel. Nancy, Bess, and George were amused at the thought of digging for hidden pirate treasure with this implement.

The bald bather had walked up, curious to see what was going on. When he realized that they were planning to dig with the toy shovel, he said, "I have a spade in my trunk and would be glad to lend it to you."

He hurried to his parked car and returned a few minutes later with the spade. He handed it to Bess and looked at her with an admiring smile. It made her blush.

"Thank you," she said and pushed the spade into the sand. She worked for a while. Then, when the hole was about a foot deep, she handed the spade to Nancy.

"Your turn," she declared.

While the day-camp children, Mrs Turnbull, and the bald-headed man watched, Nancy continued to dig. When her arms got tired, she looked at George.

"You're next if I don't hit something," she said, and shoved the spade down once more. There was a slight clang of metal against metal. Nancy exclaimed, "I hit something hard!"

"It must be the treasure!" Tessie cried out, jumping up and down.

·13·

Doubloons!

NANCY lifted Tessie into the hole, and she dug the objects out with her toy shovel. As she handed up a battered tin knife and spoon, she squealed in delight. "Did pirates leave these?"

"I don't know," Nancy replied.

"They could have been utensils dropped by a picnicker and buried in the sand," George pointed out.

Bess examined the pieces carefully. "I'm sure they're very old," she said. "They're probably from a pirate ship."

"Can I keep them?" Tessie begged.

"Maybe," Nancy replied.

Tessie looked for more treasure, but reported that there was nothing. Nancy helped her climb out, then offered to dig deeper. A few minutes later, she stopped suddenly and stepped out.

"Tessie, go down and feel around in the sand."

In a few seconds the little girl handed up a coin. Nancy looked at it and exclaimed, "This is a doubloon! A Spanish doubloon!"

Tessie wanted to know what a doubloon was. Bess explained that many years ago Spanish ships sailed

97

across the ocean to Mexico, which was not far from Florida.

"They captured people and had them do all sort of work. One thing was to make coins like those they had in Spain. They were called doubloons and were made of pure gold."

Tessie tried to dig farther, but found it impossible. She had hit solid coral rock. The little girl looked up at Nancy and said, "Please lift me out and then you dig."

Nancy complied. She assumed that the coral rock had been there a long time, but suspected that something precious might have been buried before the tiny polyps had built their pile of rock on top of it.

She chipped at the coral with the spade, and presently saw a few more doubloons. She handed them up to Tessie, then Nancy broke off more of the rock. In a few moments she climbed out of the hole, but helped Tessie down.

This time the little girl exclaimed, "Oh, I found a bracelet!" and climbed out.

Nancy explained that all treasure found must be taken to police headquarters and listed. "You can't keep everything you find," she added. "It's against the law."

George scraped the hole thoroughly, but found nothing more, and came back up.

"Now I suppose we must put all that sand back," Bess said with a sigh.

"Of course," George replied. "Otherwise someone could fall in and get hurt. Here, my dear cousin, you haven't been digging for a while. You start."

Bess did not look very happy, and the bald-headed

man stepped up. "Don't worry, I'll do it for you," he offered, and took the spade.

With powerful arms he threw the sand back into the hole and soon the beach looked just as it had before.

"Thanks," Bess said. "That was very nice of you."

"Don't mention it. Want an ice cream?"

"Oh—no, thanks. I—I'm on a diet."

The man smiled and left to take his spade back to the car.

George chuckled. "How come you're turning down food?"

Bess blushed. "As I said, I'm on a diet!"

George and Nancy laughed. "Best joke I've heard in years!" George exclaimed. "If he had been young and handsome, Bess would have eaten three banana splits!"

Mrs Turnbull's children became restless now that the treasure hunt was over and asked if they could have their lunch. The woman nodded and again thanked Nancy for rescuing Tessie. She promised to take the treasure to the authorities on their way home, then beckoned her charges towards the grove. The children waved goodbye and followed the woman.

After they had gone, Nancy said, "I'm sure someone else found the rest of that treasure."

"I hope he reported it," George said, grinning.

The three friends walked along the beach.

"From Mrs Cosgrove's description," Nancy said, "this should be the way to the old lighthouse."

"You're right," George confirmed a few seconds later, when they saw the building inside a fenced area. It was about sixty feet in height, cone-shaped, and made of brick.

Several other visitors, including a group of boy scouts, had gathered in front of the gate and the girls joined them. "The tour will begin in a few minutes," the scoutmaster told them.

He had hardly finished speaking, when an attractive young woman in a ranger's uniform unlocked the gate. She admitted the visitors and led them around the lighthouse towards the water. They went up to a small porch and gathered around her as she talked about the building's history.

"This lighthouse hasn't been used for years," she said, "because others have been built farther out in the bay. However, it has an interesting background. This building is not the original one."

"What happened to that one?" a scout asked.

"It was burned."

"Was anyone in it?"

"Unfortunately, yes. The lighthouse keeper John Thompson and his black assistant. It was dangerous living out here at that time because the Indians who occupied this territory were not friendly. Many of the Seminoles had had their wives and children taken away by white people, who made them slaves. Naturally they were furious and did everything they could to retaliate.

"One night a crowd of Indians came here. A circular stairway led to the top, where the great lantern was. The Seminoles set the old wooden building on fire to prevent the keeper and his assistant from escaping. The two men hid in the tower, but bullets whizzed at them continuously. The black man was shot and killed, and the keeper was wounded. But the fire attracted the attention of two ships offshore."

"Did anyone come to rescue them?" Bess asked anxiously.

"Yes, but meanwhile John Thompson rolled a keg of powder down the stairway. When it hit the fire below, the powder exploded and the Indians ran for their lives!"

"Good!" a boy scout exclaimed. "But was Mr Thompson saved?"

"Yes, but the rescuers almost failed. When the ships got closer to the lighthouse, they sent out a lifeboat, but the crew realized that it would be impossible to climb to the top of the tower. Instead, they tried sending out a kite from which there was a stout cord for Mr Thompson to grab. Unfortunately he wasn't able to, so they tied the twine to a ramrod and fired it from a musket. This time Thompson grabbed the cord and used it to haul up heavier rope. On it two men climbed to the tower room to take care of him. He reached the ground safely."

"I'm glad to hear that," Bess said.

"The black man was buried," the ranger went on, "but I've never seen his grave. It was unmarked so the Indians couldn't find it."

She let the visitors inside the lighthouse, which had been modernized and had an upstairs bedroom. After they had inspected the sparse but comfortable furnishings, they went down again and walked outside.

"I want to show you some of the bushes around here," the ranger said, pointing to a shrub. "This is called an inkberry bush. It was used by the Indians and the early settlers to write letters with."

"How?" one of the boy scouts wanted to know.

"The liquid from its berries is just like ink," the ranger replied. From a little basket that she carried on her wrist, she took a number of small plastic bags. Each contained an inkberry. She handed them out to the visitors as souvenirs.

"These berries were also used to make a dye," she explained. "When you get home, try to write with the ink."

The boy scouts giggled. "On regular paper?"

"Sure. White paper, yellow paper. You can even use a paper bag."

Next the young woman pointed out a bush called sea grape. "This yields fruit to make jelly," she said. "But notice the leaves. They are very thick, and you can write on them." She took one off the bush, picked up a small stick from the ground, and wrote:

Thank you for coming.
I hope you had a good time.

Then she handed the leaf to the scoutmaster. He passed it on to his charges and thanked her for the interesting tour. Now she opened the gate and the visitors said goodbye.

When the girls were back in their car, George grinned. "I'll remember that sea-grape bush. If I'm ever in a tight spot out on the water, I'll write a message on one of them and let it float ashore."

Nancy laughed. "You may have to wait twenty years before someone picks it up!"

The girls drove back to Key Biscayne, chatting about their experiences on Cape Florida. When they reached the business district, traffic became congested and momentarily stopped.

Nancy watched the scene in front of her and suddenly gasped. "Bess! George!" she said. "Do you see those two men getting into that red car up ahead?"

"I see them," George said. "They look like Matt Carmen and Breck Tobin!"

"Right!" Bess agreed. "What are we going to do?"

Just then traffic began to move again. The suspects started their red sedan and pulled in a few cars ahead of the girls.

"Let's chase them!" George urged.

"Yes," Nancy said. "Only right now it's a rather slow chase."

At the next big intersection their quarry turned right. The girls followed and kept the sedan in sight. Soon the traffic thinned out and Nancy sped after the two suspects!

·14·

Periscope Pursuit

THE driver of the car Nancy was pursuing seemed to be aware that he was being followed. Not only did he put on speed, but he turned corners with squealing wheels. Nancy and her friends were convinced that the men were indeed Carmen and Tobin.

Bess, who was tossed violently from side to side in the rear seat, begged Nancy to slow down. "Please don't go so fast! We'll overturn!"

"Sorry," Nancy replied, then grinned. "This time those men are afraid of us. A sure sign of guilt. They don't want us to alert the town cops."

They reached an intersecting highway, and the men drove on to it. They were getting ahead of the girls and it was obvious that they had no intention of obeying the speed limit.

"They're worried about being caught," George said. "On the other hand, I'm sure they wouldn't want to be stopped by the police to show their licences. That would be a dead giveaway."

Nancy did not want to disobey the traffic laws, but how else was she going to catch the two suspects? She gave her car more power and it raced along the highway.

George remarked, "If we could only get close enough to see the licence number, we could report those men to the police instead of chasing them."

Nancy agreed and asked, "Did you notice anything on the licence plate?"

"Only that it was from Connecticut," George answered. "Maybe the car was stolen, and that's one reason why they want to get away in such a hurry."

The words were hardly out of George's mouth, when the girls heard a siren behind them.

"Oh, oh!" Bess said, worried.

Obediently Nancy drove to the side of the road and waited for the police car to pull alongside her. An officer jumped out and walked up to the girls.

"You're going over seventy in a fifty-five mile zone," he grumbled. "What's the idea?"

"We're chasing a car," Nancy said. "But now we've lost it. We believe one of the passengers is wanted by the Navy for going AWOL. His name is Giuseppe Matthews, but he's known under the alias of Matt Carmen or Breck Tobin."

"How do you know about all this?"

"He owns a boat called *The Whisper* and has been harassing us in Biscayne Bay. Yesterday we were at the Naval Office and saw a picture of him. You can check with Captain Smith."

The officer hesitated a moment, then said, "What did the car look like?"

"It was a red sedan with a Connecticut licence plate," George put in.

"All right. I'll take care of the matter and send out an alarm. Since you were trying to do a good deed, I won't give you a ticket this time. But from now on, leave chasing criminals to the police."

Nancy nodded. "It's just that he turned up ahead of us in the downtown traffic," she said.

"I understand. And thanks for the information."

The officer said goodbye and went back to his car. Nancy pulled out on to the highway again and to the surprise of Bess and George did not head home. Instead she went towards the waterfront.

"Where are you going?" Bess asked.

"If the two men were Breck Tobin and Matt Carmen, they're probably headed for *The Whisper*."

"Right. But what makes you think we'll catch up with them? They're way ahead of us by now."

"True. On the other hand, if they suspect we tipped off the police, they may change their minds and not go to their boat. We may be able to find *The Whisper* at a dock," Nancy reasoned.

"Pretty smart," Bess agreed. "Let's go!"

The young sleuths drove as close to the water's edge as they could, then got out of the car and walked. They looked for a red sedan, as well as *The Whisper*. After carefully scanning all the boats and parking areas, without finding either they gave up.

"I'll bet they took the boat and skipped to Crocodile Island," George said. "They probably parked the car in some garage."

"Well, it was a good try," Bess added.

Nancy drove to the Cosgrove house. Their hosts were not there. The telephone was ringing so Nancy answered it. The caller was Colombo.

"Oh, hello," Nancy said. "How are things going for you?"

"Very fine," the young man replied. "I like my

work, and the people at the club are very good to me."

"Have you heard any news from Crocodile Island?"

"Yes, I have," Colombo answered. "A worrisome piece of news. My friend Sol there got a message through to me at the YMCA. He advised me to get out as fast as I could, since Gimler had found out I was staying there and threatened to have me arrested."

"Oh, dear," Nancy said. "I'm sorry to hear you've been tracked down. Have you any idea how Gimler knew?"

"No. But I took Sol's advice and moved out right away. If you have a pencil and paper handy, I'll give you my new address and phone number."

"Good. Hold on just a minute."

When Nancy returned with a note pad, he dictated the information. Then she asked him, "Colombo, did you ever see a submarine near Crocodile Island?"

"A submarine? No. But it's strange you should ask. Sol mentioned once that he'd seen a periscope. But the sub never surfaced while he was watching, so I thought he'd mistaken something else for a periscope."

"Has Sol told you anything else?" Nancy asked.

"Yes. He overheard Gimler say to one of the workmen that he wanted no more visitors on Crocodile Island until he gave the word. He said something like 'People are too inquisitive, and not about crocodiles, either.'"

Nancy thanked Colombo for the information and then said to him, "You'd better be careful."

"I will," he promised.

Nancy reported the conversation to Bess and George, and added, "I have a strong hunch that the crocodile farm is a cover-up for some bigger operation. I wish I knew what it was."

Bess spoke up. "Do you think it involves that big pine box we saw lowered from the freighter?"

"Probably," Nancy replied. "The freighter, *The Whisper*, and the submarine are all part of it, I'm sure."

"If you're right," George said, "what do we do next?"

"Tomorrow, let's see if we can locate the periscope and try to follow the sub," Nancy suggested.

"What!" Bess exclaimed. "If you're going on another wild-goose chase, count me out!"

"Okay," said George, "we'll leave the chicken at home. If you prefer that to a great adventure, you can have it. Nancy, I like your plan. I suppose our going will depend on the tide. When Danny comes home, let's ask him."

Nancy nodded. "Also, we'll have to find out if the *Pirate* has been repaired."

Bess laughed. "I see there's no holding you back. And you know perfectly well I don't want to be thought of as a chicken. We'll all go."

"Thank goodness!" George said. "I was just beginning to think I'd have to put you in a coop."

Bess made a face at her cousin, then she changed the subject. "Here comes Danny. Let's ask him about his boat."

The young man said he was happy to tell them that the *Pirate* was in good running order once more.

"I'll look up the tide table," he said. When he returned, Danny announced that morning would be the best time to go. "Are you game to get up real early?"

"Sure," the girls chorused.

By six-thirty they were seated in the boat. Danny put on full speed and the *Pirate* bounced across the water-covered sand dunes. When they reached the green channel alongside Crocodile Island, Nancy picked up the binoculars and stared ahead.

Suddenly a broad grin appeared on her face. "I see it!" she exclaimed.

In the distance she had discovered the periscope. It seemed to be motionless. The sub evidently was lying in the channel.

Nancy asked Danny to race towards it as fast as he could. They had barely started, however, when the periscope disappeared.

"The sub is taking off!" George exclaimed. "Oh, I hope we can catch it!"

Danny followed the green waterway into the ocean. The elusive periscope had not appeared again, and the young people assumed that the sub was now in deeper water.

"Oh, heavens!" George cried out, using one of her favourite expressions. "Now we've lost it! Where did it go?"

They all knew it was futile to search in the wide expanse of ocean. The only possible way to spot the sub would be from a plane or a helicopter.

"We'd better turn back," Danny suggested. "It's a long way home, and I'm afraid we'll have to run for it to make Biscayne Bay before low tide."

He entered the channel again, putting on full speed. But when he turned into the shallow water beyond Crocodile Island he looked worried.

"Do you think we'll make it?" George asked him.

"I'll do my best," he said grimly.

There was no more conversation as the boat fairly flew on top of the water. Everything went well until they were about halfway home. Danny, who had been turning left and right to avoid the higher dunes, suddenly swerved very hard. He straightened the boat again, but within seconds it rammed into a long sandbank. The motor churned desperately for a moment, then stopped.

The impact had knocked all three girls from their chairs. They flew through the air and landed with a resounding splash in the water!

·15·
Jungle Attack

DRENCHED with seawater and covered with sand, Nancy, Bess, and George stood up alongside the *Pirate*. To Danny's amazement they were not angry. Instead, they started to laugh. George said, "Thanks for the unexpected bath!"

Bess, looking at the boat, remarked, "I guess we'll have to walk home."

"Or wait for high tide," Danny told her. "Instead of waiting, however, you could walk to that key over there and investigate the wildlife. It isn't far from here."

"Does anyone live on it?" Nancy asked.

"No, it's uninhabited."

Bess chose to stay with Danny and dry out in the hot sun, but Nancy and George were interested in seeing the key, so they sloshed through the shallow water to the mangrove-lined island.

When the girls reached it, they scrambled over roots and coral rocks. There was nothing to see but bushes and trees.

"It's a real jungle!" George said.

"I'll say it is," Nancy agreed. "Look over at that mangrove." She pointed.

111

George stared in amazement. A fish was climbing up the bark!

The two girls watched to see how high it would go. To their astonishment it disappeared in the leafy foliage above.

"This place is absolutely spooky!" George muttered.

She had barely finished the sentence when they heard a dog barking.

"There must be somebody on this key besides us," Nancy said. "But let's go on. Maybe we'll see something else unique."

The dog's barks were coming closer, and the girls wondered if he were friendly. If not, both of them would have to scramble up the next tree!

They waited for the animal to come closer. When it did, Nancy gasped. He was an Irish terrier, and on his right forepaw were six toes!

"E-fee!" Nancy cried out, recognizing the animal from Crocodile Island. "How did you get here?"

The dog came up to the girls at once, wagged his tail in delight, and barked in short yaps.

"Is your master around?" Nancy asked apprehensively.

The girls stood still, waiting for someone to appear. But no one did. The dog stayed close by, and acted so glad to see them that they were convinced there were no other human beings on the small key besides themselves.

George asked, "Do you suppose someone from Crocodile Island left E-fee here on purpose?"

Nancy shrugged. "If so, it's a pretty poor way to treat the dog. He couldn't swim back to Crocodile

Island. It's too far from here."

Puzzled, Nancy and George walked on. E-fee bounded ahead of them. Presently he ran to a little clearing and began to bark frantically. The girls hurried to the spot where he was standing.

E-fee looked up at them, gave a few quick barks, then dug furiously into the sandy soil.

"Nancy, he's looking for something," George said. "Maybe his master is buried here!"

"Horror stories again, eh?" Nancy quipped. But she felt apprehensive herself.

E-fee did not stop digging until he had made a good-sized hole. Then he looked at the girls as if to say, "Go ahead. Take a look!"

Nancy and George stepped forward and gazed into the hole. To their amazement a pistol lay inside!

"Where did that come from?" George asked. "Do you suppose E-fee's master put it there, and then went away, leaving the dog to guard it?"

Nancy thought a moment, then said, "It's a good guess, George. Perhaps the men on Crocodile Island didn't want E-fee there anymore because his barks attracted too much attention. Now that the island is closed to the public, I'd say they don't want a dog calling attention to the place if something illegal is going on there."

George got down on her knees and carefully lifted the pistol out of the hole. She examined it and found that the firearm was not loaded, and the serial number on it had been almost obliterated.

"Let's take it along," she suggested. "If nobody owns this island and a person buries a weapon, then it becomes the property of the finder."

Nancy smiled. "I love your logic. We'll take the pistol with us, but we'll turn it over to the police."

The girls filled up the hole, shoving the sandy soil in place with their shoes. Then they went on exploring. Nancy and George watched for anyone who might be on the island. E-fee followed. Since he did not bark, they felt reasonably sure they were alone.

Presently Nancy noticed that there were many twelve-inch lizards running around. Some hid in the undergrowth, but a large number of them were at a fresh-water pond containing hundreds of mosquito larvae. The lizards were eating them greedily.

The girls were so busy watching the fascinating sight that they failed to notice a swarm of mosquitoes coming their way. Suddenly the mosquitoes enveloped Nancy and George, biting furiously! As the girls tried to duck, the insects sang, divebombed, and stung them.

"Oh, dear!" George cried out. "We'd better get away from here fast!"

With E-fee at their heels, the girls ran as quickly as they could. To their dismay the mosquitoes followed!

"This is awful!" George panted. "A real jungle attack. What'll we do?"

"I've heard," Nancy called out, "that the only way to get rid of these pests is to dive into the water."

The two friends hurried towards the spot where they had entered the key. The going was rough. Despite the protection of their shoes they nicked their ankles on coral rocks and tripped on tree roots, which made them wince in pain. The mosquitoes kept buzzing round their heads, necks, arms, and legs, which were fast covered with bites.

The dog had long since outdistanced them and met the girls among the mangroves along the shore. When he saw them dive into the water, which was now deeper, he ran in after them. How good the cool water felt!

Nancy and George swam all the way to the *Pirate*. E-fee followed. When they reached the boat and stood up, Bess exclaimed, "What in the world happened to you, and where did this dog come from?"

Without being invited, E-fee climbed aboard. Nancy said, "He's a visitor from Crocodile Island."

George explained about the jungle attack of mosquitoes, and how they had found the dog.

"Jump in, girls," Danny said. "I have just the thing for you."

He opened the first-aid kit and gave each girl an antihistamine pill, followed by a drink of water. Then he handed them a tube of cream and suggested that they lather themselves with it.

They did this and soon the medication began to take effect, making them feel better.

"What an experience!" Bess said. "Tell us the rest of the story."

"We think someone from Crocodile Island buried a pistol there and then left E-fee behind."

"How did you know that?" Danny asked.

"Here's proof." George said, and pulled the pistol out of her pocket.

"What!" Bess shrank back in surprise. "Where on earth—"

"It was buried on the key," George explained. "E-fee dug it up. Since he knew where it was, we figured he saw his master bury it. We brought the pistol to give to the appropriate authorities."

"Is—is it loaded?" Bess asked, uncomfortable at the thought.

"Relax. It's empty," George said.

Danny asked whether they intended to return the dog to his master. At once George answered, "Not on your life! I'll find a nice home for him."

Danny said he was glad to hear this because he felt it would be unwise to keep the animal at the Cosgrove home. "Some of your enemies might track it down, and then we'll be in trouble. You might be accused of stealing E-fee!"

"I agree," Nancy said. "Do you think we should drop him off at the animal shelter?"

"That's a good idea," Danny replied.

Nancy now asked, "How about those mosquitoes? We have never seen a swarm like that before."

"In Key Biscayne and other inhabited keys they have mosquito control, which takes care of the problem. The insects breed only in deserted little islands like the one you were on. Lizards act as natural balancers."

George remarked, "If they eat that whole swarm, they're sure to have indigestion!"

The others laughed, then Danny said, "Usually mosquitoes are bothersome only during the rainy season. I didn't think you'd encounter any at this time of year."

"All right, we forgive you." George grinned.

"Thanks." Danny now asked, "Do you want to go periscope hunting again or do a little more sightseeing?"

"Neither!" Nancy said quickly. "All I want is a

shower and some more of that soothing lotion."

"I second the motion," George added. "Let's head for home."

After the group docked in Key Biscayne, they brought E-fee to the animal shelter. The girls felt bad about leaving him, but just then a woman and her little girl stopped and asked if they were looking for a home for the dog.

"Yes," Nancy replied.

The child was already patting the dog, whose tail was wagging happily. The little girl looked up. "Mommy, can't we take this one? I love him already."

The woman smiled and said to Nancy, "Is he gentle?"

"Oh, very, and a good watch dog."

The little girl gave E-fee a tremendous hug. Her mother said to the man in charge of the shelter, "We'll take E-fee and give him a good home. By the way, what does his name mean?"

"Dog—in Seminole," Bess answered, and the little girl giggled.

Nancy, Bess, and George left the shelter, happy that E-fee would be living with kind people instead of suspected criminals.

Their next stop was police headquarters, where George turned in the pistol and explained where it had come from. An officer dusted it for fingerprints while they waited, but unfortunately there were none except George's.

"It'll be difficult to trace the owner," the officer told them, "unless we can find a bullet fired from this gun." He thanked the young people for bringing the weapon in. Then they left.

"And now into the tub!" George said gleefully when they reached the Cosgrove home.

"After I take a shower," Nancy said, "I'll be ready for another bit of sleuthing. I'd like to see a submarine. Danny, do you think there might be one in port at the Key West Naval Base?"

"It's possible," he replied. "I don't know if they'll let you go aboard, though."

"We can try. If we tell them about the mysterious periscope at Crocodile Island, they might."

George chuckled. "Of course they will. How could anyone ever say no to Nancy Drew?"

·16·

Exciting Phone Call

AFTER the girls had bathed and changed into fresh clothes, they went into the living-room and told their hosts about the adventure on the uninhabited island.

Mrs Cosgrove was worried about the pistol, but Danny calmed his mother by telling her that they had already delivered it to the police.

Nancy said, "I'd like to learn more about submarines. Mr Cosgrove, do you know someone at the naval base in Key West?"

He nodded. "As usual, you're lucky. It happens that Captain Townsend is an old friend of mine. I'll give you a letter of introduction and if he can spare the time, I'm sure he'll show you around and answer all your questions." He smiled at Nancy. "But don't ask him to tell you any of the secrets of the US Navy!"

Nancy knew she was being teased because of her reputation as a girl sleuth. She smiled back and said, "Maybe I'll find out some secrets without being told!"

Danny called across the room, "I dare you to!"

After breakfast the following morning Mr Cosgrove wrote the letter of introduction to Captain Townsend. "Take this to his house on the base," he said.

Danny asked to be excused from the trip, because of a dentist's appointment, so the three girls drove off by themselves. When they reached the Naval Station at Key West, they were amazed at the immensity of it. Two sailors guarded the entrance gate and asked for the visitors' identification. Nancy pulled out the letter from Mr Cosgrove and showed it to them.

"Go ahead," one of the sailors said. "Take a right turn and at the next street ask someone where Captain Townsend's house is."

They followed the directions and in a few minutes pulled up to an attractive bungalow. Many varieties of flowers were in full bloom in the front yard.

Nancy parked and the girls walked to the door. They were admitted by another sailor, who took them to Captain Townsend's office in his home. Nancy showed him the letter.

"So you're a friend of the Cosgroves?" he asked. "Our families have been very close for many years. Please sit down."

The girls seated themselves in the comfortable wicker furniture. Then the captain asked what he could do for them.

Nancy said she would love to look around the base. "But before that, I want to ask you as important question."

She related the story of having seen a periscope in the green waterway at Crocodile Island. "But each time our boat approaches it, the periscope disappears quickly. Do you know of any sub in that area?"

Captain Townsend shook his head. "No. But let me make a call and see if there's any record of it."

He punched a number into his desk phone and in a few minutes had his answer. "There's no record of any sub plying those waters. Are you sure you didn't mistake a mischievous coot for a periscope?"

"You mean those little black birds that stay underwater with just their long necks and heads showing?"

"Yes."

Up to this point George had not spoken. Now she exclaimed indignantly, "Nancy and the rest of us would certainly know the difference between a coot and a periscope!"

Captain Townsend laughed. "No offence meant. I'm sorry I can't help you."

"Perhaps you can help us with another sub," Nancy said. "I'd like to see one. Are there any in port?"

"You came at a good time," Captain Townsend said. "I'm going off duty just about now, so I'll be glad to give you a personally conducted tour of the base and show you a sub."

"Oh, that's great!" Nancy exclaimed. "Thank you."

The officer stood up and led them outside. "I don't have a car here, so shall we take yours?" he asked Nancy.

"Of course," she said, and handed him the keys.

He climbed behind the wheel and drove the girls up and down the various streets of the base, pointing out office buildings, barracks, recreation centres, and the air station.

Nancy was fascinated by the very high antenna. Captain Townsend said, "From here we can send messages to every part of the world."

"By satellite?" George asked.

"Yes."

They passed the base's hospital and came to an area where helicopters were parked.

"The men who fly these birds are specially trained in anti-submarine work," the captain explained. "They survey suspicious areas and try to spot invading enemy subs."

Bess spoke. "Maybe one of them should make a run over to Crocodile Island."

"I'll see to it," the captain promised. "It would only take a few minutes." Then he teased, "But that periscope you saw had better be there!"

They passed a building where students learned how to read sonar, and another containing advanced undersea weaponry, which was used as a teaching facility for the naval personnel.

"We have a great course here in underwater swimming and diving," the officer stated. "Some of the men later go into deep-sea diving work. You've probably seen pictures of them on television."

All the girls said they had and were fascinated by the sea life the pictures showed.

Bess commented, "But some of those creatures are too dangerous for me!"

The captain laughed. Then Nancy asked if by any chance there was a nuclear submarine in port.

"No, there isn't," he replied. "Just one of the older types. Would you like to go into it and have a look?"

"I'd love to," Nancy replied, and George and Bess wanted to, also.

When they reached it, a sailor standing on the

deck saluted his superior officer. Captain Townsend offered to show the girls the interior.

The hatch was open and he led the way down the iron ladder to the deck below. As the girls gazed ahead, they noticed a long, narrow, centre passageway.

George remarked, "I never saw so many things in such a tiny space. This is like a small apartment with a whole crew living in it!"

"And everything is so neat!" Bess added. "If I could keep my room like this, my mother would be very happy."

Nancy was interested in the crews' quarters. One bunk was perched high above a tremendous black tube. As Captain Townsend saw her eyeing it, he asked, "How would you like to sleep on top of a torpedo?"

"I wouldn't!" she replied.

The "kitchen" intrigued Bess. Every inch of the galley was used, and the equipment, including stove and refrigerator, was so compact that it amazed the visitors. She asked how many men could be served from such small quarters.

"Of course that depends on the size of the sub," the captain replied. "I think this one carries a complement of about thirty men."

As the visitors proceeded, Nancy inquired about the many upright lockers. "What is kept in them?"

Captain Townsend opened one. It was full of coiled rope, most of it hanging on hooks.

Another sailor's locker held work clothes. Nancy could see several M-16 rifles in slots behind the clothing. She wondered why they were on a sub that used only torpedoes. "Perhaps the men carry them when they're on land," she thought.

The officer said that the sub contained a ship-to-shore telephone. "Nancy, would you like to call someone?"

"Oh, yes," she replied. "I'll phone Mr Cosgrove. Maybe you'd like to speak to him."

The captain placed the call and spoke to his old friend, then he handed the instrument to Nancy. Mr Cosgrove said, "An important call came for you."

"Oh!" she said. "From home?"

"No, from your friend Ned Nickerson." Nancy could feel her face reddening. "He and Burt and Dave would like to come down here and see you. Ned said he'd call again for an answer. Mrs Cosgrove and I would be happy to have them stay with us."

Bess and George were excited by the news. It would be such fun to see the boys again!

Captain Townsend said they must leave now as it was time for the crewmen to return and go through a drill.

The visitors climbed topside and went to the car. After the girls had thanked the captain profusely and left him at his home, Nancy drove off.

On the way to the Cosgroves, she said, "I have an idea. How about the boys staying with Mr Gonzales instead of at the Cosgroves'? Gimler and Sacco don't know them, so Ned, Burt, and Dave might pick up some good tips."

The other girls liked the idea, so Nancy drove to Mr Gonzales's club. They all walked inside. The man at the desk recognized Nancy and said, "Miss Boonton, are you looking for Mr Gonzales?"

"Yes, I am," she replied. "Is he here?"

Fortunately Mr Gonzales was there. He came to meet Nancy. She introduced the other girls, then asked him, "How would you like a three-man body-guard?"

Mr Gonzales burst into laughter. "Is it that bad? Have you uncovered some new evidence?"

Nancy explained why she had made the request, and he accepted her suggestion that the three boys stay with him.

"Now that you girls will have some escorts, how would you like to come to the Saturday night dinner-dance here?" Mr Gonzales asked. "The food is always excellent, and the music exactly what you like."

"We'd love to accept," Nancy said.

The man looked at her and teased, "Don't get yourself involved in some fix related to the mystery of Crocodile Island so you can't get here."

"I'll do my best," Nancy promised, grinning.

As she was about to drive out of the club grounds, Nancy saw Colombo. He apparently was headed for a bus. She stopped the car and called to him.

"Would you like a ride into town?" she asked.

"Indeed I would," Colombo replied. "Thank you so much." He opened the door to the rear seat and stepped in. "I'm glad I met you. I just received a phone call from my friend Sol. He wants me to meet him at a garage. He sounded excited."

"He didn't say why?" Nancy asked.

"No. When we get to the garage, why don't you girls wait outside? I'll go in and talk to Sol. He may have some important news from Crocodile Island."

·17·

Deadly Golf Ball

IN a few minutes Colombo brought his friend Sol outside and introduced him. To start a conversation Nancy asked him how he had managed to come to Key Biscayne from Crocodile Island.

The broad-shouldered, dark-skinned man replied, "I begged for a ride with a sightseer who wasn't allowed to land. I waded out into the water and asked him to bring me to town. I was glad he didn't ask me why sightseers were not allowed to see the reptiles that day, so I didn't have to say anything. I hate to go back, but I need the money."

Colombo asked him how he planned to return.

"I'll hire a boat and pilot to take me out there after dark. Meanwhile I want to have a good time here. You know, it's pretty dull in that place."

Colombo said, "I know. Sol, I've told you these girls are detectives. Tell them your latest news."

Sol nodded. "I think you know a good deal already. But if you can solve the latest mystery of Crocodile Island, you'll put Mr Gimler and Mr Sacco to shame. There's no doubt that they're covering up something big."

Nancy asked him if he knew what it was, but Sol

shook his head. "I overheard the bosses bragging about the huge amount of money they were making. I know very well it's not from selling crocodiles to zoos and animal parks."

Colombo suggested that maybe there were some under-the-table sales, which Sol knew nothing about.

"There could be," his friend replied. "But I see the company's books, and I'm sure they report every sale of crocodiles faithfully."

Nancy was puzzled, and asked about *The Whisper*'s comings and going. Sol knew little. "Mr Gimler often goes out in it, but he never says where. Sometimes he brings back food."

Bess remarked that it sounded secretive. "I guess Mr Gimler doesn't want anybody finding out what's going on at the island."

Sol agreed. "By the way, those of us who are still working there are likely to lose our jobs any time."

"Why?" Nancy asked.

Sol said he had overheard the bosses say that they planned to sell out. They were going to offer all their shares of stock to Mr Gonzales or some other people.

"That's strange," Nancy reflected. "Not long ago Mr Gimler and Mr Sacco were offering to buy Mr Gonzales's stock in the Crocodile Ecology Company."

No one had an answer to this puzzle. Sol changed the subject. "Whether I lose my job or not, I'd like to get away from that place. It scares me. I have a feeling that the police are going to find out that something crooked is going on at the island and arrest the top men. Then I'll be called in as a witness. Mr Gimler and Mr Sacco might even tell lies about me and I could be sent to jail!"

Nancy was shocked to hear this. "You mean that the partners are really mean and mad enough to do that?"

"I wouldn't put it past them," Sol replied.

George told him that the girls were only visitors and had very few contacts at Key Biscayne. "But if we ever hear of a job you could fill, we'll let Colombo know."

"Thank you," Sol said. "I'd appreciate it. I don't even like the men I work with out on the island. In fact, I don't trust any of them. If something dishonest is going on, they're probably in league with the bosses."

Nancy said that under the circumstances she was amazed that they had not already discharged Sol. "Unless you haven't given any indication that you're suspicious."

"Oh, I haven't," he told her. "And I don't think the other men have any idea I'm squealing on them."

"That's good," Nancy praised him. "You're sort of playing detective. Keep up the good work and report to us as often as you can."

Sol promised to do so, but said it was becoming more difficult to get away from the island. The few times he had tried it, Gimler had docked his pay.

"That's wicked!" George exclaimed. "Nobody should be expected to stay in one place and work all the time without any recreation!"

After a little more conversation, the girls thanked Sol again and left him and Colombo. As Nancy drove off, Bess asked, "Where to now?"

Nancy said she had a hunch that they should go

back to the golf club and report this latest bit of information to Mr Gonzales. At the desk the girls learned that he was playing golf.

"But he should be back soon," the clerk told them. "Why don't you go out to the porch? From there you can watch him come in on the eighteenth green."

The three friends hurried to the porch and took chairs near the railing. They had a clear view of the green and part of the fairway. Nancy, who played golf well, noticed that there were trees on one side of the fairway just before it ended at the green. "That really makes it hard," she thought. "A person would have to aim a straight shot not to hit those trees."

"Remember that beautiful golf course at the Deer Mountain Hotel, where we solved the mystery of *The Haunted Bridge*?" George asked.

"I sure do," Bess said. "Nancy won a tournament there." She giggled. "Here comes Father Time!"

An elderly man, who was almost as round as he was high and had long white hair and a flowing white beard, putted for the cup, missed it, and made a wry face.

Bess sighed. "This sure is a frustrating game."

"It is," Nancy said. "I've seen people get so mad that they threw their clubs away. Once a fellow almost hit his poor caddy!"

"Here comes Mr Gonzales," George said. "He's a good distance away from the green. I wonder how he'll make out?"

The girls watched in silence as he took his position behind the ball and swung his club in a few practice strokes. Just as he placed the club behind the ball and got ready for his approach shot, another player's ball whizzed from among the trees to his right and hit him hard on the temple. Mr Gonzales dropped his club and fell to the ground, unconscious.

"Oh!" all three girls cried out in horror.

Nancy, Bess, and George expected the other player to emerge from the woods and run up to the victim. But no one did.

"That ball must have been sent on purpose to hit Mr Gonzales!" Nancy exclaimed.

The three girls jumped up and ran towards an outside stairway.

Bess suddenly pointed. "I see somebody running beyond those trees. He's carrying a bag of clubs. He must be the one who shot that ball!"

"Maybe he's a caddy," George added.

Nancy was torn between the desire to hurry after the suspect and the need to help Mr Gonzales. By the time the girls reached the foot of the stairs, they noticed that several people had surrounded their friend. But no one was taking off after the suspect. This helped Nancy decide what to do, although the man was out of sight.

"Let's go!" she said. "We must catch him!"

"Where do you think he'll run?" Bess asked. "To the caddy house?"

"He doesn't seem to be heading in that direction," George replied. "Maybe he isn't a caddy, but a member who is running scared."

Nancy was already racing across another fairway towards a public road. The man with the golf bag suddenly came into view. He looked back and realized he was being chased. Despite the weight of the bag, he put on extra speed. Before the girls could get to him, he reached the road. A car was waiting for him. He jumped in and it roared off.

"Now we'll never know who he is," Bess wailed.

Nancy said she had seen the licence plate and repeated the number to the girls.

"What's more, the glimpse I got of the man makes me think he's the one who spied on us out at the Easton estate!" She added, "Since we can't chase him, let's return to the clubhouse and phone the police."

The girls hurried back and told the manager what they had seen and asked him to call headquarters and give the licence number. He did so, and the sergeant on duty promised to send two officers out at once.

While they were waiting, Nancy asked how Mr Gonzales was. The manager replied, "He's still unconscious, but a doctor is with him. He's in a room down the hall."

Bess decided to go there and see if she could find out anything further. Nancy and George remained in the lobby. When the police officers arrived, the manager introduced them as Parks and Joyce.

"This young lady saw a man with a bag of clubs running away. She'll give you the details," the manager said.

The girl detective described how the suspect had fled in a car, adding that she had managed to see the licence plate. "Headquarters has the number."

"Yes, we know it," Parks said. "Can you tell us anything else about the man?"

"Yes," Nancy replied. "I think he's the same person who was spying on me and my friends while we were watching the crocodiles at the Easton estate. He was peering at us from behind some mangroves, so I caught only a glimpse of his face. He had shoulder-length black hair and beady eyes. He might be part Indian. I'm afraid that's all I can tell you about him."

"That's more than people usually notice," Officer Joyce complimented her. "Thank you for the information."

While he had been talking, Lieutenant Parks picked up the manager's phone and called headquarters. He asked the sergeant on duty to look up the licence number Nancy had given him.

"It's urgent," she heard him say.

They all waited for an answer, which came in a few minutes. When the manager heard the name of the owner, he showed utter astonishment. "That's my name! It's my car! It must have been stolen!"

Immediately he called the parking-lot attendant, who phoned back in a few minutes. "Your car is not here! I didn't notice anyone take it. I'm sorry, sir."

The manager hung up. Just then another phone rang. The call was for the officers. Lieutenant Parks picked up the instrument. He said, "That's good. You say the suspects got away?"

The officer put down the phone and reported to his listeners that a few minutes earlier the car had been found abandoned about five miles from the club.

"In that case," Joyce said, "we'll have to depend on this girl's description to nab the fellow. We're to look for a man with a bag of golf clubs. He has long black hair, beady eyes, and could be part Indian."

While this conversation had been going on, Bess

had been waiting outside the room where Mr Gonzales was for the doctor to appear. In a few minutes he came outside. She asked how the patient was.

"He has regained consciousness," the physician reported, "but has a terrible headache. I've ordered an ambulance to take him to the hospital. No one is to see him, either here or at the hospital."

Bess said thank you, turned, and hurried back to repeat this message to Nancy and George. She heard Lieutenants Parks and Joyce discussing the case. Parks declared that he was sure the suspect would have dumped the golf clubs as soon as possible. As to his being part Indian, there were so many of them around that it would be almost impossible to identify the man they were looking for.

Joyce shrugged. "I guess we're at a dead end on this case."

Nancy spoke. "Maybe not," she said. Then, turning to the manager, she requested, "Will you see if Colombo has returned?"

·18·

Snakes

THE manager, Mr Burley, learned that Colombo was back and sent for him. He asked him to meet Nancy, Bess, and George in the tropical garden.

"Did something happen?" he questioned, when they met and sat down. He looked worried.

"I'll say it did," George replied. "Mr Gonzales was hit on the head with a golf ball, which was deliberately aimed at him. It knocked him out and now he's in the hospital."

Colombo stood up, walked in a circle, and spoke Spanish so fast that the girls could not understand him. Finally he sat down again and said, "That is very bad. Please tell me more about it."

Nancy took up the story, and when she finished describing the attacker, Colombo said, "He sounds like a man named Sam Yunki, who used to be a caddy at this club. Then he worked at Crocodile Island a short time. I don't know where he is now."

"When he was at the island," Nancy asked, "was he one of the workmen who was close to Mr Gimler?"

"Yes, he was. Very close. I'm sure Yunki's the one

who threw the golf ball at Mr Gonzales. He's an excellent shot."

"Did you know him well?" Bess inquired.

"No," Colombo replied. "I was never allowed to be near him."

"That's understandable," George said. "Gimler and his partner wouldn't have wanted you to become a pal of his."

Nancy went into the clubhouse to tell this latest news to Mr Burley. When she told him about Sam Yunki, he said, "I remember hearing about him. He was surly and unco-operative. That is—unless people paid him handsomely or tipped him generously."

Nancy asked Mr Burley if he knew that Yunki had worked at Crocodile Island after leaving the club.

"No, I didn't," he said. "I heard he left here unexpectedly and no one knew where he went, not even the other caddies. Well, I'll notify the police at once."

Nancy rejoined her friends, who said Colombo had already gone back to work. As the three girls walked to the parking lot, George said, "We really picked up a good clue!"

When they reached home, their hostess was smiling. "I have another message for you girls," she said. "Nancy, your friend Ned called again. I invited the three boys to come down as soon as they could. It didn't take them long to make up their minds. They'll be at the Miami airport this afternoon."

Nancy gave the woman a hug. "How sweet of you to invite them! You know we wanted to farm them out as bodyguards for Mr Gonzales, but now he won't need them. He's in the hospital."

"What!" Mrs Cosgrove cried out in alarm.

Nancy and the girls told her about the day's events.

"Oh, I'm so sorry," Mrs Cosgrove said. "I hope Mr Gonzales isn't seriously hurt."

Bess said, "We'll call tomorrow and find out. The doctor said they would need to make some tests."

Nancy, Bess, and George went upstairs to get ready. They gave their hair special attention and put on pretty dresses before going to meet the boys.

Miami airport was crowded, but the girls had no trouble finding the athletes from Emerson College. At once the couples paired off to exchange kisses. Then, while the boys were collecting their baggage and later as they all rode to the Cosgrove home, the girls told them of their adventures to date.

"I'm relieved that you've made such progress in your sleuthing," Ned teased. "We didn't want to come here to join a wild-goose chase."

George said, "I haven't seen any geese around, but there are crocodiles, alligators, snakes, fish that climb trees—"

"Oh, stop your kidding," Burt interrupted.

"You'll see," George told him.

A few minutes later the young people reached the Cosgrove house. After dinner, Dave said, "Danny, what do you think our chances are of getting on to Crocodile Island? I can't wait to see a crocodile. Nancy told us that recently it has been closed to visitors."

Danny offered, nevertheless, to take them all in the boat the following morning and try to land on the key. "It may be open," he added cheerfully.

The seven young people set off early and headed directly to Crocodile Island. Nancy suggested that if visitors were allowed ashore, Ned, Burt, and Dave should go without the girls.

"No one there knows you, so you could look around without making the owners suspicious. Perhaps you can pick up some clues we've missed."

Unfortunately the planned visit did not take place. When they reached the island, prominently displayed signs prohibited visitors. Furthermore, there was no activity around the place.

The lack of activity puzzled Nancy. "I can't understand it," she said. "I wonder if something happened."

Danny shrugged. "If we can't go ashore, we can't find out. Tell you what. Suppose I take you boys to an uninhabited key so you can see exactly what one looks like. The girls haven't seen the island either." He smiled. "I can almost guarantee that you won't find any mosquitoes."

The girls laughed and then told the boys about the jungle attack.

Danny went on to say that the key ahead was reputed to have been a slave hide-out. "I mean an Indian-slave hide-out."

Ned remarked, "We haven't been here twenty-four hours and I've learned a lot I never knew before."

George grinned. "Oh, hadn't you heard? We three girls and Danny are walking encyclopedias! Just ask us anything you want to know about this place."

"Okay," said Burt. "How deep is the water in Biscayne Bay?"

George did not hesitate a second. "It runs from

nothing to approximately twenty feet."

Burt was startled and turned to Danny. "Is she putting us on?"

"No, she's not. George is telling the truth. At low tide some of the sand isn't covered at all. The deep-water channels vary from twelve to thirty feet," he explained.

"Wow!" Burt said. "I never would have guessed. That's interesting."

When they reached the key, Danny stayed in the boat while the others went ashore. As they scrambled over the mangrove roots, the boys seemed to have trouble.

"This stuff is something!" Dave cried out. "I just turned my ankle."

"You have to get used to it," Bess told him. "And make sure you don't turn your whole leg!"

The young people found it difficult to walk across the coral rock, mangrove, and spiny plants, which grew in profusion. About quarter of a mile from shore they spotted a tumble-down thatched-roof hut.

Ned remarked, "I thought Danny said this place was uninhabited."

"I'm sure it is," Nancy said. "No one could possibly live in that cabin."

They all struggled up to the hut and stared. Its roof was sagging and the building, made of mangrove branches, was ready to fall apart.

"I've seen enough," Dave announced. "Now I can be a walking encyclopedia myself on the subjects of mangrove trees and coral rocks."

Bess was about to say something, but screamed instead, "Look out!"

"What's the matter?" George asked her.

Bess continued to scream and pointed at the branches of trees over their heads. Large black snakes were falling from them in profusion!

Everyone ran, and the reptiles missed all of them except Ned. One slimy creature landed on his shoulders and instantly wound itself around the young man's neck.

"Ugh!" he cried out, trying to pull the snake away.

Burt and Dave jumped to help him. Burt grabbed the snake just behind its head, while Dave closed his fingers around the body near the end of the tail.

Bess was still screaming, with the result that all the other snakes scurried off into the underbrush, apparently frightened.

Within seconds Burt and Dave yanked the reptile from Ned's neck and shoulders. They flung it away, and with swift humping motions, the snake crawled out of sight.

"Thanks, fellows," Ned said. "I'm glad that thing didn't fasten its fangs in my throat!"

Bess's continued screaming had brought Danny dashing through the bushes.

"What happened?" he asked.

George told him, and he said, "Don't worry, Ned. Those snakes are harmless. They live in the water part of the time, but come ashore to hunt for food. I guess they climb the trees to sleep and dry off."

Nancy told Danny his passengers were ready to return to the boat. After they had reached it and climbed aboard, the boy pointed out a police launch in the distance.

"I wonder where it's going," he said.

Nancy asked, "Isn't that the direction of Crocodile Island?"

"Yes, it is," he replied. "Want to follow it and see what's happening?"

"You bet," everyone replied.

As they neared the crocodile farm they saw the police launch pull up to the pier. Four officers jumped out and went ashore. Nancy and her friends could hear indistinct voices. They assumed the police were ordering everyone on the island to come out of hiding. When no one appeared, the officers blew whistles. At the same time, the men spread out on the island.

"I wish we could do something to help," Nancy said.

Danny suggested that they go around to the other side of the island and see if any of the suspects were trying to escape in a boat. He put on power and presently the *Pirate* was rounding the tip of the key.

"Look!" George exclaimed. "There's a boat and men are climbing into it!"

Nancy and Bess cried out together, *"The Whisper!"*

"Oh, they're getting away!" Bess wailed. "What'll we do to stop them?"

"We should tell the police!" George declared.

·19·

Triple Sleuthing

"AFTER them!" Burt shouted, and Danny quickly guided the boat towards the fleeing boat.

The Whisper was a more powerful craft, however, and stayed well ahead of them. They followed it through the green waterway and it became smaller and smaller in the distance. By the time they reached the ocean, *The Whisper* was only a tiny dot.

Nancy heaved a sigh. She felt completely defeated. "I was so sure we would close in on those men," she said. "Now they've slipped through our fingers!"

Ned patted her shoulder lightly. "Don't give up," he said kindly. "We're bound to get a break."

George said. "I think the break is coming right now!" She looked into the sky. A helicopter was making its way towards their boat.

"It's a police helicopter!" Burt pointed out.

The helicopter hovered just above them and the young people in the boat could see the officers aboard. They were shouting through a megaphone, but those on the water could not understand a word.

"Too bad we don't have a ship-to-shore or ship-to-ship telephone," Danny said.

The only way Nancy could get a message across to

the men above was to point in the direction *The Whisper* had taken. She made motions with her hands to indicate that it was going very fast. Then she put her finger to her lips, hoping the men might translate it to mean "whisper!"

She could see the pilot bobbing his head and assumed he understood what she meant—that they should follow the suspect boat to the ocean. The 'copter turned and set off in that direction.

Dave spoke up. "Too bad we can't be on hand to witness the capture. I'll bet the men in *The Whisper* put up a real fight."

Bess said, "Well, I for one would just as soon not witness a battle. Let's go back."

The boat returned to Crocodile Island. The police launch was gone, but two officers stood on the dock and invited the young people to come ashore. They introduced themselves as Patman and Fifer.

"Aren't you Danny Cosgrove and these girls detectives?"

"Yes."

"We've made some arrests," Patman reported. "For one, we caught the man named Yunki."

"Oh, the one who hit Mr Gonzales with a golf ball?" Bess cried out.

"Yes." Putnam said they had found him hiding among some bushes. He had readily confessed to hitting the deadly shot towards Gonzales. But Yunki also said that he had not done it of his own accord. Gimler and Sacco had hired him to do not only this but several other illegal jobs. Yunki was well paid for his dastardly work."

"Where is he now?" Ned asked.

Patman told him that the police launch had taken away Yunki and all the other workers, who admitted helping Gimler and Sacco in some illegal secret work. However, they would not say what it was. Two of the men had escaped.

"It's important that we catch them. They're the ones who made phone calls and acted as spies whenever necessary."

"As far as we know, they are still on the island. They are Gimler and Sacco's special henchmen named Stryker and Jackson. Unfortunately for them they were not quick enough to follow Gimler on *The Whisper*, which set off in a hurry when you people showed up at the key."

Nancy asked if Gimler had gone off with Matt Carmen and Breck Tobin. Patman nodded. "Yunki told us that. We sent word for a police helicopter to go out and intercept the craft."

The listening group also learned that the fake Mr and Mrs Cosgrove and their daughter, who had posed as Miss Boonton, had been arrested. They were part of the Gimler-Sacco gang. The weapon E-fee dug up belonged to Sacco, who buried it so the police would not find it if they visited Crocodile Island. He left the dog on the deserted key because E-fee had almost bitten one of the men on *The Whisper*, whose cruelty he hated.

Nancy looked at the police officers and asked, "Did I understand you to say that you think two of the workmen are still on the island?"

"Yes. A couple of Sacco's special buddies, and bad, both of them. They have records."

"Where did they go?" Nancy asked.

"We don't know," Patman replied. He walked off to join his fellow officer in another hunt.

Nancy said to her friends, "Why don't we start a search?"

"Great idea!" Ned agreed.

The others were eager to begin but Bess was cautious. "Maybe the men are armed. If so, we're walking into danger!"

Ned hurried off to ask the officers about the firearms. Patman replied, "According to Yunki they were not armed— didn't have time to go for any. I doubt that you'd be in any danger if you want to look around. Fifer and I must stay within sight of the beach until the launch returns. It took all the captives to jail."

Nancy had followed Ned and was alarmed at its import. She asked quickly. "Was one of the prisoners a man named Sol?"

Patman pulled a pad from his pocket and consulted it. "I have the list of prisoners here. There's no one named Sol on it."

"I'm glad," Nancy said, "that he's not with Gimler and Sacco. We've talked to him. He's very nice. Probably he didn't come back to the island after being in Key Biscayne."

Nancy and Ned returned to their friends. She suggested that they separate into couples and make their search on the island some distance from one another. "We'll be couple one, George and Burt, two; and Bess and Dave, three. In case of trouble call out your numbers instead of your names.

"And, Danny, how about your going round the island in the boat? If you see anyone or anything suspicious, sound your horn."

"Okay," he agreed.

The three couples started off on their search. Bess and Dave stopped for a few minutes to look at the crocodiles, and Bess remarked, "If all the workers are gone, who's going to take care of these reptiles?"

Dave grinned. "How would you like the job?"

Instead of answering, Bess made a face at him.

Just then one of the old male crocodiles grunted, then hissed, and opened its jaws wide. Within seconds he closed them with such a resounding snap that the couple jumped.

Bess and Dave waited no longer. They took off for a copse of mangroves to start their hunt for the missing suspects.

Meanwhile, Burt and George tramped through a jungle area, looking up into the trees, behind bushes, and on the ground. They stopped every few minutes to listen, but everything was quiet and there was no sign anywhere of the wanted men.

They came to a low coral cave and stopped. "Isn't that attractive?" George whispered. "I wonder if those men are hiding inside."

"I'll look," Burt said.

"No! They might trap you and attack!"

"I'll be careful. Just follow me, but wait when I get to the entrance."

The two advanced without making a sound. Slowly they neared the entrance. Then Burt picked up a stone and threw it inside. There was no reaction from within.

He cautiously peered around the rocky opening and saw the small interior. The walls were jagged and arranged in a moon-shaped pattern, but there was no cement or any other indication that the cave was man-made.

"It's empty," Burt reported. "Anyway, it's not much of a hiding place."

George looked inside. "Isn't that coral fascinating?" she said. "Think of the millions of tiny polyps climbing up and dying to form layer after layer of coral."

"Yes," Burt said. "But don't get sidetracked. Never mind the coral now. Let's look for those missing men."

The couple went deeper into the jungle. Rabbits and raccoons scurried away from them. Suddenly the stillness was broken by a loud noise. Something was crashing through the underbrush ahead of them. George wondered if it was an animal. Then they heard human voices.

"They may be the suspects!" Burt whispered. "Come on!"

All this time Nancy and Ned were searching along the waterfront, thinking the men might have hidden a second boat among the mangroves and would try to reach it. Suddenly Nancy stopped short.

"Look!" she said, pointing to a periscope out in the green waterway.

"It's moving in the direction of the island!" Ned said, excited. "Maybe it'll dock here!"

"Let's return to the pier," Nancy suggested.

She and Ned quickly made their way back, careful to remain shielded by trees at all times. Just before they reached the open areas, the submarine surfaced! It slid in noiselessly. The hatch opened, and two men appeared. They jumped to the dock and disappeared in the direction of the main building.

Nancy and Ned wondered if the men were aware of the recent events on the island. Obviously they were not worried about being seen. Or were they just desperate?

Nancy decided on a bold move. "Ned, are you game to go aboard and hide?"

"Sure thing."

"Wait just a second," Nancy said. She plucked a leaf from a trailing sea-grape bush. Next she picked up a small sturdy stick and scratched out the words, "Going aboard. Couple one."

She jabbed the leaf on to a tree twig and beckoned Ned to follow her. Quickly the two went to the open hatch and climbed down the iron ladder.

"Where can we hide?" Ned asked, looking around.

Nancy pointed to the upright lockers and opened one. It contained a coiled rope similar to the one she had seen on the sub in Key West.

Ned checked the adjoining locker. Behind some clothes, many boxes were stacked neatly from the floor to the ceiling. Each one was stamped *High Speed Cameras. Bridgeport, Ct.*

"That's a lot of cameras for a few guys," Ned remarked.

"Right," Nancy said, now suspicious. "Open the next locker."

Ned did, and found similar boxes concealed behind raingear. Further search revealed guns, grenades, and explosives in each locker! Ned shook his head in disbelief, and Nancy's eyes were wide with amazement.

"Ned!" she exclaimed. "Now I know what the secret of Crocodile Island is! Gimler and Sacco are taking expensive high-speed cameras out of the US. They're smuggling them to someplace, maybe Mexico!"

As the two hurried back to the ladder, Ned put a hand on Nancy's shoulder. "You're right. And this means we're in great danger. We'd better get out of here before—"

Just then they heard voices. Two men were conversing rapidly and walking towards Nancy and Ned. The couple, who did not want to be seen, quickly went into the first two lockers. Nancy hid behind coiled ropes. Ned managed to squeeze in behind the raingear and stood next to the boxes of cameras.

They left the doors slightly ajar so they could see who was coming. The two men they had seen leave the sub, re-entered it. Quickly one of them turned a handle, which slowly closed the hatch. The other man rotated a wheel that retracted the periscope. Then he started the engine and the sub moved away.

Nancy and Ned held their breath, wondering what would happen next. The man at the wheel suddenly laughed. He said confidently, "We pulled that one off all right. No more bothering with Gimler and Sacco! Next stop Mexico!

·20·

Submarine Prisoners

"MEXICO!" Nancy thought.

She and Ned were terrified when they realized that they were being taken out of the country with no chance to call for help. They tried to keep calm and figure out some way to outwit these men.

The prisoners listened attentively when the men resumed their conversation. One said, "I had no idea when we went into shipping stolen cameras with Gimler and Sacco that we could make so much money. I don't know why we ever bothered with the small amount we got out of the Crocodile Ecology Company."

The other man said, "You forget, Williams, that we needed a cover. I'd say we just got out of there in time. That nosey girl detective and her friends are just too smart."

In spite of their predicament, Nancy and Ned smiled at this remark.

Williams said, "Nothing to worry about now, Captain Frederick. We're rid of the bunch."

The men talked about what they were going to do with all the money they had made.

Frederick said, "I'll show those relatives of mine in

149

Mexico what I can do, even if they thought I was a no-good." He laughed raucously. "How easy the whole operation was! We stole a lot of cameras from the factory in Connecticut and bought a whole lot of others cheap on the black market. And sold them at a three hundred per cent profit."

Nancy and Ned almost suffocated in the lockers but did not dare miss a word. They learned that the cameras were shipped out at night to a freighter going south. Then they were transferred to *The Whisper*, which carried them to the submarine. Then *The Whisper* returned to the key, which was home base. Whenever the submarine came there, the periscope would be hoisted. If any visitors were on the island, an alarm would be sounded and the sightseers sent away.

Williams said, "It's too bad we couldn't fill that order for five hundred cameras. If the buyer in Mexico had only given us a little more time, we wouldn't have had any trouble."

The men were silent for a while, then Williams said, "We won't be tying up for some time. I think I'll put away this rope we're not using. It's in the way."

He stepped to the locker in which Nancy was hiding and yanked open the door. The girl detective tried to slump to the floor so she would not be seen, but it was impossible.

Upon spotting her, Williams cried out a volume of expletives. He reached in roughly, grabbed Nancy's arm, and pulled her out into the passageway.

The captain also exclaimed and then said to Nancy, "How did you get here?"

She did not answer.

"I said, how did you come aboard this sub?" the captain demanded.

Still Nancy made no reply.

"I'll make you answer!" Frederick cried out, exasperated, and grabbed hold of her with both arms. He was so strong that she thought he would crush her ribs.

At this second a voice said, "Let her alone!"

Ned!

The sub's captain let go of Nancy and stared at the young man. "Who are you?"

Ned said nothing. By this time Williams and Frederick were jabbering loudly and arguing about what they should do with their stowaways.

"We can't take them into Mexico!" Williams said.

"You're right," the captain agreed. "What do you suggest? That we go topside, open the hatch, and push them out into the water?"

Ned spoke up. "You'd better not do that," he said, then decided to try a bluff. "Did you know that we're being followed by helicopters?"

The men looked stunned. Williams rushed to raise the periscope above the water. After turning it in various directions, he said, "I don't see any helicopter."

The captain, angry, yelled at Ned, "You were just trying to bluff us. Well, we're not going to fall for it."

After a pause Williams said, "I have an idea, Captain. We both like money. Why don't we hold these two snoopers for ransom?"

Captain Frederick thought this over and finally agreed it was not a bad idea. "Just how can we work it?" he wondered.

"I'll think of something," his fellow officer said. "Give me time."

Nancy and Ned were glad of the temporary reprieve. Their thoughts went back to Crocodile Island. Where were the rest of their friends? Had they found Nancy's note? If so, had they done anything about it?

All this time the two couples had been very busy. George and Burt had finally startled Stryker and Jackson, who were hiding in the jungle. They managed to corner them, then talked to the men from a distance.

"It's no use to try getting away," George called. "All the others on this island have left. They didn't even wait to take you along. Now you have nothing. They have the money and won't dare come back here because of the police. In fact, there are policemen on the island now, hunting for you."

"What?" Stryker exclaimed, then gave a sneering smile. "You're trying to trick us!"

Burt spoke up. "It's no trick. You don't have a chance."

The couple continued to coax the men to come out of hiding, but several more minutes went by before they consented to do so. Burt told them to walk ahead. He and George would follow.

All the way to the pier on the other side of the island the couple was very watchful in case the men should try to get away. Apparently the fugitives felt beaten because they did not attempt to run or fight.

When the two captives saw the officers on the pier, they knew Burt and George had been telling the truth. The captives raised no objection when they were placed under arrest.

Some time before this, Bess and Dave, having found no trace of the suspects, had started back towards the pier. As they were making their way along the waterfront, Bess grabbed Dave's arm.

"Look! There are Nancy and Ned! Nancy is writing something on a leaf."

The couple were too far away to distinguish what it might be, but started to run forward as fast as they could over the mangrove roots.

When they reached the note, Bess and Dave read it quickly. *Going aboard. Couple one.*

"Going aboard what?" Dave asked.

He and Bess ran faster. A few moments later they saw Nancy and Ned hurry across the pier.

Bess exclaimed, "There's the sub! Oh my goodness, they're climbing down inside! We must stop them!"

Before the couple could get near enough to shout to their friends, they saw two men dash from the main building and get on to the submarine. Quickly they descended and closed the hatch. The ship submerged and took off.

Bess was in tears. "Oh, Dave, what's going to happen now to Nancy and Ned?"

Dave wasted no time in conversation. "Where's the office?"

"I'll show you," Bess said and the two sped off to the little building.

The door was open. Dave looked around for what he wanted to use, then began to send a radio message to the Coast Guard. In as few words as possible, he described what had taken place on Crocodile Island.

Within seconds a return message was received. Two Coast Guard cutters would be sent out at once. One would go directly to Crocodile Island. The other would go after the submarine.

"We will also send out two helicopters. Try to have someone tell them which direction the sub and the speedboat took," the Coast Guard operator said.

About this time the two policemen who had gone into the jungle returned. They were amazed to hear what had happened and thanked Dave for sending out the alarm. The officer had hardly finished speaking when they saw the two suspects being ushered into the area by George and Burt.

Patman and his companion looked astounded. "You caught them?"

George could not help quipping, "Yes, and with no guns!"

The officers gave the two prisoners a long look, then advised them of their rights to seek legal counsel. The two men exchanged worried glances but did not answer.

"Where does the sub go?" Patman asked. No reply.

Bess felt that treating the men gruffly was accomplishing nothing. She tried a softer, more kindly approach.

Smiling at them she said, "What about your families? Surely you care for them and would like to get back to them as soon as possible. You can't hide out forever."

One prisoner stared at her. "Are you some kind of preacher?" he asked. "You sure talk like one. But what you say makes good sense. I'll tell what I know after Gimler and Sacco are caught. They ran out on us, so I won't mind squealing."

Just then the group heard a motor and turned to see the police launch coming. After it docked and the two prisoners were taken aboard, the officer in charge, Lieutenant Royce, said, "*The Whisper* was spotted and the Coast Guard picked up Gimler, Sacco, Carmen, and Tobin."

"Great!" said George. "But what about the submarine? Two of our friends are prisoners on it."

"A 'copter and two Coast Guard revenue cutters are after it," he replied. "They got directions from Danny Cosgrove. He followed *The Whisper* in the *Pirate*. The speedboat got away, but he spotted the sub as it came out the channel. Danny made hand signals to the 'copter. I'll see what else I can find out."

He leaped ashore and went at once to the office. In a few minutes he was back.

"Good news," the officer said. "Your friends are safe and are on their way back. The smugglers have been arrested. They wouldn't talk, but Nancy Drew and Nick Nickerson told their story for them, and for Gimler and Sacco. The freighter's captain is also in custody."

"Wonderful! Wonderful!" Bess cried out and the whole group clapped. Bess, George, Burt, and Dave hugged one another in their exuberance.

Lieutenant Royce smiled as he boarded the launch and said, "Nancy, Ned, and Danny will meet you at the Cosgroves. A 'copter will pick you all up. Goodbye!" He waved and gave orders to shove off.

In a short time the helicopter landed and soon Nancy's friends were back in Key Biscayne. There was a joyful reunion, and an exchange of stories far into the night.

Of course, Nancy, though happy at the successful outcome of the mystery, hoped another would soon come her way.

The following afternoon she and her friends went to see Mr Gonzales in his hospital room. He was sitting up and declared he felt much better. "But let's not talk about me," he said, after Nancy introduced the others. "Tell me everything."

After he had heard all the details and thanked the young sleuths, Nancy said, "There's one question I have. When you told us not to come down here, was it because you were intimidated by Gimler and Sacco?"

"Yes," he admitted. "I see now why they didn't want you to investigate them." He smiled. "But I'm mighty glad you came. Thank you all for your superb work. And now," Mr Gonzales said, "I have a surprise for you. I have taken over ownership of Crocodile Island. I want you to greet the new manager and his assistant."

He waved towards the corridor. Through the doorway walked two smiling young men—Colombo and Sol! Nancy and the others cheered softly and congratulated them.

"Thank you," said Colombo. "And now Sol and I must get back to feed our pets, the crocodiles of Crocodile Island."

The Secret of Red Gate Farm

First published in a single volume in hardback in 1989 by
William Collins Sons & Co Ltd.
First published in paperback in Armada

· 1 ·

A Strange Fragrance

"That Oriental-looking clerk in the perfume shop certainly acted mysterious," Bess Marvin declared, as she and her two friends ended their shopping trip and hurried down the street to the railroad station.

"Yes," Nancy Drew answered thoughtfully. "I wonder why she didn't want you to buy that bottle of Blue Jade?"

"The price would have discouraged me," spoke up Bess's cousin, dark-haired George Fayne. Her boyish name fitted her slim build and straightforward, breezy manner. "Twenty dollars an ounce!"

Blonde, pretty Bess, who had a love for feminine luxuries, laughed. "I *was* extravagant, but I just couldn't resist such yummy perfume. After all, Dad gave me money to buy something frivolous, so I did!"

Nancy by this time was some distance ahead. "Hurry, girls, or we'll miss the next train to River Heights!" In her active life the attractive, titian-haired young sleuth had learned that being on time was important.

The three eighteen-year-old girls continued their

frantic pace until the railroad station finally came into view.

Once at the station, they set down their packages to rest their arms. "Whew!" Bess sighed, looking at her watch. "I didn't think we'd make it, but we have two minutes to spare. And this would be one of July's hottest days!"

Nancy was pensive, still contemplating their encounter with the mysterious woman in the Oriental perfume shop. She had realized the Blue Jade was much too expensive, and the unwillingness of the young woman to part with it had stimulated her interest. Instinct had told Nancy that there must be some special reason why the saleswoman had been so reluctant to sell the Blue Jade.

Then another idea struck her. "You know," she said aloud, "it's possible that saleswoman deliberately raised the price of the perfume."

George frowned. "But why? You'd think she'd be thrilled to make such a good sale."

"Yes," Nancy agreed. "That's what perplexes me. There's something very strange about it and I'd certainly like to know what it is!"

"Oh, Nancy," teased George, "there you go again, dreaming up another mystery!"

Nancy's blue eyes sparkled as she thought of the prospect. The young sleuth had already solved serveral mysteries, some of them for her father, Carson Drew, a famous criminal lawyer. Among the cases on which Nancy had worked were *The Secret in the Old Clock* and *The Secret of Shadow Ranch*.

The girls heard the train approaching the station.

As it came to a halt they quickly gathered up their packages and hurried aboard.

"What a day!" Bess exclaimed as she pushed on through the cars. The train was crowded, and the girls walked through several cars before they found any vacant seats.

George and Bess began discussing their many purchases. Bess gloated in particular over the bottle of exotic perfume. Even though the package was wrapped, it gave off a slight fragrance which was very pleasant.

George took a quick inventory of their purchases, then laughed. "Bess, it's a good thing we got you to leave that last department store or you wouldn't have had enough money left to buy your ticket home," she stated bluntly. "You should practise self-control, the way I do."

"Self-control!" Bess retorted. "I suppose you call a new hat, two dresses, three pairs of stockings, and a handbag self-control!"

George mustered a smile and decided to drop the subject.

Nancy leaned her head back against the cushion, and as she relaxed, studied the faces of the nearby passengers. She thought that the thin, sweet-looking girl who occupied the seat just opposite looked very tired, worried, and even ill. Nancy judged the girl to be her own age.

"Why are you so quiet, Nancy?" Bess demanded suddenly.

"Just resting," Nancy returned.

She did not tell her friends that she had become

interested in the nearby passenger, for George and Bess often teased her about her habit of scrutinizing strange faces. However, it was Nancy's lively interest in people that was largely responsible for involving her in unusual adventures, and she was always on the alert for a new mystery.

Bess eyed her perfume package longingly and finally ripped off the paper. "I can't stand it any longer." She sighed. "I must try some of this delicious-smelling stuff!" She opened the bottle and dabbed a couple of drops behind each ear. Then she offered it to George. "Try some. It's really lovely – makes me think I'm in the mystic Orient."

George could not keep from making a face. "No *thank* you!" she replied firmly. "It's not my type!"

Nancy and Bess laughed. Then Bess offered some to Nancy, who accepted willingly. Bess again took out the stopper and was leaning over to put some perfume on Nancy when the train lurched and jogged her arm.

"Oh!" Bess cried in horror. The perfume sprayed over Nancy, as the bottle fell to the floor.

"Such a waste of money!" George muttered as she picked up the half-empty container.

"What a shame!" Nancy exclaimed. "It's your perfume, Bess, and now I have a lot of it on me."

Bess groaned. "I should've waited till I was home to open the bottle. I'm lucky there's some left!" Carefully she placed the small vial in her handbag.

By now the concentrated odour of Blue Jade had permeated the car, and passengers in nearby seats flung open the windows.

"I'm glad we're getting off at the next stop." Nancy giggled. "Everyone is laughing at us."

Nancy had become so engrossed with the spilled perfume that she had forgotten about the pale young woman who occupied the opposite seat. Now, as Nancy turned her head, she was startled to see that the girl had slumped down in a dejected heap.

"She's fainted!" Nancy exclaimed, moving quickly across the aisle.

She shook the girl gently, but there was no response from the frail figure.

"Bess! Ask if there is a doctor in the car!" Nancy cried urgently.

By this time other passengers in the car were aware that something had happened, and were crowding about, asking unnecessary questions and getting in the way. Nancy politely asked them to move back.

There did not appear to be a doctor in the coach, but as Nancy rubbed the girl's wrists, she was relieved to see that she was showing signs of recovering consciousness.

George quickly raised the window so that the fresh air fanned the girl's face. Leaning against the seat, she looked deathly pale.

"What can I do?" George asked.

"Stay here while I get some water," Nancy answered. "She's coming around now. I think she'll be all right in a few minutes."

Nancy hurried to the water cooler at the far end of the car. As she was trying to fill the paper cup, a man who had been standing near the doorway came toward her. He made a pretence of waiting his turn to get a drink, yet she realized by the intent look on his face that something had startled him. He was deliberately studying her! Was it because of the perfume? She fairly reeked with it!

Nancy was not prepared, however, for what came next. The man edged closer to her, glanced quickly about to see that no one was close by, and muttered in a guttural tone:

"Any word from the Chief?"

Nancy was taken completely by surprise. She knew she had never seen the man before, for she would not have forgotten such a cruel face. His steel-grey eyes bored straight into her. Nancy was so bewildered she could think of nothing to say.

The stranger realized at once that he had made a mistake. "Excuse me, miss. My error," he murmured, starting for the car ahead. "But that perfume – Well, never mind!"

· 2 ·

Mysterious Numbers

Nancy stared after the stranger and wondered what he could have meant.

"Evidently he mistook me for somebody else," she thought. "But even so, his actions certainly were peculiar."

What message had he expected to receive from her? Who was the Chief? How strange that the man should speak of the perfume as though it had been the cause of his mistake!

If Nancy's mind had not been occupied with the frail girl's condition, she might have wondered more over the strange encounter. She dismissed it for the moment. Quickly filling a cup with ice water, she rushed back to George and Bess, who were giving first aid to the girl.

"Do you feel better now?" Nancy asked. "Here, drink this."

"Thank you," the girl murmured, gratefully taking the cup. "I feel much better now," she added quietly. "It was very kind of you to help me."

"It must have been the perfume that made you faint," George declared. "A little is all right, but half a bottle is overpowering."

"I'm sure it wasn't the perfume," the girl returned quickly. "I haven't felt well since I first boarded the train early this morning."

"What a shame," Bess said. "I'll get you some more water." She soon returned with a second cup.

"By the way, Nancy" – Bess turned to her friend – "who was that man who spoke to you at the water cooler?"

"You noticed him?" Nancy asked, surprised.

"Yes," Bess said, "but I didn't recognize him."

"Nor did I," Nancy remarked. "The whole thing was quite mysterious. He simply approached me and said: 'Any word from the Chief?'"

"The Chief!" Bess and George chorused. "What Chief?"

"I have no idea," the young sleuth admitted. "But evidently it was this strange perfume that attracted his attention, or so he said."

"I wonder what the perfume could have to do with it?" Bess looked perplexed.

By this time the train was slowing down as it approached the River Heights station and Nancy and her friends realized they must hurry or they would miss their stop.

"I'm afraid that we must interrupt this conversation and say good-bye," Nancy told the girl reluctantly. "We get off at River Heights."

"River Heights!" The girl glanced anxiously out the window. "I get off here too! I had no idea we were so close."

"We'll help you," Nancy offered. "Do you really feel well enough to walk?"

"Yes, I'm all right now."

George and Bess collected the miscellaneous packages, while Nancy helped the stranger along the aisle. The girl hesitated uncertainly as she stepped from the train.

"I'm not very familiar with River Heights," she said to Nancy. "Which direction should I take to go to the centre of town?"

"You're still too shaky to walk any distance," George spoke up. "Have you no friend here to meet you?"

The girl shook her head.

"Then why don't you come home for a snack with us?" Nancy suggested. "I left my car parked here by the station, and I can drive you back."

The girl started to protest, but Nancy and the others urged her on, and soon they were all settled in Nancy's blue convertible.

"I haven't even told you my name," the strange girl said, leaning back wearily. "I'm Joanne Byrd. I live with my grandmother at Red Gate Farm about ten miles from Round Valley. That's where I took the train."

Nancy introduced herself and her friends as she started the car and headed it toward the Drew residence in another section of the city.

"How nice it must be to live on a farm!" Bess remarked. "And Red Gate is such a pleasant-sounding name."

"Red Gate *is* a lovely place," Joanne said feelingly. "I've lived there with my grandmother ever since I can remember. We don't have the money, though, to keep up the farm. That's why I left home today – to find work here."

"Do you have something in mind?" Bess questioned.

"I came in response to a particular advertisement," Joanne replied, but did not say what it was. A faraway look came into her eyes. "We simply must raise enough money to pay the longstanding interest due on the mortgage of our farm or Gram will lose it."

"Surely no one would be mean enough to take over your farm," Bess murmured sympathetically.

"A bank holds the mortgage. It has no choice. Gram knows very little about money matters, so she takes anyone's advice. Years ago she was advised to buy another farm and sell it at a high price. All at once values crashed and she couldn't meet the payments on her extra farm, so it went back to the original owners. Then she had to put a heavy mortgage on Red Gate, too, and if she loses that, she'll be penniless."

As Joanne finished her story, Nancy turned the car into the Drews' driveway.

"Come in, everybody," she invited. "Perhaps we can think of a way to help Joanne."

The three girls followed Nancy into the house, where they were greeted by the Drews' pleasant housekeeper. Hannah Gruen had been like a mother to Nancy ever since the death of Mrs Drew when Nancy was a child. Nancy asked Hannah to make some sandwiches for them all, then led the girls to the living room.

"You must be nearly starved," Nancy said to Joanne a moment later. "I know I am."

"I am rather hungry," Joanne confessed. "I haven't had anything to eat since last night."

"What!" the other girls chorused.

"It was my own fault," Joanne said hastily. "I was too excited this morning to think about food."

"It's no wonder you fainted," Nancy said. "I'll ask Hannah to fix you something hot."

Nancy returned from the kitchen with a tray of appetizing sandwiches and a bowl of soup. Joanne ate heartily. Nancy and her friends joined in, for they had had only a light snack while on their shopping expedition.

"I do feel better," Joanne announced when she had finished. "It was so good of you to bring me here."

"Not at all," Nancy said softly. "We'd like to help you all we can."

"Thank you, but I believe everything will work out all right if only I get this position." Joanne glanced anxiously at the clock. "I'll really have to go now or I'll be too late to make the call this afternoon. Could you tell me how to get to this address?"

She handed a folded scrap of newspaper to Nancy. "This particular ad for an office girl caught my eye since it asks for someone who has had experience on a farm."

Nancy found the advertisement to be rather conventional, but it was the name at the bottom of the paragraph that held her attention.

"Why, this ad says Riverside Heights!" she exclaimed. "You should have stayed on the train until the next stop!"

"I thought Riverside Heights and River Heights were the same place!" Joanne Byrd cried in distressed surprise.

"Riverside Heights is only a few miles away," Nancy explained, "and the names are confusing even to people who live near here, so it's a natural mistake."

"Oh, dear, I don't know what to do now," Joanne said anxiously. "If I don't apply for that position this afternoon, I'll probably lose my chance of getting it."

Nancy had taken a liking to the girl and wanted to help her. Not only was Joanne half sick from lack of food, but she had worked herself into a nervous state.

"You must let me drive you to Riverside Heights," Nancy insisted. "It'll only take fifteen minutes and you'll have plenty of time to apply for the position."

Joanne's face brightened instantly, but she was reluctant to accept the favour. "I've really troubled you enough."

"Nonsense! We'll start right away!" Nancy turned to Bess and George. "Want to come along?"

Bess and George both declined, since they were expected home. The cousins gathered up their packages and all the girls went to the car. Nancy dropped Bess and George at their own homes, then took the highway leading to the next city.

"I do hope I get there in time," Joanne said worriedly. "The job will mean so much to Gram and me!"

"You'll get there," Nancy assured her. "Have you ever applied for a job before?"

"No. I've always helped Gram run the farm until now," Joanne explained. "I felt I was more needed there than anywhere else. We keep a farm hand, but a great deal of the work still falls upon me."

The girls soon reached Riverside Heights, and Nancy had no trouble finding the address mentioned in the advertisement. It was in a run-down section of the city, but Nancy did not mention this to her companion.

"Here we are," Nancy said cheerfully, stopping the car in front of a dingy-looking office building.

Joanne made no move to get out of the car, but sat nervously pressing her hands together.

"I'm a terrible coward," she confessed. "I don't know what in the world to say when I go in. I wish you'd come with me."

"I'll be glad to," said Nancy, as she turned off the ignition and locked the car. They entered the building. There was no elevator, so the girls climbed the dimly lighted stairway to the third floor. Soon they came to Room 305, which had been mentioned in the advertisement.

"There's no name on the door," Nancy observed, "but this must be the right place."

As they stepped into the reception room, Nancy noted that it was dirty and drab. The two girls glanced at each other, exchanging expressions of disappointment.

At that moment a man came from the inner office and surveyed the girls sharply. He was tall and wiry, with hostile, penetrating eyes and harsh features. His suit was bold in pattern and colour, and his necktie was gaudy.

"Well?" he demanded coldly.

Joanne found sufficient courage to take the advertisement from her pocket.

"I – I saw this in the paper," she stammered. "I came to apply for the position."

The man stared at Joanne critically, then at Nancy.

"You lookin' for the job too?" he asked.

Nancy shook her head. "No. I'm here with my friend."

The man looked at Joanne again and said with a shrug of his shoulders, "Go on in the other room. I'll talk to you in a minute."

Joanne cast Nancy a doubtful glance and obediently stepped into the inner office.

"Look here," the man addressed Nancy, "wouldn't you like that job? I could use a good-lookin' girl like you."

"I'm not looking for work, thank you," Nancy returned aloofly.

The man was about to make a retort when the telephone rang. He scowled and went over to the table to answer it. As he lifted the receiver he looked nervously back toward Nancy.

"Hello," he growled into the phone. "This is Al. Shoot!"

Nancy listened to his end of the unbusinesslike conversation and watched him reach for paper and pencil and begin to scribble down a line of figures. This in itself would not have seemed so peculiar, except that he continued to eye Nancy suspiciously.

He kept on copying figures. All the while Nancy watched him curiously.

"OK, Hank," he muttered just before he hung up. "You say you've found a girl? . . . Fine! We can't be too careful in this business!"

All this time Nancy was wondering what kind of transactions went on in this office. There had been no indication on the door of what business the man was engaged in and nothing in the room gave her any clue. She realized now that Joanne's chances of getting the position were slim, and Nancy was actually relieved. She was very suspicious of the whole setup.

"I was just taking down some stock-market quotations," the man remarked lightly as he crossed the room toward Nancy.

"This isn't an investment house, is it?" she asked.

"No, you wouldn't call it that exactly," he answered with a smirk. "We run a manufacturing business."

"I see," Nancy murmured, though she really did not understand at all. "What do you manufacture?"

The man pretended not to hear and moved on to the inner office where Joanne was waiting. In haste to escape further questions, he forgot to pick up the sheet of paper with the numbers on it.

Nancy was curious about the telephone conversation and could not resist the temptation to take a peek at the notation. She stepped silently over to the telephone table and glanced at the sheet. Strung out across the top and bottom of the page were numbers. The top row read:

$$16\overline{5}3 \; 112 \; 129 \; 156\overline{2} \; 16 \; 882 \; 091 \; 56\underline{18}$$

"Stock quotations, like fun!" Nancy told herself. "Why did he lie about it? He must have been afraid I'd discover something!" As usual, Nancy was intrigued at any hint of a mystery. She studied the row of odd figures. Suddenly it dawned on her that they might be a message in code!

Nancy looked quickly toward the inner office. The door was open, but the man sat with his back toward her. She did not dare pick up the paper. If only there was enough time to copy the code!

With one eye on the office, Nancy took a sheet of paper and frantically scribbled the numbers, carefully keeping them in their right order. She could hear Joanne's soft voice, then her prospective employer talking loudly, and realized the interview was coming to an end.

She had copied only the top row of numbers, but dared not spend any more time at it. She put the copy into her bag and slipped back into her chair just a moment before Joanne and the man emerged from the inner room. He glanced toward the tele-

phone, gave a start, and rushed across the room.
With a muttered exclamation he grabbed the paper
and thrust it into his pocket.

Nancy's heart was beating madly as she forced
herself to remain outwardly calm. He stood with a
cold look on his face, his eyes fixed on Nancy.

·3·
Work on a Code

Had the man heard her rush from the telephone table? Nancy wondered. Was he suspicious of her actions during his absence? If so, what reason did he have and what business deal was he hiding in this dingy excuse for an office? Nancy pretended not to notice his penetrating, questioning eyes, but she was ill at ease.

The hostile man spoke up. "You girls better get out of here!" he blurted. "I got no more time to waste. And don't bother to come back!"

Nancy and Joanne looked hastily at each other and moved toward the door. Once outside the building, Nancy breathed a sigh of relief and turned toward Joanne, who was close to tears.

"Don't feel bad because you didn't get the job," Nancy said gently as they walked to the car. "You wouldn't have wanted it, I'm sure."

"That man was detestable!" Joanne shuddered. "I had just given my name and address when he started to shout. You must have heard him."

Nancy nodded. "I think he had already found another girl to work for him," she said. "At least I heard him say something like that over the phone."

"I knew I wouldn't get the job." Joanne sighed dejectedly. "He told me I wasn't the type!"

"I'd count my blessings if I were you," said Nancy soberly. "There's something strange going on in that office and I'd like to know what it is."

"Why, what do you mean?" Joanne asked quizzically.

"Well," Nancy began carefully, "I'm not sure my suspicions are just, but I have a hunch there's something shady about the telephone message he got when you were in the inner office." Nancy explained about the series of numbers on the sheet of paper and how she suspected they might form some sort of code.

"At any rate," Nancy went on, "we can't be sure of anything, so this must remain confidential."

Joanne nodded and fell silent.

Many thoughts raced through Nancy's mind as she remembered the day's encounters. First there had been the perfume shop and its mysterious saleswoman, then the curious man on the train who had been attracted by the strange fragrance. And now, this crude, gruff man in Room 305!

"What should I do now?" Joanne asked forlornly. "I can't go back to Red Gate Farm and let Gram down. I simply must find work!"

"Why not come home with me?" Nancy suggested as they paused beside her car. "I'll be glad to have you as my guest for the night, and in the morning you'll feel better and can decide what to do then."

Joanne shook her head proudly. "Thank you, but

I wouldn't think of letting you go to any more trouble. I have a little money. I can find a boardinghouse and I'll keep on looking for work here."

Nancy saw that Joanne was disappointed and discouraged and hated to leave her on her own, but finally conceded. "I guess you're right," she admitted. "But at least let me help you hunt for a place to stay." Joanne accepted the offer gratefully.

Even with the car, it was difficult to locate a pleasant room. Joanne could not afford a high-priced place, and the cheaper ones were unsatisfactory. Finally, however, they found a suitable room on a quiet street and Nancy helped Joanne get settled.

"I may be driving over this way tomorrow," she said. "If I do, I'll stop in to see what luck you've had."

"I wish you would," Joanne invited shyly. "I'll need someone to bolster my morale."

"All right, I will," Nancy promised.

After a few words of encouragement she said good-bye, then drove slowly toward River Heights, her mind again focused on the various events of the day.

"I don't know what will happen to Joanne if she doesn't find work," Nancy told herself. "It would be a shame if her grandmother loses Red Gate Farm. I wish I could do something, but I don't know of any available jobs."

It was nearly dinnertime when Nancy reached River Heights. As she passed the Fayne home, she saw George and her cousin Bess on the front lawn and stopped to tell them about Joanne's unsuccessful interview.

"Isn't that too bad?" Bess murmured in disappointment. "She seems such a sweet girl. I'd like to know her better."

"I promised I'd drive over to see her tomorrow," Nancy told the girls. "Why don't you come along?"

"Let's!" George cried enthusiastically. "I love going places with you. We always seem to find some sort of adventure!"

Nancy's blue eyes became serious. "I'd say this has been a pretty full day! I can't seem to forget that mysterious saleswoman in the Oriental perfume shop or the strange man on the train. I wasn't going to say anything to you about this, but something odd happened this afternoon in that office."

Nancy then related the mysterious actions and behaviour of the man named "Al."

"You mean you think his telephone conversation was a little on the shady side?" Bess asked, wide-eyed.

"It seemed that way to me," Nancy answered. "I doubt very much that it's a manufacturing business and those numbers I copied from his pad were anything but stock-market quotations!"

"Well, here we go again! Never a dull moment with Nancy around!" George laughed gaily.

"Don't be too impatient, George," Nancy advised with a grin. "We don't have proof that any of today's incidents is really cause for suspicion."

At this moment a foreign-make car went by. Nancy glanced casually at the driver, then gave a start. He was the man who had spoken to her on the train!

He slowed down and stared at the three girls and at the Fayne home. Nancy felt at once that he was memorizing the address. He gave a self-satisfied smile and drove on. Nancy noted his licence number.

"I almost feel as if I'll hear from him again," she told herself, then revealed to the girls, who had not noticed the car's driver, that he was the man who had confronted her on the train.

"He's still interested in you," Bess teased.

But George found nothing to laugh about. "I don't like this, Nancy," she said seriously. "I remember he had a hard, calculating face."

Nancy, too, remained serious. A disturbing thought had suddenly occurred to her.

"Why," she told herself, "that man must have been trailing me. But I wonder for what reason?"

She determined, for the moment at least, not to mention her suspicions aloud and dropped the subject of the mysterious man. Presently she bade Bess and George good-bye, climbed into her convertible, and drove home.

"I think I'll ask Dad what he thinks about that man Al's mysterious telephone message," Nancy decided as she hopped from the car.

She had often taken some of her puzzling problems to her father. He, in turn, frequently discussed his law cases with his daughter and found Nancy's suggestions practical.

"You look tired, dear," Carson Drew observed

as she entered the living room and sank into a comfortable chair. "Have a big day shopping?"

"I can't remember when so much ever happened to me in one day." Nancy smiled despite her fatigue.

"I suppose I'll be getting the bills in a few days," her father remarked teasingly.

"It wasn't just the shopping, Dad," Nancy returned gravely.

Nancy now plunged into the story of the Oriental shop and the dropped perfume bottle, of her encounter with the stranger on the train, and the strange fact of having seen him a short while ago in a foreign-make car.

"What do you make of it?" she questioned.

Mr Drew shrugged. "What did he look like?"

"The man seemed very polite, but he had a cruel look in his eyes." Nancy gave a brief description of him.

"Hm," Mr Drew mused, "I can't say I like the sound of this."

"I wouldn't wonder about it," said Nancy, "except that the girl in the shop seemed so reluctant to sell the perfume. Why do you suppose she cared whether someone bought it?"

"Maybe she was instructed to save it for special customers," Mr Drew suggested.

"Dad, you may have something there!" Nancy exclaimed.

She told her father about Joanne Byrd and described the office which they had visited together.

She ended by showing him the figures which she had copied.

"This was almost all of the message," she explained. "I didn't have time to copy the rest. Can you figure it out?"

Carson Drew studied the sheet of paper. "I'm not an expert on codes," he said finally, "but I suspect this might be one, since the man lied in saying these figures are market quotations."

"Can you decipher it?" Nancy asked eagerly.

"I wish I could, but it looks like a complicated one. It would probably take me days to figure out what these numbers stand for. Why don't you work on it yourself?"

"I don't know too much about codes," Nancy declared, "but perhaps I can learn!"

"I have a book you might use," her father offered. "It may not help much, since every code is different. Still, all codes have some features in common. For instance, in any language certain words are repeated more frequently than others. If you can figure out a frequency table, then look for certain numbers to appear more often than others, you may get somewhere."

"I'd like to try," Nancy said eagerly.

"This will be a good test for your sleuthing mind," her father said teasingly. "If you don't figure out the code, you can always turn this paper over to an expert."

"Not until I've had a fighting chance at it myself," Nancy answered with spirit.

"I'd really like to help you with this mystery,"

her father said, "but I'm so tied up with this Clifton case I just can't tackle anything else right now."

Immediately after dinner Mr Drew retired to his second-floor study to work on his law case. Nancy went to her bedroom to read the book on codes. When she finished, the girl detective took out the sheet on which she had copied the numbers and studied the figures intently.

"I'm sure the numbers stand for letters of the alphabet," Nancy told herself. "They must have been arranged in some pattern."

For over two hours Nancy tried combination after combination and applied it to the code. Nothing showed up until she hit upon the plan of four letters of the alphabet in sequence by number, the next four in reverse. Alternating in this manner and leaving two in the end bracket, Nancy scrutinized what she had worked out:

A	B	C	D	E	F	G	H	I	J	K	L	M
1	2	3	4	8	7	6	5	9	10	11	12	16

N	O	P	Q	R	S	T	U	V	W	X	Y	Z
15	14	13	17	18	19	20	24	23	22	21	25	26

"I've hit it!" she thought excitedly.

· 4 ·

A Switch in Jobs

16$\overline{5}$3 112 129 156$\overline{2}$ 16 882 091 56<u>18</u>
 C a l   l i   ng   m ee   ti   ng

The numbers with the marks above or below
them stymied Nancy completely. Most of the others
fell neatly into place and spelled:

"Calling meeting," Nancy repeated. "But where?
And by whom?" She yawned, weary from her long
concentration. "My brain's too fogged to figure out
anything more," she told herself. "I'll tackle this
another time."

The next morning Nancy and her father enjoyed
a leisurely breakfast. He praised her for hitting
upon the key to the code but agreed that solving
the rest of it would be difficult.

"Keep at it," he advised smiling fondly at his
daughter. "By the way, I won't be home to lunch
or dinner today because of this Clifton case."

"I thought I'd visit Joanne and try to cheer her
up," Nancy said. "Do you, by any chance, know
anyone who's looking for an office girl?" she added.

Mr Drew shook his head. "No. I'm afraid I
don't. But if I hear of anything I'll let you know."

186

"I feel that Joanne isn't the type to be in the hectic business world," Nancy remarked. "If it weren't that she wants to help her grandmother, I doubt that she'd even try for a city position."

After Carson Drew had left for his office, Nancy busied herself around the house, helping Hannah. When the housework was finally done, Nancy settled herself in an easy chair and delved into the code book once more. But she found no new hints to help break her own set of numbers.

Nancy, Bess, and George had planned to start for Riverside Heights early in the afternoon, so as soon as the luncheon dishes had been cleared away, Nancy was off to pick up the other girls. By two-thirty they had reached Joanne's rooming house.

The landlady answered Nancy's knock on the front door and informed her that Joanne had left two hours before to see about a job. She would be back at three o'clock. The woman invited the girls in, but the living room looked so dark and dreary that they preferred to wait outside in the car.

"It's too bad Joanne has to stay in a dismal place like that," Nancy remarked, "especially when she's accustomed to farm life."

"I sure hope she finds something," Bess added. "Maybe luck will be with her today."

Within fifteen minutes the girls spotted Joanne at a distance. She did not notice the car, and unaware that she was being observed, walked slowly toward the rooming house, her head drooping dejectedly.

"She didn't get the job," George murmured. "I feel so sorry for her."

As Joanne approached, Nancy called to her. Joanne glanced up quickly and mustered a smile.

"No luck today?" Bess questioned.

"None at all," Joanne answered with a sigh. She came over to the car and stood leaning against the door. "I tried half a dozen places, but I couldn't land a thing. I'll just have to try again tomorrow."

In the face of such spirit on Joanne's part, the girls could do nothing but encourage her, though secretly they feared she would have no better luck the next day.

"How about coming for a short ride?" Nancy invited.

"I'd love it," Joanne accepted eagerly. "It's so hot and stuffy in my room – " She hesitated, then added, "Of course, I guess it is everywhere these days!"

Nancy took a road that led out of the city and soon they were driving past cultivated fields of corn and wheat. Gradually, Joanne became more cheerful.

"It's so good to be out in the country again!" she declared, gazing wistfully toward a farmhouse nestled in the rolling hills. "That place looks something like Red Gate Farm, only not half so attractive. I wish you all could visit me there sometime!"

"So do we!" Nancy said enthusiastically. "Wouldn't it be wonderful to hike over hills and breathe in the fresh clean air?"

"I've always wanted to spend a vacation on a

farm," Bess declared longingly. "Just imagine having cream an inch thick!"

"Just what you need for reducing!" her cousin teased her.

"You wouldn't have to worry about that." Joanne smiled. "We keep only one cow."

When the girls later left Joanne at the door of her boardinghouse, they had the satisfaction of knowing she was in a more cheerful frame of mind.

"We'll keep in touch with you, Joanne," Nancy promised as they said good-bye.

"I have a feeling we'll be seeing a lot more of each other," Joanne called after them. "So please do call me Jo! I'd much prefer it."

"Jo it is!" they agreed merrily. "Good-bye for now."

Nancy and her friends had just started back to River Heights when Nancy checked her gas gauge and decided to stop at a filling station. The girls were idly watching passers-by when suddenly a young woman, walking with mincing steps because of her extremely high heels, attracted Nancy's attention. Nancy gasped in recognition.

There was no mistaking the distinctive Oriental features. The clerk in the perfume shop!

Nancy turned to her companions. "Look at that girl who just crossed over. Isn't she the same one who sold you the perfume, Bess?"

"You mean the one who tried *not* to sell me the perfume, don't you?" Bess joked. "Yes, she's the same girl!"

Their eyes followed the girl up the street. She had not glanced toward them, but had passed the filling station and continued on.

"Now, what can she be doing here?" Nancy wondered. She got out of the car and stood watching the girl, who entered an office building a short distance farther up the street.

"That's funny," Nancy said to her friends, who were peering from the car windows. "I think that's the very place where Jo applied for a position!"

"You don't suppose that perfume girl has two jobs, do you?" George questioned.

"I'd sure like to find out," the young detective answered.

Just then the attendant approached. Nancy paid him and stepped back into the car.

"We must try to follow her," she declared, starting the motor. They pulled up near the office building into which the young woman had disappeared.

"You two wait here and keep watch," Nancy said. "If I'm not back in a few minutes, you'd better come and see what's going on."

"Aye, aye, sir!" George said mockingly. "We're at your service! But be careful!"

Nancy alighted, hurried up the street, and went into the building. The halls were deserted. Evidently the girl had gone into one of the offices. But which one? As Nancy stood uncertainly staring up and down, she spotted a handyman coming down the corridor.

"Did you see a girl come into the building just a moment ago?" she inquired.

"Oriental?" the man demanded, resting on his broom.

Nancy nodded eagerly. "Yes, she looks rather Oriental."

"Oh, you mean Yvonne Wong."

"Do you know her?" Nancy said, thinking that with the name Yvonne, the girl was probably part French.

"No, but I heard that man she works for, with the loud voice and the swell clothes, call her by that name."

"She works here?" Nancy inquired in surprise.

"Guess so. She must be a new girl. Came here yesterday."

"I see," Nancy murmured, thinking Yvonne Wong had managed a rather sudden change of jobs. "Could you tell me in which office she works?"

Her questions evidently had begun to annoy the handyman. "In 305. If you're so interested," he said brusquely, "why don't you go in and ask her what you want to know?"

"Thank you," Nancy responded with a polite smile, turning away. "I won't trouble you any further."

Nancy had taken only a few steps when she thought of one more question and came back. "By the way," she said in a casual tone, "what sort of office is 305?"

The man regarded her suspiciously. "How should I know?" he demanded bluntly. "They don't pay me to go stickin' my nose in other folks' business. I got my own work."

Nancy could see that she was not going to learn any more from the man, so she left the building and joined Bess and George, who were waiting anxiously at the door.

"Well, what did you manage to find out?" Bess queried, as the three girls walked toward the car.

"Quite a bit," Nancy answered meditatively. She was certain that she could not have been mistaken. Yvonne Wong was the same girl who only yesterday had waited on them in the Oriental shop. Why had she changed positions?

"Well," George broke into her thoughts, "don't keep us in suspense!"

Nancy answered all their questions as she drove toward River Heights, explaining that the young woman's name was Yvonne Wong and that she was a new girl in the office – the same office Nancy and Joanne had visited.

"But what about Yvonne's job at the Oriental perfume shop?" asked George.

"I don't know," Nancy admitted, "and the handyman wouldn't give me any indication as to the type of business it was!"

Nancy recalled the strange telephone call which had been made while she and Joanne were in the office. She distinctly remembered that some mention had been made of a girl who had been found for the position, and that the man who called himself "Al" had said that one "couldn't be too careful."

"I wouldn't be so suspicious about Yvonne," Nancy added, "except I have a feeling she didn't get that job by chance. She must have been chosen because she was especially suited to the situation – whatever that is."

"There's something underhanded about the whole thing, but we haven't much to go on," Bess declared.

Nancy agreed. "Some clue may turn up. Anyway, we have Jo to think about for the time being."

It was getting dark as Nancy dropped off Bess and then George at their homes.

It rained so hard the following day that Nancy stayed indoors and tried to figure out the remaining symbols of the code. Using the same alphabetical key, 16 was M, $\bar{5}$ equalled H, $\hat{2}$ could be B, and 18 stood for R.

"MHBR," Nancy pondered. "That doesn't make any sense. Perhaps those marks over and under the letters are a second code," she reasoned. "If only I could decipher *them*, I might know who's calling what meeting, and where."

The next morning a bright sun shone. While Nancy was busy with chores around the house, the phone rang and she went to answer it.

"Hello, Nancy," said a quiet voice. "This is Jo. How are you?"

"Oh, Jo, I'm fine," Nancy replied eagerly. "Did you find a job?" she asked hopefully.

"Not yet," Joanne answered sadly. "But I have some other news."

"I hope it's good," Nancy said.

"I just talked with my grandmother on the phone. I must go home right away. She told me that soon after I left, a man called and made an offer to buy Red Gate. His price was so low, she didn't accept. He was very persistent, though, and gave her five days to think it over."

"Yes?" Nancy prompted.

"Well," the other girl went on, "in the meantime, Grandmother decided to try raising money by taking in boarders. She placed an ad in the paper that same day."

"Good for her!" Nancy exclaimed. "Has she had any replies?"

"No," Joanne said worriedly. "Even though the ad hasn't run very long, Gram's discouraged. I'm afraid she has changed her mind and intends to take that man's offer. She said he's coming to Red Gate tomorrow at five o'clock and bringing papers for her to sign."

There was a pause, then Joanne burst out, "Nancy, I just can't let Gram go through with this, and if I'm not there, she'll accept the man's offer. She mustn't give up Red Gate Farm yet! That's why I must get home and persuade her not to sell."

"By all means," Nancy agreed. "I suppose you'll take the train to Round Valley in the morning?"

"That's the horrible part, Nancy," Joanne said dejectedly. "I'll have only enough money for train fare half the way after I pay my room rent."

"No need to do that, Jo," Nancy said eagerly. "You get your bag packed and be ready to leave at ten o'clock tomorrow morning!"

· 5 ·

Money, Money!

As Nancy reflected on her plan, another idea occurred to her. She was sure that Bess and George would love the chance to spend a vacation on a farm, since they had both mentioned it the other day. Nancy did some mental arithmetic and came to the conclusion that three steady boarders who paid their bills regularly might help to lessen the amount of the mortgage interest payments that threatened Red Gate.

"And also keep Mrs Byrd from selling the place," Nancy thought. "I hope Dad agrees to my making the trip."

That evening at dinner Mr Drew said, "I'll be out of town for a week or so, Nancy. Do you think you can get some of your friends to stay with you?"

"I have an even better idea," Nancy replied, and smiled.

She outlined her plan to help Joanne Byrd. Her father consented enthusiastically, proud as always of Nancy's desire to assist others.

It was not so easy to convince Bess and George, when Nancy telephoned them. They both wanted to help Joanne and agreed that a week or two in the country would be very pleasant, but there were complications. If George went, it meant she would lose out on a camping trip. Bess had planned to visit an aunt in Chicago, but admitted that the trip could be postponed.

"There's one thing about it," George said laughingly as she finally agreed to give up the camping trip. "I've never been with you yet that we didn't run into an adventure or mystery! Maybe a trip to Red Gate will be exciting."

Bess and George had no trouble in getting their parents' consent. It was decided that Nancy would pick up Joanne first, then come back for the cousins, since River Heights was on the way to Round Valley.

Nancy packed her clothes that night after telephoning the plans to Joanne. As she was closing the suitcase, her eyes fell upon the copy of the coded message which lay on the dressing table.

"I'd better take it along and work on it whenever I have the chance," she decided.

Nancy got up early the next morning and had breakfast with her father. After exchanging fond good-byes with him and Hannah, she hurried to her car.

It was close to ten o'clock when Nancy reached Riverside Heights. She stopped at a downtown service station and had her convertible filled with gas and checked for oil. Then she drove to Joanne's boardinghouse.

Her passenger was waiting. Nancy was glad to find that Joanne seemed to be in better spirits.

"It'll be such fun, all of us going together,"
Joanne said, "and I know Gram will be happy to
have you stay as long as you like."

"Only on the condition that we are paying
guests," Nancy insisted.

"We'll see about that later," Joanne said,
smiling.

They put her suitcase into the trunk of the car
and soon were on their way back to River Heights.
Assured by Joanne that they would be welcome at
Red Gate, the cousins brought out their suitcases
and put them in the luggage compartment.

George took Nancy aside and said excitedly, "A
little while ago a man phoned here and asked for
Miss Fayne. When I answered, he said, "Listen,
miss, tell that snoopy friend of yours to *stop* her
snooping, or she'll be sorry!" Then he hung up
without giving his name."

Nancy set her jaw, then smiled. "Whoever he is,
he has a guilty conscience. So my suspicions were
well founded."

"Who *do* you think he is?" George asked.

"Either the strange man on the train who followed me here, or some accomplice of his."

"I'm glad for your sake we're going away,
Nancy," stated George.

"Let's not say anything about this to Jo," Nancy
advised, as she and George walked back to the car.

"It's a perfect day for our trip to the country,"
Joanne said excitedly.

George could see by the expression on Joanne's
face that a visit to Red Gate Farm with her new

friends was far more important to her than any other plans the girls might have had.

"I agree one hundred per cent!" George answered happily as she stepped into the car.

"And I'll be so glad to get out of this heat," Bess chimed in with a sigh. "I spent practically the whole night dreaming about the cool, refreshing breezes in the country."

As Nancy steered the convertible in the direction of Round Valley, she said with an eager smile, "We're off to rescue Red Gate Farm!"

Nancy and her friends thoroughly enjoyed the scenic route to Round Valley. They stopped for a quick lunch and then continued their drive. The winding roads led through cool groves and skirted sparkling little lakes. Each hilltop brought a different and beautiful view.

Gradually the worried expression completely left Joanne's eyes, and colour came into her thin face. She began to laugh heartily at the antics of Bess and George. As they rode along she told the girls a great deal about her home.

"You'll like Red Gate, I'm sure," she said enthusiastically. "We haven't any riding horses, but there will be plenty of other things to do. We can explore the cave, for one thing."

"Cave?" Bess questioned with interest. "How exciting! What kind is it? A home for bears or a pirate's den?"

Joanne laughed. "There's a large cavern located on the farm. No one knows how it came to be there, but we think it must have been made a long time ago by an underground river."

"You must have explored it before this!" Nancy exclaimed.

"Oh, yes, of course, though I'll admit I never did very thoroughly, and I haven't been near the cave for years. As a child I was always afraid of the place – it looked so dark and gloomy. Lately I've been too busy working around the farm."

"We'll have to put that at the top of our list!" George declared. "I love spooky things."

"Well, I'm not so sure *I* do," Bess admitted

Nancy laughed. "We may even find hidden treasure in the walls."

"I wish you could." Joanne sighed. "It certainly would come in handy."

The hours passed quickly as the travellers alternately sang and chatted. "Why, it's almost four o'clock!" George announced in surprise.

"We've made good time," Nancy remarked.

Bess spoke up plaintively. "I'm half-starved. It's been *ages* since lunch. I could go for a gooey sundae."

The others laughed, but agreed they were hungry too.

"Let's watch for a roadside stand," Nancy proposed. "I'll have to stop soon for gas, anyway."

"We'll come to one soon," Joanne spoke up. "We're in Round Valley now."

A few minutes later she pointed out a combination filling station and lunchroom which looked clean and inviting. Nancy turned the convertible into the driveway and parked out of the way of other drivers who might want to stop for gasoline.

The group entered the lunchroom and took seats at one of the small white tables. They all decided on chocolate nut sundaes topped with whipped cream.

"Here goes another pound." Bess sighed as she gave her order. "But I'd rather be pleasantly plump than give up sundaes!"

Though there were few customers in the room, the woman in charge, who also did the serving, was extremely slow in filling the orders. Twice Nancy glanced at her watch.

"If you'll excuse me," she said, "I'll step outside and get the gasoline. It will save us a little time in getting started. Don't wait for me if our sundaes come."

She drove the car over to the pump and asked the attendant to fill the tank. Before he could do so, however, a large, high-powered sedan pulled up to the other pump, coming to an abrupt stop almost parallel to Nancy's car.

"Give me five and make it snappy!" a voice called out impatiently.

The attendant glanced inquiringly at Nancy Drew. "Do you mind?" he asked.

"Wait on them first if you like," she said graciously.

Nancy observed the passengers with interest. There were three rather coarse-looking men, accompanied by a woman.

Nancy could not see the face of the driver, for it was turned away from her. But suddenly he opened the door of his car.

"I'm goin' inside and get a couple bottles of ginger ale," she heard him grumble to his companions.

As he stepped from the automobile and turned, Nancy saw his face. He was the mysterious man who had spoken to her that day on the train!

In view of the telephone call George had received, Nancy did not wish to be observed. She turned her head quickly, leaned down, and pretended to be studying a road map. "I hope he doesn't recognize me!" Nancy thought. "Or see my licence plate!"

To her relief, the man walked in front of the convertible without a sideward glance. At that moment the woman alighted and walked toward the lunchroom, passing close to Nancy's car. She was tall and slender, with blonde hair that was almost shoulder length. Nancy's attention was suddenly arrested when she detected on the stranger a familiar scent — Blue Jade perfume!

After the driver and the blonde woman had entered the lunchroom, Nancy gazed at the two men who remained in the automobile. They were the sort Carson Drew would describe as "tough customers."

The blonde woman soon reappeared and got back into the sedan. Then the driver came out carrying the cold drinks. Without looking in Nancy's direction, he addressed the attendant harshly.

"Say, ain't you finished yet?"

He turned to one of the men in the car and handed him the bottles of ginger ale.

"Hold these, will you, Hank? I got to pay this bird!"

Nancy started. "That man in Room 305 called one of his friends 'Hank' over the telephone," she said to herself. "Could he be this person?"

Her attention was drawn back to the driver, who was paying the attendant. He took a thick roll of bills from his pocket, and with a careless gesture peeled off a ten-dollar bill.

"Aren't you afraid to carry such a wad around, sir?" the attendant questioned, gazing admiringly at the thick roll.

The driver laughed boisterously. "Plenty more where this comes from. Eh, Hank?"

"You bet! My roll makes his look like a flat tyre! Just feast your eyes on this!" He flashed an even larger roll of bills in the amazed attendant's face.

The filling-station man shrugged. "I'll have to go inside to get your change."

The moment he had disappeared, the third man in the car muttered to his companions, "You fools! Do you want to make him suspicious? Pipe down!" He spoke in a low tone but the wind carried his voice in Nancy's direction.

"Maurice is right," the driver admitted. "The fellow is only a cornball, but we can't be too careful."

The attendant returned with the change. The driver pocketed it and drove off without another word. Nancy instinctively noted the licence number of the car. On impulse she went to a phone booth and dialled her friend Chief McGinnis of the River Heights Police Department.

"I'll ask him to let me know who owns both the sedan and the foreign-make car that slowed down at George's house," she determined. "Then I'll find out about the driver, the woman wearing the Blue Jade, the men named Maurice and Hank, and maybe the man in Room 305!"

·6·
A Worrisome Journey

"Some class, eh?" the attendant remarked to Nancy as she came back to her car. "Must be millionaires."

"Or racketeers," Nancy thought. As soon as her gas tank was filled, she paid the bill and hurried back into the lunchroom. The girls already had been served.

"What took you so long?" Bess asked.

"Another car drove up and I had to wait," Nancy answered simply. She sat down, thoughtfully eating her sundae.

"What's the matter with you?" George demanded presently. "You've hardly said a word since you sat down."

Nancy looked around and saw that no one was seated near their table. In whispers she told what had happened.

"Oh, dear," said Bess, "maybe that man on the train found out where we're going and is on his way there too!"

"Don't be silly," George chided her cousin. "If he's in some shady deal around River Heights, he'd be glad to have our young sleuth out of the way."

Joanne looked a bit worried, but all she said was, "I think we'd better be on our way. I *have* to be there before that man comes to buy the farm. I must talk Gram out of it!"

The girls finished the sundaes and picked up their checks, but Nancy insisted upon paying.

"I want to break this twenty-dollar bill Dad gave me," she said. "I've spent most of my smaller bills."

The waitress changed the bill for her without comment and the girls left the lunchroom. As they climbed into the car, Nancy glanced anxiously at the sky. There was a dark overcast in the west.

"It does look like rain over my way," Joanne observed. "And we leave the paved road and take a dirt one about five miles from the farm."

"I'm afraid it's going to be a race against time," Nancy warned, starting the car. "A bad storm on a dirt road won't help matters at all!"

The girls now noticed a change in the countryside. The hills had become steeper and the valleys deeper. The farms dotting the landscape were very attractive.

Nancy made fast time, for she was bent on beating the storm. The sky became gloomier and overcast. Soon the first raindrops appeared on the windshield. "We're in for a downpour all right!" Nancy declared grimly, as she turned on to the dirt road.

Soon there was thunder and lightning, and the rain came down in torrents.

"Listen to that wind!" Bess exclaimed. "It's enough to blow us off the road!"

The next minute everyone groaned in dismay, and Nancy braked the car. Across the road stood a wooden blockade. On it was a sign:

DETOUR
BRIDGE UNDER REPAIR

George read it aloud in disgust. An arrow on the sign indicated a narrow road to the right. As Nancy made the turn, Joanne gave a sigh.

"Oh, dear," she said, "this back way will take us much longer to reach Red Gate."

The detour led through a woodland of tall trees. Daylight had been blotted out entirely, and even with the car's headlights on full, Nancy could barely see ahead. Again she was forced to slow down.

Suddenly a jagged streak of lightning hit a big oak a short distance from the car. It splintered the tree.

"Oh!" screamed Bess. "This is terrible!"

Nancy pretended to be calm, but she really was very much worried. She decided it would be safer to get away from the dangerous line of trees, any one of which might crash down on them!

"How long is this stretch of woods?" she asked Joanne.

"Oh, perhaps five hundred feet."

"We'll have to chance it." Nancy drove as quickly as she dared in the darkness. The girls breathed sighs of relief when open country was reached.

But Joanne's fears were not yet over. "Watch out!" she advised. "There's a sharp, treacherous curve very soon, just before we take the turnoff for the farm."

By now the brief storm had moved off to a distant sky and it was easier to see the boundaries of the slippery road. Nancy rounded a curve, but as the car took the turn, the wheels on the right side sank into the thick mud of a ditch, bringing the car to a lurching halt.

The unexpected mishap stunned the girls for a moment. Finally Bess found her voice. "Now what?"

Nancy endeavoured to drive the car out of the ditch, but it was useless. "Well" – she sighed – "we may as well jump out and examine the car. Keep your fingers crossed."

They found the convertible at a lopsided angle. The right wheels, however, were firmly anchored by the mud. The four girls attempted to push the car, but without success.

"I'll look in the trunk," Nancy said, "to see if there's something to help us."

Nancy found two pieces of heavy burlap. Bess and George put them in front of the two back wheels for traction. Then they gathered and broke up some brush to make a mat for each tyre.

"I hope this works," Joanne said, taking her place to assist in pushing the car. "There probably won't be anyone else using this desolate road who could help us. "I – I'm afraid we won't reach the farm in time!"

Nancy stepped into the car and started the motor, easing the gas and slowly rocking the convertible back and forth. Inch by inch the tyres crept forward, finally catching on the burlap and brush and rolling out of the ditch.

"We've done it!" Bess shouted proudly.

"With a little outside help!" George panted with a grin. The girls laughed from sheer relief.

They started off again, more slowly than before. But they had gone only a mile when a new storm seemed to be coming up. In less than five minutes complete darkness descended again, bringing another deluge of rain. Deafening thunderclaps instantly followed vivid forks of lightning.

Of necessity, Nancy once more kept the automobile at a snail's pace. It was impossible to see more than a few feet ahead. Anxiously Joanne kept glancing at her watch. "It's five-fifteen," she announced nervously.

Nancy tried to assuage the worried girl's fears. "This storm may have delayed your grandmother's caller."

The wind and rain continued unabated. As the convertible climbed the brow of a hill, there was a brilliant flash of lightning. George, who was seated in front with Nancy, screamed, "Don't hit her!"

Nancy jammed on the brakes so quickly that the rear of the car skidded around sideways in the road.

"Who?" she demanded, horrified.

"The woman in the road! Didn't you see her? Maybe she's under the car!"

Heartsick, Nancy jumped out one door, Bess another. They peered under the car, alongside it, in back of it. They could see no one.

"Are you sure you saw a woman?" Nancy inquired.

Just then another streak of lightning illuminated the sky, and Bess called out, "There goes someone running across that field!"

Nancy glanced quickly in that direction and saw the running figure of a woman. At that same moment the woman looked back over her shoulder, revealing a thin, haggard face. Nancy judged her to be in her early fifties.

All four girls stared in mystification. Nancy and Bess returned to the car and the journey was resumed.

"Why would any sane person be walking in such a storm?" Bess spoke up finally.

"She's headed in the direction of the cavern," said Joanne, and explained that they were now nearing the farm. "Maybe she's one of those strange people over there!"

Nancy and her friends were immediately curious. Before they could ask what Joanne meant, the car reached the crest of a steep hill and Joanne cried out:

"There's Red Gate Farm!" She pointed to the valley below them.

The storm had let up and the sun was coming

out. The River Heights girls could clearly see the forty-acre farm, with its groves of pine trees and a winding river which curled along the valley. Everything looked green and fresh after the heavy rain.

'It's beautiful!" exclaimed Bess.

"And cool – and peaceful," Joanne added excitedly.

"Don't count on much relaxation with Nancy around," George advised their new friend. "She'll find some adventure to occupy every waking hour!"

"Yes," Bess agreed. "Adventure with mystery added."

Nancy smiled. She reflected on the two mysteries she had already encountered; the unsolved case of the Blue Jade perfume and the strange code.

As the car descended into the valley, the girls caught a better glimpse of the farm with its huge red barn and various adjoining sheds and the large, rambling house, partly covered with vines. There were bright-red geraniums in the window boxes, and a freshly painted picket fence surrounding the yard.

Nancy stopped the car in front of the big red gate which opened into the garden. "Oh, I hope it's not too late!" Joanne cried as she sprang out to unlatch the gate.

· 7 ·
Nature Cult

Nancy drove in to Red Gate Farm and parked. She consulted her watch and noted with dismay it was quarter to six. By now the farmhouse door had opened, and a grey-haired woman in a crisp gingham dress and white apron came hurrying out to meet them. Her blue eyes were bright as she welcomed Joanne warmly.

"My granddaughter told me how kind you all were to her in the city," she said to Nancy and her friends. "I can't thank you enough."

"Gram!" Joanne exclaimed. "I can't stand the suspense. Did you sell the farm to that man?"

Mrs Byrd shook her head. "Mercy! I was so excited at your coming back I forgot to tell you. He phoned a little while ago and said that because of the storm he'd rather come here tomorrow – he could wait one more day."

Not only Joanne, but her visitors, heaved sighs of relief. Further discussion of the subject was deferred when Mrs Byrd insisted the girls freshen up for supper.

They entered the large, rambling house, and a little later everyone sat down in the plainly furnished but comfortable dining room. Mrs Byrd appeared very happy as she bustled about, serving the delicious meal of hot biscuits, sizzling ham, sweet potatoes, and coffee. The girls had not realized how hungry they were.

"Nothing like driving through a storm to work up an appetite." George grinned.

It was not until dessert – freshly baked lemon meringue pie – that Joanne mentioned again what was uppermost in her mind. "Gram," she said gently, "*please* call up that man and tell him you don't want to sell our farm. *Please*. We'll find a way to stay here, somehow. I'm sure there'll be answers to your ads for boarders."

Nancy quickly spoke up. "Yes, Mrs Byrd. It certainly would be a shame to give up Red Gate. And besides, George, Bess, and I would like to be paying guests for a while – if you'd like us to stay, that is."

"Of course I want you all here as long as possible. But I really can't accept any money," Mrs Byrd protested. "You have been so wonderful to Jo."

"If you won't let us pay our share, we'll have to return home tomorrow," Nancy insisted.

Mrs Byrd finally relented and declared with a smile: "I believe I was just waiting to be dissuaded from taking that Mr Kent's offer. I'll call him right now. He gave me his telephone number."

The girls followed her into the kitchen, and sat down while Mrs Byrd went to the phone there and put in the call.

"Mr Kent? I've decided not to sell Red Gate Farm – at any price . . . No. I . . . No . . . Absolutely." The woman winced and held the phone away from her ear.

Nancy and her friends exchanged glances. The man was evidently incensed and was speaking so loudly they could hear his voice easily. Finally Mrs Byrd put down the receiver.

"Well, I'm glad that man isn't going to own Red Gate," she declared. "He certainly was unpleasant. He even said I might regret my decision."

Joanne's face was radiant and she hugged her grandmother. "I feel so much better now." She turned to her new friends. "Somehow, I know you're going to bring us luck, Nancy, Bess, and George."

Suddenly Mrs Byrd said, "Goodness! I've forgotten to look in our mailbox today."

"I'll go." Joanne hurried outside and was back in a minute, several envelopes in her hand.

Gram! One of these is from the Round Valley *Gazette*. Do you think – ?" Excitedly she handed the mail to her grandmother.

The girls watched eagerly as Mrs Byrd tore open a long, bulky envelope and took out a number of enclosed letters. She looked at them quickly. A smile spread over her face.

"Gram, are they answers to the ad for boarders?" Joanne asked excitedly.

Mrs Byrd nodded. "I can hardly believe it! Two people are arriving the day after tomorrow. First, a

Mrs Salisbury, then a Mr Abbott. Several others will come later this month."

"Wonderful!" Nancy said, and immediately offered her assistance in getting rooms ready.

"Count Bess and me in too," said George.

Joanne and her grandmother at first demurred, but were outvoted. "Very well." Mrs Byrd smiled. "Tomorrow afternoon will be time enough to get things ready."

Later, as the guests bid her good night, Mrs Byrd said:

"Jo was right. You three girls *have* brought us luck. Bless you!"

George and Bess were shown to the room in which they would sleep. Nancy was to share Joanne's bedroom.

"Oh, how sweet it smells in here," Joanne commented, as Nancy unpacked.

"That's some of the Oriental perfume which splashed on my clothes in the train," said Nancy. "It certainly is strong and lasting!"

When Nancy awoke the next morning, warm sunlight was streaming through the windows. Joanne had already gone downstairs. Nancy's first thought was to phone Police Chief McGinnis and find out about the owner, or owners, of the cars driven by the suspicious man. After dressing hurriedly she went to the first floor and placed the call.

"Good morning, Nancy," the officer said. "Here's the information you wanted. Both cars were rented from drive-yourself agencies by a man named Philip Smith, a native of Dallas, Texas. They've been returned."

Nancy thanked the chief and hung up. "That clue wasn't any help," she thought. "None of those suspicious men talked like a Texan. The name Philip Smith was probably phony, and made up on the spur of the moment. Also, a forged driver's licence might have been used."

Presently Bess and George came down and the girls enjoyed a delicious breakfast of pancakes and sausages. Afterward, Joanne took the girls on a tour of the farm. She showed them the lovely gardens, a large chicken house, and her pet goat, Chester.

A turkey took a dislike to Bess and chased her to the farmhouse porch, much to the amusement of the onlookers! Joanne came to the rescue and chased the turkey away.

"Our farm isn't very well stocked," she admitted as she led the way to the barn. "We keep only one cow and one work horse. Poor old Michael should be retired on a pension, but we can't afford to lose him yet!"

Joanne cheerfully hailed the hired man. Reuben Ames was about forty years old, red-haired, and rather quiet in manner. He acknowledged each introduction with a mumbled "Pleased to meet you, miss," and extended a work-worn hand for each girl to shake. Reuben shifted uncomfortably and then returned to the barn.

"Reuben is as good as gold, even if he is bashful," Joanne told the girls. "I don't know what we'd do without him."

"We'd better keep an eye on Bess," George teased. "She'll be breaking another heart."

Bess made a good-natured retort as the girls started for the orchard. George demonstrated her agility by climbing the nearest apple tree. Once back at the farmhouse, Nancy asked curiously, "Jo, please tell us more about the cave that you spoke about yesterday. I'm bursting to know all about it."

"Well, the cave is on a piece of land along the river which Gram rents out."

"Oh, then I suppose it'll be impossible for us to visit the cavern," Nancy commented.

"I don't see why we can't. It's still our land." Joanne frowned. "A queer lot of people are renting it, though."

"How do you mean?" Nancy questioned, recalling Joanne's remark of the previous day.

"They're some sort of sect — a nature cult, I think, and part of a large organization. At least that's what it said in the letter Gram received from their leader. Anyway, this group calls itself the Black Snake Colony."

"Pleasant name," Bess observed cynically.

"I'm not sure what they do," Joanne admitted. "We've never even spoken to any members. I suppose they believe in living an outdoor life."

"You can live that way without joining a nature cult," George said dryly. "I suppose they dance when the dew is on the grass and such nonsense!"

"Believe it or not they *do* dance!" Joanne laughed. "But only nights when the moon is out.

I've seen them from here in the moonlight. It's an eerie sight. They wear white robes and flit around waving their arms. They even wear masks!"

"Masks!" Nancy exclaimed. "Why?"

"I can't imagine. It all sounds senseless. But the rent money is helpful."

"Do they live in this cavern?" George asked in amazement.

"No, they live in shacks and tents near the river. I've never really had the nerve to visit the place. Of course if you girls went along — "

"When can we go?" Nancy asked excitedly.

"I'll speak to Gram," Joanne offered.

"It's odd you've never spoken to any of the colony members," Nancy remarked thoughtfully. "Who pays the rent?"

"It's sent by mail. They even leased the land that way."

"Didn't it strike you as a peculiar way of doing business?" Nancy asked.

"Yes," Joanne admitted, "but I suppose it's part of their creed, or whatever you call it. They probably don't believe in mingling with people outside the cult. That's often the case."

Directly after lunch the girls helped the Byrds straighten and clean the rooms for the expected boarders. They hung curtains, newly made by Mrs Byrd, and put fresh flowers in each room.

At the end of the afternoon they were very pleased with the result.

"All you girls have worked hard enough," Mrs Byrd said. "You go rest while I fix supper."

She was insistent, so Joanne led her friends to the porch. Bess stretched out in the hammock and picked up the day's newspaper. The others chatted. Suddenly Bess gave an exclamation of surprise.

"Nancy," she asked tensely, "what was the name of that girl who sold me the perfume?"

"Wong," Nancy answered in amazement. "Yvonne Wong. Why?"

"Because there's an article in the paper that mentions her name!" Bess thrust the newspaper into Nancy's hands, indicating the paragraph. "Wow! This is something! Read it yourself!"

· 8 ·
Hillside Ghosts

Nancy read aloud:

"'The Hale Syndicate, which has been engaged in the illegal importation of Oriental articles, has been dissolved by court order.'" Nancy looked up and said, "I don't see what that has to do with our perfume friend Yvonne Wong."

"A great deal," Bess declared. "Read on and you'll find out!"

"Oh!" Nancy exclaimed a few seconds later. "Yvonne was employed by the syndicate as a clerk in their shop. She hasn't been indicted, because of insufficient evidence, and the top men have skipped!"

Bess nodded, realizing the impact of her important discovery. "That perfume store we visited must have been owned by the syndicate!"

"How long ago was the fraud discovered?" George asked.

"The article doesn't say," Nancy returned. "It has just now been made public."

"It doesn't surprise me that the Wong girl was mixed up in some underhanded affair," George remarked. "I didn't like her attitude from the beginning!"

"Nor did I," Bess added. "And I liked her less after Nancy found out she had received the job Jo wanted."

"I'm certainly glad I *didn't* get that job." Joanne smiled. "I'd much rather be here."

"Do you suppose Yvonne knew the work of the syndicate was dishonest?" Bess asked with concern.

"I'm sure of it," George answered flatly. "But it looks as if she and the others slipped out quickly when the federal authorities became aware of the racket."

All this time Nancy had been staring into space. It had occurred to her that Yvonne Wong might still be employed by the suyndicate. Undoubtedly the name and offices had been changed to throw off the federal authorities. Was Room 305 now the syndicate's headquarters?

Nancy immediately thought of the coded message she had brought with her. "The third number in it, 5, was the letter H," she told herself. Then she reflected on the recent newspaper article about the syndicate.

"This 'H' might stand for Hale!" she thought excitedly. "And the line over it might mean that someone by this name is important – the ringleader, perhaps! I must talk to Chief McGinnis again. I may have stumbled on to a clue to those missing Hale Syndicate men!"

After supper she phoned the chief and propounded her theory. "Well, Nancy," he said, "it sounds as if you might have picked up a clue, sure enough. Send me a copy of that code and I'll get busy on it."

After Nancy completed the call, she and the other girls studied the code once more.

Gazing at the 16 and the 5, Nancy suddenly said, "M – M – why that *could* stand for Maurice! Maybe that man's name is Maurice Hale!"

"Now I'll sleep better," Bess sighed. The girls went to bed happy and excited.

The next day everyone's attention was focused on a new boarder. Shortly after church services, Mrs Alice Salisbury and her daughter Nona arrived in an expensive sedan. Mrs Salisbury walked with a cane, and complained loudly of her arthritis as the girls helped her into the house.

Nona waited only long enough to see that her mother was made comfortable. Then she announced that she must hurry back to the city nearby, where she lived.

"Mother was born on a farm," she told Mrs Byrd as she stepped into the car, "and she simply pines for the country. I thought this arrangement might be ideal since she's never entirely happy with me in the city. I'll drive down to see her weekends. I do hope she'll be happier here at Red Gate Farm."

Joanne and her friends hoped so too, but they were not at all certain, for it became increasingly apparent that Mrs Salisbury could not be happy anywhere. She found no fault with the immaculate farmhouse or the lovely view from her bedroom window, but she constantly complained of her various aches and pains. She talked incessantly about her many operations. She had a sharp tongue and delighted in using it.

"She wouldn't be so bad, if only she'd stop talking operations," George burst out. "Makes me feel as though I'm ready for the hospital myself!"

By the time the girls had adjusted themselves to Mrs Salisbury, the second boarder arrived. He was Karl Abbott, a diamond-in-the-rough type of man. In spite of his sixty-three years, he boasted that he was as spry as his son Karl Jr, who had brought him.

Karl Jr, who worked in a nearby city, was a personable young man. The girls, particularly Bess, were sorry he could not remain with his father.

The girls liked Mr Abbott very much, but they were appalled by his tremendous appetite. "I wish we could turn him out in the yard to forage for himself," Joanne sighed several days later as she peeled her second heaping pan of potatoes. "It's all I can do to keep one helping ahead of him!"

At first Mr Abbott insisted upon remaining in the kitchen, teasing the girls as they worked and sampling the food. Then he fell into the habit of sitting on the front porch with Mrs Salisbury and chatting with her for hours. Frequently they became involved in violent arguments about trivial matters just for diversion.

After one of their disagreements Mrs Salisbury would maintain a stony silence which was refreshing. But Mr Abbott would once again take refuge in the kitchen!

In spite of such slight annoyances, the days at

Red Gate Farm passed very pleasantly. Nancy would go into town on various errands for the boarders and sometimes Mrs Byrd.

One day she had just returned to the farm from a shopping trip and on her way to the house stopped at the mailbox.

"There might be a letter from Dad," she thought, and drew out a stack of mail.

She took it all into the house, where Mrs Byrd asked Nancy to distribute the letters. As she was sorting them out, she came to one addressed to the Black Snake Colony.

"Look!" Nancy exclaimed. "This letter belongs to the nature cult. The mailman must have put it in our box by mistake."

"What will you do?" asked Bess seriously. "Drive over with it?"

"Of course not," growled Mr Abbott, who had just entered the room. "You keep away from those outrageous people. Take it back to the post office."

Nancy studied the postmark. It was very blurred. Could it be Riverside Heights, or was she mistaken? Her curiosity about the mysterious cult was now even more aroused. Perhaps she could deliver the letter in person! But she got no further in her plan, for just then a neighbour passed on his way to town. Mrs Byrd handed him the letter to remail.

Nancy felt disappointed, but was determined to find out in some way what was going on "over the hill." "If I can only be alone with Bess and George a little later, maybe we can come up with some plan," she thought.

There had been a letter from Mr Drew, informing Nancy that he had returned home. "At least Dad's making progress on *his* case!" she said to herself.

Then Nancy hurried off to the barn where the "city slickers," as Reuben called them, were to have a milking lesson.

"It's no trick at all!" Bess insisted. "Give me that pail and I'll show you just how it's done."

Reuben handed over the bucket, and Bess marched determinedly up to the cow.

"Nice bossy," she murmured, giving the animal a timid pat on the neck.

The cow responded with a suspicious look and flirt of her tail. As Bess set down the milking stool, the cow kicked it over.

Bess sprang back in alarm. "You can't expect me to milk a vicious cow!" she exclaimed.

Joanne and Reuben exploded with laughter.

"Primrose is an extremely smart cow," Reuben drawled. "She won't stand being milked except from the side she's used to!"

Reluctantly Bess picked up the overturned stool and went around to the left side. The cow leisurely moved herself sideways.

"I give up! Here, you try it, George."

"Oh, no, Bess. I wouldn't spoil your fun for anything!"

After a great deal of manoeuvring, Bess succeeded in handling the whole procedure to the satisfaction of Primrose. Nancy came last, and she, too, was a bit awkward. When Reuben finally sat down to do the milking, the girls watched him with admiration. "It just takes practice," he said, smiling.

That evening Mrs Salisbury and Mr Abbott had their usual disagreement and both retired early. Mrs Byrd soon followed, leaving the girls alone on the porch.

"Do you think there will be any activity on the hill tonight?" George asked suddenly.

"I'm not sure," Joanne answered. "But it's a good clear night and the moon is full, so the setting is perfect for it."

"I'm dying to see what those nature enthusiasts look like," added Bess. "Just so they don't come too close!"

It was a lovely evening and Nancy had been only half listening to the chatter. She remained silent and thoughtful. The letter addressed to the Black Snake Colony was still very much on her mind.

"What's up, Nancy?" Bess finally asked, noticing her friend's silence.

"Three guesses," Nancy replied with a laugh. "I'm still curious about that envelope I had in my hands this afternoon. I'm almost certain that blurred postmark read Riverside Heights."

"Even if it did," George remarked, "it could have been written by almost anyone and simply *mailed* in Riverside Heights."

"I suppose you're right," Nancy agreed. "I guess I'm trying too hard. But let's walk over toward the hill."

The four girls started off. They crossed one field

in front of the house and were just climbing a rail fence to the next one when Nancy cried out:

"Am I seeing things? Look! Over there on that hill!"

Following her gaze, the girls were astonished to see shadowy white figures flitting about in the moonlight.

"Ghosts!" Bess exclaimed.

"Ghosts nothing," George retorted. "There's no such animal!"

"Don't be alarmed," Joanne said with a smile. "I imagine the members of the nature cult are having one of their festive airings by the light of the moon!"

The girls watched the cult members go through their mystic rites.

"They're not doing much of anything," Nancy observed, "except flitting around."

Within ten minutes the ceremony apparently was concluded. The white figures clustered together for a moment, then moved off across the hillside.

"I wonder where they're heading," Nancy mused. "Back to their tents?"

Joanne had been watching intently. Now she shook her head. "I don't think so. I forgot to tell you – the cave has another opening on the slope of the hill, near the river. The colony members are going in that direction."

Immediately Nancy's curiosity was aroused. Did this mean the white-robed group intended to go into the cave itself? If so, why? To continue the ceremony?

"It certainly was a short performance," Bess remarked as the mysterious "dancers" vanished from sight. "I wonder if the ritual has any significance."

"That's what I'd like to know," Nancy said quietly. "And that's what we must find out!"

"Not tonight!" Joanne said firmly. "Grandmother will be very upset if we don't come right back."

Reluctantly Nancy gave up the idea. The girls started for the farmhouse, but Nancy kept looking back over her shoulder, determined not to miss anything. However, the hillside remained uninhabited and still.

As the girls drew near the road, the motor of a car broke the silence and headlights appeared. The automobile slowed down in front of the farmhouse as if about to stop. Then suddenly the car went on. Why? Nancy wondered. Had the driver seen the girls and changed his mind?

· 9 ·
Black Snake Colony Member

Nancy was too far away from the car to see its driver or licence plate. Thoughtfully she went to bed, but lay awake for some time, feeling completely baffled over the many mysterious happenings.

By morning she felt eager for action. Ever since her arrival at Red Gate Farm, Nancy had wanted to visit the cavern on the hillside. The strange moonlight ceremony and the unidentified car which had hesitated in front of the house only intensified her interest in the place.

She broached the subject of a visit there to Mrs Byrd, but Joanne's grandmother frowned on the idea. "I'll worry if you go," she said. "Those folks are probably harmless, but we don't know much about them. I wish now I had never rented the land. The neighbours are saying I was foolish to do it in the first place."

"And so you were!" Mrs Salisbury, who had overheard the conversation, chimed in. "You'll ruin the value of your farm. Why, people around are saying dreadful things about the members of that cult. Even Reuben is afraid to go near the place!"

"I'm not," Nancy announced. "I think it would be fun to investigate."

Mrs Salisbury snorted. "Fun! Girls these days have strange ideas of fun! First thing you know, Mrs Byrd, she'll be wanting to join the colony!"

"Nonsense." Mrs Byrd smiled.

In order to avoid further dissension, Nancy dropped the subject of the cave. But that afternoon she set out alone on a hike. Making her way to the woods which skirted the river, Nancy struck a well-worn path and decided to continue along it.

She had walked only a short way when the sound of a faint cry came to her. Nancy halted in the path and listened intently. The cry was not repeated.

"Maybe I imagined it," she said to herself.

Nevertheless, Nancy quickened her pace, looking about her as she walked. As she rounded a bend a few minutes later, she was startled to see a woman hunched over on the ground, writhing in pain.

"What's the matter?" Nancy cried out, hurrying over to her. Then the girl's eyes widened. This was the woman she had seen running across a field the night of the storm.

"I tripped on a root in the path," the woman murmured, rocking back and forth in pain. "My ankle – it's broken."

Nancy dropped to one knee and quickly examined the injured ankle. It was swelling rapidly, but all the bones seemed to be in place.

"See if you can stand," she advised.

With Nancy's help the woman managed to get to

her feet, but winced as she tried to take her first step.

"It isn't broken," Nancy said gently, "but you have a bad sprain."

"Oh, what'll I do now?" the woman moaned.

"Do you live far from here?" Nancy asked.

The stranger looked at her rather queerly and did not answer at once. Nancy thought she had not understood, so repeated the question.

"About a quarter of a mile up the river," was the mumbled response. "I'll get there all right."

"You're scarcely able to walk a step," Nancy said with a troubled frown. "Please let me run back to the farm and bring help."

"No, no," the woman protested, clutching Nancy fearfully by the arm. "I don't want to be a bother to anyone!"

"Nonsense! You shouldn't be walking at all. It won't take me a minute to get someone to help you."

The woman shook her head stubbornly. "My foot feels better now. I can walk by myself."

She started off, but nearly collapsed by the time she had taken three steps.

"If you won't let me go for help, then at least let me take you home."

Again the woman protested, but Nancy took hold of her arm and placed it over her own shoulder. With Nancy's support, the woman made slow and painful progress up the path.

"This is killing you," Nancy said, dismayed that

the woman was so foolishly stubborn. "I can get our hired man to carry you – "

"No!" the woman objected vehemently.

Her unwillingness to accept help puzzled Nancy. As they made their way slowly along, she became aware that her companion's distress was not entirely due to pain, but partially to Nancy's own presence. This mystified Nancy, but she could not turn back as long as she knew the woman really needed her.

"I don't remember seeing any houses along the river," Nancy said after a time. "You're not a member of the nature cult, are you?"

A half-cynical expression crossed the woman's face, then one of sadness. "Yes," she returned quietly, "I'm one of the members."

Nancy took time to scrutinize her companion more carefully than before. She wore a blue gingham dress which was plain and durable, and certainly did not appear to be a costume. The woman did not speak or act as Nancy imagined a member of the cult would. She seemed like any other person.

"It must be healthful to live an outdoor life," Nancy remarked, feeling that some comment was necessary. "I've often looked over at your tents and thought I should like to visit the colony some time."

The woman stopped abruptly in the path and faced Nancy, an odd look on her face.

"You must never come near!"

"Why not?"

"It wouldn't be safe!"

"Not safe!" Nancy echoed in astonishment. "I don't understand."

"I – I mean the members of the cult don't want folks prying around," the woman said hastily.

"I see. The rites are secret?"

"That's it," the woman said in obvious relief.

"But why couldn't I visit the colony sometimes when ceremonies aren't being held?" Nancy persisted.

"You mustn't come near the hillside – ever!" the stranger warned.

The two continued up the path. To Nancy it was apparent that her questions had disturbed the woman, for several times she caught her looking distressed and worried.

As they approached the hillside colony, and before they were within sight of the tents, the woman stopped short.

"Thank you for your help," she said quietly. "I can make it alone from here."

Nancy hesitated. The woman's firm tone told her it would do no good to protest. She was not going to let Nancy come any nearer the camp!

"At least let me find something that you can use as a cane," Nancy said.

She searched along the path and found a branch that was strong enough. The woman accepted it gratefully. Her face softened and she stood for an instant, looking intently at Nancy.

"You're a good girl to help a stranger like me. I wish – " The woman turned away abruptly.

"Remember," she advised sternly over her shoulder, "don't ever come near the camp!"

Still perplexed, Nancy watched the woman hobble away. It took her a long time to reach the top of the hill, but at last she disappeared from sight.

"I can't understand why the poor thing acted the way she did," Nancy said to herself as she sat down on a log to think. "What harm could it have done if I'd gone with her to the colony? The cult must have some very important secrets!"

The more Nancy considered the matter, the more baffled she became.

"The woman didn't look as though being a member of the Black Snake Colony made her very happy," Nancy thought. "If they're so afraid that someone will discover their secrets, they must be doing more than just flitting at night in white robes! Maybe that's only to keep people from guessing what really goes on there!"

As Nancy reached this startling conclusion, she jumped up and walked briskly toward Red Gate Farm.

"There's one thing certain," she said to herself with a chuckle. "Now that the woman has forbidden me to go near the camp, I can't resist finding out what's happening there!"

Nancy was just approaching the farmhouse when she heard the phone ringing. She hurried inside and answered it.

"Yes, this is Nancy Drew," she replied to a strange man's question.

"One moment."

While Nancy waited, she wondered who the caller might be. Was someone going to threaten her to desist in her detective work?

"Oh!" she said as the next speaker announced himself as Chief McGinnis. A sense of relief came over the girl.

"I have some news, Nancy," the officer said. "It's discouraging. Nothing on the code or the missing men." Then he chuckled. "We need another clue from you."

Nancy realized her old friend was teasing. "Glad to help," she said gaily. "What's the assignment?"

"To find out where the Hale Syndicate moved to after it left Room 305."

"Then that was their headquarters!" Nancy cried excitedly.

"Temporarily. But they left no forwarding address," the police chief said.

"If we could decipher the rest of the code we might be able to trace them," Nancy said. "Anyhow, I'll be on the lookout for any clues. At least it shouldn't be too hard to find Yvonne Wong."

Chief McGinnis agreed and assured Nancy he would let her know if there were any new developments. Then he asked, "And what are you doing? Any mysteries up your way?"

"There might be." She told him the little she had been able to glean about the mysterious nature cult. She described the unusual moonlight ceremony the girls had witnessed and the appearance of the unidentified car.

The police chief whistled in amazement. "Sounds as though you *do* have another mystery up your sleeve! Have you come across any possible clues to what the cult is worshipping, Nancy?"

The girl detective hesitated a moment before telling Chief McGinnis about her curious conversation with the woman she had assisted in the woods. She decided to mention it, and added that although the woman had readily admitted to being a member of the cult, she had given Nancy no reason for her firm warning to stay away from the meeting place.

"Black Snake Colony, eh?" the police chief said reflectively.

"Yes," Nancy replied. "Have you ever heard of it?"

"No, but let me look in a report we have here on all cults. I'll call you right back."

Nancy waited eagerly for the phone to ring. When it did she snatched up the receiver. "The Black Snake Colony is not listed," Chief McGinnis told her.

"You mean it's a phony?" Nancy asked excitedly.

· 10 ·

Plan of Attack

Chief McGinnis refused to comment on the possibility that the Black Snake Colony might be a phony group.

"They may not have been in existence long enough to be known," he replied. "But you might try to find out what you can and let me know."

"I'll do that," the young detective agreed.

After Nancy had put down the phone, she reflected for a long minute on the new twist to the hillside mystery, then walked out to the porch, where Mrs Salisbury, Mr Abbott, and the three girls were seated.

Nancy had not planned to tell them of her experience, but her face was so animated it revealed her thoughts. They besieged her with questions until finally she revealed her meeting with the woman member of the strange nature cult.

"Told you not to come near, did she?" Mrs Salisbury cackled. "Well, I hope you intend to follow her advice."

Nancy laughed and shook her head. "I'm more interested than ever in what's going on up there on the hillside. I'm ready for a little adventure right about now!"

"So am I," George chimed in.

Joanne nodded vigorously, while Bess, always more cautious, agreed rather halfheartedly.

"Better stay away," Mr Abbott advised, for once not contradicting Mrs Salisbury. "You can't tell what may be going on there."

Nancy was tempted to comment, but instead she forced a smile and said, "It seems to me that this matter may be of deep concern to Jo and her grandmother, if not to me."

Mrs Byrd had stepped to the porch door in time to get the gist of the conversation, and at once spoke up.

"I think Nancy is right," she declared thoughtfully. "Of course, I don't want the girls to go looking for trouble, but I'm beginning to think someone ought to investigate those mysterious people. If anything questionable is going on, I want to know about it. I'll ask the Black Snake Colony to move out, even if I do lose the rent. Why, I might get into trouble myself if they stay."

Mr Abbott and Mrs Salisbury fell into an injured silence. Nancy gave her friends a sly wink, and in a few minutes they all quietly withdrew to the spring-house to discuss their plans. Here, she told the girls about her conversation with Chief McGinnis.

"Something peculiar is going on at those cult meetings, I'm sure," Nancy went on, "and I must find out about them if I can. Do you all want to join me in the investigation?"

"Of course," Joanne and George said.

"Do you think it'll be safe?" Bess asked.

"I'm not making any rash promises." Nancy laughed.

Bess gave a little shiver. "I don't like it, but count me in."

"How can we visit the colony without being caught?" George asked.

"That's the problem," Nancy replied. "We must make our plans carefully. Before we do anything, I suggest we find out about the robes the cult members wear. We may need to wear similar ones to help us in our investigation."

"There's only one way to find that out," Joanne said. "Some night when they're having a ceremonial meeting, we can sneak through the woods and try to get a closer look at what's going on."

Nancy nodded excitedly. "The double entrance to the cave will be perfect!" she said. "If we can't sneak into the meetings any other way, we can get into the cave at the end they don't use."

"Sounds terribly risky to me!" Bess commented.

"Oh, for Pete's sake," George said scornfully. "Don't be such a wet blanket, Bess!"

Her cousin opened her mouth to retort, but Nancy interposed quickly to forestall any further argument.

"We'd better not tell our plan to anyone except your grandmother, Jo," she advised. "Otherwise, Mrs Salisbury and Mr Abbott will try to talk her out of letting us investigate."

After a light supper and some rather forced conversation on trivial matters, the girls retired. They had tried to keep silent about the activities of the nature cult, but their secretive manner did not escape the notice of Mrs Salisbury and Mr Abbott.

"You're up to something," Mrs Salisbury remarked the next morning. "And if I were Mrs Byrd, I'd put a stop to it at once!"

Mrs Byrd, however, went on serenely with her work, being careful not to interfere with the girls' plans. They maintained a close watch of the hillside, but for two days seldom saw anyone in the vicinity.

"I think they've holed in for the rest of the summer," George declared impatiently at breakfast. " Either that, or they've moved out."

"The cult's still there," Joanne reassured her. "The rent cheque arrived in the morning mail."

"By the way, where do these nature people get their food?" Nancy queried. "They can't live on blue sky and inspiration."

"I think friends must bring food to them in automobiles," Joanne answered. "Several times I've seen swanky cars drive up and park near the hillside."

"The cult members must be fairly well off, then," Nancy said thoughtfully. "I'm getting tired of marking time. I wish something would happen soon. If it doesn't, I think I'll investigate that cave, anyway!"

That night the girls were late in finishing the dishes. By the time they had put everything away it was quite dark. When they went out to the porch, they were relieved to find that the boarders had gone to their rooms.

The girls sat talking quietly for some time. The moon was high, and Nancy, from force of habit, glanced eagerly toward the distant hill.

"Look, girls!" she exclaimed. "They're at it again!"

The four girls could see white objects moving to and fro, apparently going through a weird ritual. Nancy sprang to her feet.

"We'll have to hurry if we want to see anything," she said. "Come on! We'll take the short cut!"

They dashed across the lawn, flung open the gate, and ran through the woods. Nancy led the way up the river path, then to the sparsely wooded hillside. Not until they were close to the camp did she stop.

"We'll have to be very careful," she warned in a whisper. "Scatter and hide behind trees. And don't make a sound."

The girls obeyed, Bess staying as close to George as possible. Nancy found a huge oak tree well up the hill, and hid behind it. From this vantage point she could see fairly well.

Nancy had been there for less than five minutes when she heard the sound of several cars approaching. They came up the woods road and stopped at the foot of the hill, not far from the nature camp.

Several men stepped from the cars. Nancy was too far away to see their faces, but she did observe that they quickly donned long white robes with head masks, and joined the other costumed figures who were on the brow of the hill.

For nearly ten minutes the members of the cult flitted back and forth, waving their arms and making weird noises. Then they moved single file toward the cavern and vanished.

Suddenly Nancy felt herself grasped by an arm. She wheeled sharply and then laughed softly.

"George! For goodness sake, don't ever do that again! You scared me silly!"

"What do you make of it, Nancy?"

"It's the strangest thing I've ever seen. I haven't been able to figure it out."

"What should we do next?" asked Bess, who had joined them.

"Let's follow them into the cave!" George proposed rashly.

"And be caught?" Nancy returned. "No, this is serious business. I think it's time to go home and plan our own costumes."

"I wonder why so many people came here in automobiles?" Joanne mused, as the girls walked off slowly.

"That's what I've been wondering," Nancy replied soberly, "but I think I might know."

"Why?" her friends demanded.

"It looks to me as if only a few persons are actually living in the Black Snake Colony. Apparently they want to give the impression that the organization is a large one, so they have these other people come the night set for the ceremonials."

"There were certainly a lot of men in those cars," added Bess.

"Why should they go to all that trouble?" Joanne asked doubtfully.

"I don't know," Nancy admitted, "unless it's because they're trying to hide something they're doing here." She changed the subject. "I think we'll be able to make costumes like theirs if you'll give us some old pillow cases and sheets, Jo. When we visit the cave, we must disguise ourselves to make our scheme work!"

· 11 ·

A Midnight Message

"When shall we visit the cave?" George asked.

"As soon as we can," Nancy answered. "Of course we must help Jo and her grandmother with the work."

Since there was no further evidence of activity on the hillside, the girls went to bed.

The next morning George remarked, as she helped Nancy make her bed, "What do you suppose those men do between ceremonials? It certainly is strange how much time they spend in that cave!"

"What puzzles me is those automobiles that were on the hillside," Bess said. "Why did they come? Surely those men were here for something besides ballet dancing. What's your guess, Nancy?"

"I'm afraid I haven't any answer. But I mean to find one for Mrs Byrd's and Jo's sakes."

The three girls learned that Reuben was due to be absent most of the day and offered to do his chores. During the morning they picked cherries and took them to town to sell at a local market. When they returned, a small, strange car was standing in the driveway. Loud voices were coming from the living room.

"I don't have to sell and I won't sell!" Mrs Byrd said with finality in her tone.

"That's what you think," a man said sneeringly. "You're going to lose this farm and I can buy it cheaper from the bank. Why don't you sell it to me and make a little profit? Then you can go to the city and take life easy."

"We don't want to go to the city," Joanne spoke up. "We're getting along all right here. More boarders are coming soon and we are paying off our back mortgage interest. So we don't have to sell."

Outside, Nancy, Bess, and George looked at one another. The insistent buyer again! Fervently they hoped that Mrs Byrd would not weaken in her decision. A moment later they felt relieved.

"I will say good afternoon, Mr Kent," Mrs Byrd said. "Thank you for your offer, but I cannot accept it."

"You'll be sorry! You'll regret this!" the caller stormed. He came out the screen door, slamming it viciously behind him.

Nancy stared in surprise. Mr Kent certainly was one of the most ill-mannered men she had ever seen! And also, she thought wryly, one of the most tenacious! Why was he so determined to buy the Byrd home?

Mr Kent, his face red with anger, stepped into his car and sped off, but not before he gave Nancy and her friends a baleful look. "Nice disposition," George commented sarcastically.

"I hope he never shows up again," Bess said firmly.

The girls found Mrs Byrd and Joanne quite shaken. "I can't understand that man's persistence," the woman said.

Nancy was sure the matter was tied in with the cult on the hillside but did not mention this theory. She merely said, "Try not to worry about Mr Kent. I doubt that he'll return."

Soon the incident was forgotten as preparations for supper were started and the farm animals were fed. George elected to take care of gathering eggs from the henhouse. Bess gave the horse hay and water.

"I'll get the cow," Nancy offered, and went off toward the pasture to drive Primrose in.

But the cow was not there. Nancy walked around the fence surrounding the field to see if there was any opening through which the animal might have wandered. Finally she found one, and saw hoofprints leading toward a patch of woods.

Nancy dashed off among the trees. She had never been that way before, but there was only one path to follow. Several times she paused to listen and thought she heard the faint tinkling of a cowbell somewhere ahead of her.

It was rapidly growing dusky in the woods and Nancy hurried on. Again she stopped to listen. She could hear the cowbell distinctly now.

"Primrose can't be far ahead," she thought in relief, and went in that direction. Nancy finally caught sight of the Jersey contentedly munching grass on the hillside beyond.

Nancy stopped short and gave a gasp of astonishment – the sound of the cowbell had brought her to the mouth of the cave!

"I can hardly believe it!" she almost exclaimed aloud. This must be the other opening near the nature camp Jo told me about!"

Eagerly Nancy rushed toward the cave. But no sooner had she peered into the dark entrance than she was startled by the crackling of a twig behind her. Nancy wheeled to find a man standing not three feet away from her!

He seemed to have risen from the bushes which half hid the opening of the cave. Instantly it flashed through Nancy's mind that he had been stationed there to see that intruders did not enter.

"What're you doing here?" he asked, his voice as cold as steel.

Nancy recoiled. The man stood in the shadows of the shrubbery so that she could not see his face distinctly. But at the sound of his voice she knew instantly she was in danger.

"I must persuade him I wasn't spying," she thought desperately.

"Better speak up!" the man snarled. "What're you doin' here, girlie?"

"I was hunting for that cow," Nancy replied as casually as possible. She pointed to the Jersey, which was grazing a short distance away.

She held her ground defiantly. There was a moment's silence. Nancy could feel that the man was staring at her, as if undecided whether or not to believe her.

"So you were after the cow?" the lookout growled. "Then why are you by this cave?"

"Why, I was just wondering what was inside," Nancy said innocently. "Surely there's no harm in looking."

"You've no business around here!" the man snapped. "This property belongs to the members of the Black Snake Colony."

"Oh!" Nancy exclaimed in pretended awe. "Then you must belong to the colony. How very interesting!"

The man made no response to Nancy's remark. Instead, he muttered:

"Round up that old cow of yours and get out of here! And don't come trespassing again!"

Nancy knew she would gain nothing by arguing. Obediently she overtook the cow and headed her back toward Red Gate. The man watched until Nancy disappeared into the woods.

As soon as she had started the cow down the path, however, Nancy quietly retraced her steps. She reached the edge of the woods just in time to catch a glimpse of the man entering the cave.

"That proves he's one of the Black Snake group," she told herself. "He was acting as a guard for them."

For an instant Nancy was tempted to follow, but common sense told her not to press her luck. The lookout seemed determined enough to make trouble for her if she took the chance. Reluctantly, the young sleuth turned back toward the farm.

It was clear to Nancy that the entire business of the Black Snake group was anything but open and aboveboard! Obviously they were afraid that some of the countryfolk would attempt to investigate.

When Nancy finally reached the barn and Joanne began to milk Primrose, the other girls plied their friend with questions.

"We were beginning to worry," Joanne said in relief. "I wouldn't have let you go alone if I'd known this cow of ours would stray so far."

"I'm glad I went," Nancy said quickly.

She then told the others what had taken place near the mouth of the cave. They gasped in astonishment upon hearing of her encounter with the lookout.

"Weren't you frightened when he sprang up out of nowhere?" Bess asked, giving Nancy an admiring glance. "I'd have fainted on the spot!"

"That's an easy way out if I ever heard one!" Nancy commented with a laugh.

"Girls don't faint these days," George scoffed. "Probably you'd have screamed and brought all the members down on you. They'd have dragged you off and put an end to you!"

"Thanks, George," Bess muttered. "You say the nicest things!"

"Well, girls, talk all you like," Nancy added, "but don't lose your nerve altogether. I still want to get a closer look at that cave!"

"Not tonight!" Bess said firmly.

Nancy smiled. "I hope there won't be a ritual on the hillside tonight. We've been too busy to get our costumes ready."

The girls watched but the distant landscape remained dark. Finally they went to bed. Not long afterward, Nancy was roused from a fitful slumber by the stopping of a car not far from her window. She hopped from bed and went to peer out. A tall, slender woman who wore her hair piled high was walking to the front door.

Nancy leaned out the window and called, "What is it you wish?"

"Nancy Drew. Is she here?"

"Yes, I'm Nancy."

"I have a letter for you." Nancy did not recognize the woman's voice. But she might be disguising it.

"From whom?"

"Your father."

"Why are you bringing it now?"

"It's an urgent message," the strange woman said. "I'll leave it on the doorstep."

She dropped the letter, hurried into the car, and the man at the wheel drove off. Heart pounding, Nancy put on her robe and slippers and hurried down to the front door.

· 12 ·

Secret Service Agents

The stopping of the car at the house had awakened Mrs Byrd who slept on the first floor. She met Nancy in the hall and asked what was happening.

Quickly Nancy told her, then opened the door. On the porch lay a plain envelope with Nancy's name typed on it.

"This seems like a peculiar way for your father to get in touch with you," Mrs Byrd remarked. "Why didn't he phone if it's urgent?"

"I don't understand it myself," Nancy answered, as she tore open the letter.

The message was typewritten and was succinct. Nancy was to return home at once. Her father needed her. She was not to try to communicate with him. He could not explain why. It was signed "Dad."

Nancy read the letter to Mrs Byrd. "Oh, I couldn't let you start out at this time of night alone," the woman said at once. "You must wait until morning."

"This whole thing doesn't seem like Dad," Nancy reflected. "He wouldn't send a terse note like this even if he *were* in some kind of trouble."

Mrs Byrd was very much concerned. "It seems to me he would have called you on the phone in an emergency," she offered thoughtfully.

"Yes," Nancy agreed, "that's why this puzzles me so. But don't you worry about it, Mrs Byrd. This is something I'll have to try to figure out myself."

"But, my dear," Mrs Byrd repeated, "it's impossible for you to do anything about it at this hour."

Nancy carefully studied the note again. Suddenly she became aware of a familiar scent of perfume. The young detective held the envelope to her nostrils. It had been handled by someone who used the distinctive Blue Jade scent which Bess had purchased!

Instantly Nancy was alerted. "It wouldn't surprise me, Mrs Byrd, if this letter is a phony! I'm going to call Dad, even though it's an unearthly hour to waken him."

She picked up the receiver in the hall. No sound reached her ears. "I'm afraid the line is dead," she told Mrs Byrd. "Does this happen often?"

"It has never happened before," Mrs Byrd said. "I made a call after supper and everything was all right then."

Nancy stood in perplexed silence. Had her father tried to get her, found the line out of order, then given the note to the couple? The woman might have carried the letter in a handbag which contained a purse-size bottle of the Oriental perfume.

"In that case I ought to start for River Heights," Nancy thought. But a feeling of suspicion about the whole thing overpowered her. It might be a trap. The telephone line could have been cut. One or more persons might try to capture her on the road.

"But why?" Nancy asked herself repeatedly. She came to the conclusion that the Hale Syndicate was at the back of the incident. They must have found out she had reported her suspicions to the police and somehow had learned where she was staying.

She turned to Mrs Byrd and said, "I'll wait until seven o'clock, then try the phone again. If it still isn't working, I'll go to town and call Dad."

"Thank you, dear." Mrs Byrd patted Nancy on the shoulder. "But don't go anywhere alone. Take Bess and George with you."

"I will."

Promptly at seven o'clock Nancy tried to get in touch with her father but the phone still was not working. Joanne was already up, but Nancy roused Bess and George. The three girls were astounded to learn about the note.

"We'll get breakfast in town," Nancy told Mrs Byrd as she prepared to drive off with her friends. "And if I don't have to go to River Heights, I can do your shopping, too. Suppose you give me the list."

Halfway to town, George said suddenly, "Nancy, isn't your gasoline tank nearly empty?"

Nancy nodded. "I'm glad you reminded me. Watch for a station and we'll stop."

Presently Bess sighted one on the main road. "It's the same place we stopped to eat on our way to the farm," she said.

"So it is," George remarked.

"I can phone from here," Nancy decided.

She turned in at the gravel driveway, but as two other cars were ahead of her, she drew up some distance from the pump.

"How about getting breakfast here after you phone?" Bess suggested.

The girls agreed. Bess and George entered the lunchroom while Nancy went to an outdoor phone booth. She had her father on the wire in a few moments.

"Dad, did you send me a note last night?"

"Why, no."

Quickly his daughter explained her question. The lawyer said grimly, "It's plain to see someone wants to harm you in one way or another. Please be very careful."

Nancy promised and said, "Anyway, I'm glad you're all right."

After Nancy hung up, she dialled the phone company to report that the Byrd line was out of order. A few minutes later she joined Bess and George at a table and whispered the result of her conversation with Mr Drew.

"Oh, Nancy, this means you're in danger!" Bess said worriedly.

"I thought at least I'd be safe at Red Gate Farm," Nancy said.

"I wonder," George muttered.

The girls were the only customers in the restaurant. No one came to wait on them. From an inner room, evidently used as an office, they could hear excited voices.

"Something's wrong," Nancy said to her companions.

Just then two men came out of the office in company with the gasoline-station attendant and the woman who served as waitress of the restaurant. The woman was talking excitedly.

"We found the twenty-dollar bill in the cash register at the end of the day. It looked like any other money, and we didn't suspect anything was wrong until John took the day's receipts to the bank. And of all things they said the bill was counterfeit and they'd have to turn it over to the Secret Service!"

"Yes," one of the agents spoke up, "we've just come from the bank and it's a counterfeit all right. There's been a lot of this bad money passed lately. The forgery is very clever."

"What am I going to do?" the woman cried. "We were cheated out of twenty dollars! It isn't fair to hard-working people like John and me. Aren't you Secret Service agents going to do something about it?"

"We're doing all we can," one of the men replied. "We don't have much to go on."

"It was a girl who gave me the bill," the woman explained. "There were several of them in the party. I'd recognize – Oh!" she shrieked. "There's the very girl!" She pointed an accusing finger at Nancy Drew.

Nancy and her friends stared in astonishment. They could not believe what they had just heard.

"Arrest that girl!" the woman screamed. "Don't let any of them get away – they're all in on it together!"

"Just a minute," one of the agents said. "Suppose you explain," he suggested to Nancy.

The excited woman, however, was not to be calmed. She rushed toward Nancy and shook her fist at the girl. "Don't deny you gave me that phony bill!" she almost screamed.

"I neither deny nor affirm it," Nancy said, turning to the agents. "I did give the woman a twenty-dollar bill, but how do you know it was the counterfeit?"

"It was the only twenty we took in that day," the waitress retorted.

Nancy's thoughts raced. "I'll take your word for it," she said quietly.

Opening her purse she took out another twenty-dollar bill. The woman snatched the money and handed it to one of the Secret Service men. "Is this good?" she asked crisply.

The agent examined the bill. Then he looked at Nancy. "Where did you get this?"

"From my father. He gave me both bills, as a matter of fact. One was for car emergencies."

Instead of giving the bill to the woman, the man put it into his pocket. "This is serious business, young lady. The bill you just gave me is also counterfeit!"

Nancy was thunderstruck. Bess and George

gasped. Before any of them could speak, the lunch-room woman cried out, "She's one of the gang! Arrest her!"

For the first time the station attendant spoke up. "Take it easy, Liz. These girls don't exactly look like counterfeiters."

Liz sniffed. "People don't usually go around paying for sundaes with twenty-dollar bills!" she said tartly.

"My father gave me the money because I was going on a vacation."

"A likely story!" the woman sneered.

"It's the truth!" George spoke up indignantly. "The idea of accusing my friend of passing bad money on purpose! It's ridiculous!"

"Ridiculous, is it?" the woman retorted angrily. "You'll sing a different tune when you're in jail!"

"You can't have Nancy arrested. She didn't realize it was counterfeit money!" Bess protested. "George and I have some cash. We'll pay you twenty good dollars to make up for the bad one."

As the cousins pooled their funds and handed over the money, the woman quieted down. "Maybe I was a little hasty," she admitted. But she was not entirely cowed. "How about your father?" she asked Nancy. "How come *he* had counterfeit bills?"

Nancy said she did not know, but certainly he had not acquired them dishonestly.

One of the Secret Service men said, "Suppose you tell us who you are, and – "

"I'll tell you who she is!" came an authoritative voice from the doorway.

· 13 ·

A Hesitant Hitchhiker

Unobserved by the girls, an automobile had driven up and parked near the filling station. A tall young man had alighted and started for the lunchroom. Upon hearing the amazing conversation inside, he had halted. Then, realizing Nancy was in need of help, he had stepped inside.

"Karl!" Nancy cried out. She had never before been so glad to see anyone!

"It looks as if I just got here in the nick of time." Karl Abbott Jr smiled.

"They're trying to arrest us!" Bess exclaimed.

"You're kidding!" Karl cried in astonishment.

"It's no joke," Nancy returned earnestly, then told him of her predicament.

"Look here," Karl said bluntly, turning to the two Secret Service agents, "you can't hold these girls."

"Who are you?" one of the agents demanded.

"My name is Karl Abbott, and these girls are friends of mine. As it happens, my father is living at Red Gate Farm in Round Valley, where they also are staying. I was on my way there when I thought I'd stop for a bite to eat. Lucky I did, too!"

257

"These girls may be friends of yours," the unpleasant woman spoke up shrilly, "but this girl had better explain why she gave me counterfeit money!"

"If you're accusing these girls of deliberately trying to pass counterfeit money, you're crazy!" Karl Abbott cried out.

"You're willing to vouch for the honesty of this young lady's father as well?" the agent asked.

"Most definitely. This is Nancy Drew. No doubt you've heard of her father, the famous lawyer. If you haven't, you soon will!"

"Not Carson Drew of River Heights?"

"Yes," Karl replied.

"Why didn't you tell us who you were?" the restaurant owner asked.

"You didn't give me a chance to tell you anything!" Nancy retorted. "And you didn't seem ready to believe what I did have to say."

The two agents looked at each other. One asked to see Nancy's driver's licence, then with a smile he said, "Too bad you have such a loss because of the counterfeit money. The outfit which is distributing the twenty-dollar bills is a clever one.

"The money is turning up in many places. I'll get in touch with your father to find out where he was given the bills. Incidentally, we understand a few women are mixed up in the racket. That's why we detained you."

"Let's get out of here!" George urged.

The girls hurriedly left the lunchroom with Karl.

The government agents leisurely followed them outside.

As Nancy was about to step into her car, she thought of something. It occurred to her that by some remote chance the investigators might be interested in the phony message which she had brought with her.

"This may or may not have anything to do with the case," she told them, handing over the scented note. "But the signature is a forgery, and the perfume has some mystery to it."

She gave a brief account of her own involvement with the mystery, beginning with her encounter on the train with the man who had mentioned "the Chief," and ending with the code.

"If the rest of the code can be deciphered," Nancy concluded, "that might give us the answer to everything, including the Hale Syndicate's whereabouts."

"So you're the young detective Chief McGinnis mentioned in his reports to us," one of the agents said admiringly. "What you've done so far is really astounding. Chief McGinnis didn't mention you by name. He probably figured you would prefer him not to.

"Your deductions seem very sound, Miss Drew, and I'd advise you to be careful. That Hale gang may think you know too much already. I'll take this note and pass it along to a handwriting expert. Perhaps Yvonne Wong was the person who delivered it."

Nancy shook her head. "From what I could see of the woman, I know she wasn't Yvonne."

After the agent had wished Nancy luck on the solution of the mystery, she said good-bye to the men, and, with the others, went back to her car.

Although Karl Abbott was eager to continue on to Red Gate Farm to see his father, he expressed concern about the three girls and their upsetting experience. He asked for a detailed account of the events which had led to Nancy's predicament. He was most interested and sympathetic when the girls told him the whole story.

"Well," he said admiringly, "I guess I won't worry too much about you girls. You certainly aren't easily daunted by emergencies."

After Karl Jr and the trio had exchanged good-byes, the young man got into his car and drove on to the farm.

Bess turned to her companions. "Where to? I'm more starved than ever."

"It's only a short way to town from here," Nancy replied. "We can get breakfast there and then do our shopping."

Soon the girls reached Round Valley. When they finished eating, Nancy looked at Mrs Byrd's list.

"There's really not much on it," she commented. "Two of us could do the shopping. Suppose you girls take over and I'll go buy the material for our costumes."

"Material?" Bess queried.

Nancy laughed. "If we're going to join the Black Snake group in one of their rites, we'll need ghost costumes, and I've decided it wouldn't be fair to Mrs Byrd to ruin four of her sheets and pillowcases."

Suddenly George said, "What are we going to use for money?"

Nancy had only two dollars. Bess and George between them counted six.

"That will pay for the meat and groceries," Bess said. "I guess our costume material and the other errands will have to wait."

The food shopping was soon finished and the girls returned to Red Gate Farm.

Joanne met them at the kitchen door. "Guess what?" she burst out. "The telephone repairman was here. He said our line had been cut!"

Nancy nodded. "By those people who were here last night."

"I suppose so. Oh, Nancy, I'm so worried for you. And Karl Jr tells us you've had another adventure this morning. He said you'd explain."

Nancy, with lively interruptions from Bess and George, related the girls' recent experience.

"I gave those Secret Service men the note and told them the Hale Syndicate might be mixed up in some way with the counterfeiters. The syndicate may be the distributors of the phony bills."

"Well, do let the authorities take care of it," Joanne urged. "I want you girls to have a good time while you're here."

"Oh, I'm having a wonderful time," Nancy assured her. "By the way, I think we should work on our costumes for the hillside ceremony. Could you repay us the money we spent today so I can buy more material? We decided it isn't fair to use your grandmother's good linens."

"Oh, yes, right away. I'll get it from Gram. And I think there are a few more groceries she needs."

Joanne returned in a few minutes and handed over the money to which she added enough for the marketing. Nancy headed for town. She had gone about a mile when she sighted a woman hurrying along the side of the country road. She was limping slightly.

"I'll offer her a ride," Nancy decided. "She seems to be in a great hurry."

She halted the car and called, "May I give you a lift to town?"

The woman glanced up, startled. Nancy was surprised to see that she was the woman from the Black Snake colony whom she had helped several days before on the river trail! What she was doing so far from her camp Nancy did not know, but she was determined to make the most of the opportunity at hand.

"Please get in," Nancy urged, as the woman hesitated. "I'm sure your foot must be paining you. I notice that you are still limping."

"Thanks," the woman returned gratefully, hobbling over to the car door which Nancy held open for her. "I am in a hurry to get to town."

Before stepping inside she looked quickly over her shoulder as though fearing that someone might observe her actions.

She sighed in relief and settled back, looking very pale and exhausted.

"You weren't intending to walk all the way to town?" Nancy asked in a friendly, conversational tone.

The woman nodded. "I had to get there somehow."

"But aren't the members of your colony permitted to use any of the cars I've seen around the camp?" Nancy questioned, watching her companion closely and hoping that she might tactfully glean some information.

"We aren't allowed much freedom," the woman answered.

"You shouldn't be walking on that foot yet," Nancy protested. "You're apt to injure your ankle permanently."

"It's nearly well now," the woman told her, avoiding Nancy's eyes. "They didn't know at the camp that I was going to town. I – I left in a hurry."

Again the stranger cast an anxious glance over her shoulder. "She obviously thinks she's being followed," Nancy thought to herself. "Perhaps she's even running away!"

Nancy wanted to ask her companion a number of questions but the woman's aloofness discouraged her. Deciding on an entirely different course, the young sleuth pretended not to pay particular attention to the woman. For some time they drove along in silence. Nancy could see that her passenger was gradually relaxing and losing her fear.

"Am I going too fast for you?" Nancy inquired, thinking the time was right to launch the conversation.

"Oh, no," the woman returned quickly. "You can't go too fast for me." She hesitated, and then added, "I have an important letter to mail."

"Why don't you drop it in one of the roadside mailboxes?" Nancy suggested casually. "The rural carrier will pick it up and save you a long trip."

"I want to get it off this morning if I possibly can."

"I'll be glad to go to the post office and mail it for you," Nancy said, purposely drawing the woman out.

"Thank you, but no," the woman mumbled. "I – I'd feel better if I did it myself." As Nancy did not reply, she said, "I don't mean to be ungrateful for all you've done – really I don't. It's only that I mustn't get you into trouble."

"How could I get into trouble by helping you?" Nancy asked with a smile.

"You don't understand," her companion replied nervously. "There are things I can't explain. The leaders of the colony will be very angry with me if they find I have left even for a few hours, and especially that I've mailed this letter to my sister. The cult forbids communication with the outside world."

"I can't understand why you tolerate such rigid supervision," Nancy said impatiently. "Why, the leader of the cult must treat you as prisoners!"

"You're not far from wrong," the woman confessed.

"Then why don't you run away?"

The question startled the woman. She glanced sharply at Nancy, then as quickly looked away.

"I would if I dared," she said finally.

"Why don't you dare?" Nancy challenged. "I'll help you."

"No, you mustn't get mixed up in this. Perhaps later I can get away."

"I don't see what anyone can do to you if you decide to leave the colony," Nancy went on. "Surely you're a free person."

"Not any more," her companion returned sadly. "I'm in it too deep now. I'll have to go on until Fate helps me."

"I wouldn't wait," Nancy advised bluntly. "Let me help you – right now!"

·14·

Disturbing Gossip

The strange woman in Nancy's car seemed to waver for a moment, as if about to accept the girl's offer of help. Then she shook her head.

"No, I won't drag you into it!" she said with finality. "You don't know what you'd be getting into if you helped me. Why, if they even learn that you've aided me in mailing this letter – "

Nancy saw the woman shudder. For one fleeting instant she, too, felt afraid – afraid of something she could not define.

The young sleuth realized that the woman was trying to warn her of danger. Nancy knew the wise thing to do was forget all about the nature cult and the strange things which apparently went on in the hillside cave. Yet, she felt that she was on the verge of discovering an important secret.

Nancy's companion was obviously relieved when the car rounded a bend and brought them within sight of town. "If you'll just drop me off at the post office, I'll be most grateful," the woman said.

"May I take you back with me?" Nancy asked. "I'll be returning in less than an hour."

"No, I'll walk back."

Nancy saw that it was useless to protest and let the matter rest. She made no comment.

After leaving her passenger in front of the post office, Nancy continued down the main street to the supermarket. Later, while she waited in the check-out line to pay for her groceries, two women took their places behind her. They were talking earnestly together, and did not pay any attention to Nancy. She, in turn, did not notice them until one of the shoppers began to speak on a startling subject.

"It beats me the way those people carry on," she heard one of them say. "You'd think Mrs Byrd would turn them out!'

Instantly Nancy became alert.

"I suppose she needs the money," the other woman responded, "but someone should speak to her about it. The idea of those folks capering around in bedclothes! They must be crazy!"

"That's just what I think!" the first woman remarked. "If I lived near that farm I wouldn't feel safe! And I don't think it's decent for a law-abiding community like ours to have folks like that around. I'm going to get a big group together and call on Mrs Byrd to tell her what we think of her!"

"I'll certainly join you," the woman said.

Nancy felt the situation was becoming serious; that the criticism of Mrs Byrd would grow even sharper. If the two women carried out their threat, the consequences might be very unpleasant. Prospective Red Gate boarders might change their minds! The colony might take reprisals!

"One thing is certain," Nancy decided. "Our

costumes must be ready by tonight in case the colony members have a meeting."

She paid for the groceries and went directly to the material shop, where she bought several yards of white muslin, then started for home.

Driving back to Red Gate Farm, Nancy kept a sharp lookout for the woman from the Black Snake Colony, but she was nowhere along the road. "I wish I could have talked to her more. It might have helped in my plan to attend the ceremony."

Joanne, Bess, and George were just returning from the woods with pails brimming over with luscious-looking berries when Nancy drove into the barnyard. As they started to help her carry in the packages, Karl Abbott Jr rushed gallantly from the house to assist. He glanced curiously at the soft, fat one which Nancy kept tucked under her arm, but she did not give any explanation of its contents. Besides, the elder Mr Abbott and Mrs Salisbury were within hearing distance.

Immediately after a late lunch and some pleasant conversation with the guests, Nancy excused herself and summoned the other girls to her room. There she unwrapped the material and brought out scissors, needles, and thread.

"We must work like mad," she said, "in case there's a meeting tonight."

With great excitement and anticipation she cut out the first costume which was to serve as an entering wedge to the nature-cult ceremonial. As Nancy worked, she told the story of her adventure with her passenger and the conversation of the women in the market.

Joanne was alarmed. "Oh, Gram must never hear of this!" she exclaimed. "She'd be heart-broken!"

The others agreed. "We won't tell Mrs Byrd any more than we have to," George said. "I do hope we can solve the mystery before something ugly happens!"

For the next few hours their needles flew furiously. At last the costumes were finished. The four friends could not control their laughter as they tried them on.

"You certainly look as if you're ready for Hallow-een!" George told Nancy.

"Do you think I'll pass?"

"In the moonlight they won't be able to tell you from a full-fledged member of the cult," Bess declared. "Let's see you go through the mystic rites."

To the delight of her chums, Nancy danced around the room, waving her arms wildly and making weird moans.

"Jo!" a voice called. "Dinner's ready!"

Startled, the girls scrambled out of the white robes and hastily hid them. They tried to compose their faces as they hurried downstairs, but merely succeeded in looking guilty.

"Seems to me you girls spent a long time locked up in your rooms." Mrs Salisbury sniffed suspiciously.

"Planning some kind of mischief, no doubt." Mr Abbott wagged his finger playfully at the four girls.

George had a hard time keeping a straight face, and hastily took a sip of milk. Bess could not restrain a giggle, whereupon Mrs Salisbury gave her a sharp look.

"Humph!" she exclaimed. "I must say I'll have to agree with Mr Abbott this time. I'm sure you four *are* up to some prank."

Even Nancy and Joanne had to smother tell-tale grins. They only smiled pleasantly, but offered no explanation.

Actually, the girls were so excited over their prospective adventure they could scarcely do justice to the excellent meal Mrs Byrd had prepared. Karl Jr, as usual, was a charming companion.

He had many amusing anecdotes to tell, and Nancy was happy to observe that Joanne seemed to be enjoying it all immensely.

Indeed, by the time dessert was finished, Nancy and her chums realized that they had temporarily forgotten counterfeiters, syndicates, and even the nature cult on the hill.

Everyone was sorry, a little later, when the young man announced that he must leave.

"I wish I could stay," he said regretfully, letting his eyes rest especially long on Nancy, "but I must get back to the city tonight. I'll try to run down again in a few days to see Father. Take care of yourselves," he added to the girls.

After Karl Jr had gone, and the girls were washing the dishes, George said teasingly, "You can't tell me 'Father' is the only attraction at Red Gate Farm! He has his eye on Nancy!"

"Silly!" Nancy laughed.

"He scarcely took his eyes off you all evening," George insisted. "You made quite a hit this morning with that rescued-heroine bit."

"Oh, honestly, George!" Nancy blushed. "You never give up, do you?"

"Karl Jr wouldn't be so bad," Bess added, "but imagine having Mr Abbott for a father-in-law!"

"You do the imagining," Nancy said lightly. "I'm going outside and look at the hillside."

All the girls watched until late in the evening, but the mysterious place remained dark and deserted. Disappointed, the girls went to bed.

They awakened early the next morning, for they had gradually become accustomed to farm hours. When they learned from Mrs Byrd that Reuben was not feeling well, the girls eagerly helped with the various outdoor chores. It was noontime before they realized how much time had passed.

"You girls should have some relaxation this afternoon," Mrs Byrd said. "How about a swim down in the brook? There's a spot that used to be known as the old swimming hole. It's fairly deep."

"That sounds wonderful," Bess declared.

Jo declined, but at two o'clock Nancy, Bess, and George set off in bathing suits. For two hours they swam, floated, and sun-bathed on the shore. Every once in a while Nancy or George would mention some angle of the colony, Hale Syndicate, or counterfeiting mysteries.

But immediately Bess would say, "Shush! We're relaxing. We may have a big night tonight."

Finally the girls started for the farmhouse. To reach it they had to cross a field in the corner of which lay a heap of large stones, apparently raked there when the acreage was cultivated.

George, grinning, climbed across the stones, saying, "This life is making me rugged. I – Oh, ouch!" she cried loudly, then added, "A snake! It bit me!"

· 15 ·

Masqueraders

Nancy and George turned just in time to see a brownish snake slither off in a wiggling motion and disappear among the stones

"Oh, George!" Bess cried. "Was it a poisonous one?"

"I'm not sure," she answered, "I – I hope it wasn't a copperhead."

"We'd better not take any chances," Nancy declared, whipping a handkerchief from her beach robe. "Let's put on tourniquets, Bess."

Like lightning the two girls tied their handkerchiefs tightly above and below the puncture marks made in George's calf by the snake's fangs.

Then Nancy took a tiny pair of scissors from her bag. "I wish I had something to sterilize these with," she said.

"Will perfume do?" Bess asked, and took from her bag the tiny bottle of Blue Jade.

The liquid was poured on to the scissors, then Nancy deftly made a crosscut incision near the punctures. Blood spurted out, and with it, she hoped, any serum the snake might have injected.

George stoically had not made a sound, but

finally she said, "Thanks, girls. Your quick first aid probably made it possible for me to go to the ceremonies tonight – if they have them."

"I think you'd better not step on your foot, or stimulate circulation," Nancy advised. "Suppose Bess and I carry you."

George started to protest but finally consented. Seated on a "chair" made by the intertwined hands of Nancy and Bess, George was carried toward the farmhouse.

The trip, though awkward and slow, went at a steady pace. George maintained her Spartan attitude. She not only refused to complain but teasingly asked Bess, "Aren't you glad I don't eat as much as you do?"

"I don't know what you mean," Bess replied, puzzled.

"Well, if I loved desserts as you do," George teased, "I wouldn't be such a featherweight to carry!"

Bess gave her cousin an indignant glance. "How do you like that for gratitude! Next time I lug you all the way home – !"

Nancy interrupted with a grin, "I guess we all do our share of eating dessert. Anyhow, we've made it, girls. Red Gate Farm is just ahead!"

As they came up to the house, Mrs Salisbury, who was in the garden, exclaimed, "Oh, gracious! What happened?" Mr Abbott and Mrs Byrd hurried from the house.

"Just a precautionary measure," Nancy explained, and told of the snake incident.

George was carried indoors and laid on a couch. Mrs Byrd quickly called the family physician. He arrived shortly, and examined George's wound.

The doctor nodded approvingly as he bathed it with an antiseptic and removed the tourniquets.

"Excellent first-aid treatment," he announced. "You'll be fine, young lady. I'd advise you to rest for several hours."

"Thank you. That's good news." George gave a relieved grin.

For the remainder of the afternoon she was made to lie inactive. When dinnertime came, George got up, declaring, "I never felt better!"

"But take it easy in case we go out tonight," Nancy pleaded with her.

To allay suspicion on the part of the other boarders, Bess and Joanne were posted as guards across the road. If they saw the beginning of rites on the hill, the girls were to give birdcalls. In the meantime, Nancy and George waited in George's room, the costumes ready to be picked up at a moment's notice.

Suddenly Nancy leaped from her chair and flew into her own bedroom. "What's eating you?" George called.

"Oh, why didn't I think of it before? How stupid of me!" Nancy said, returning with a piece of paper in her hand.

"What *are* you talking about?" George demanded.

"That snake today. The way he wriggled. It looked just like the mark over the numeral 2 in the coded message!" Nancy cried excitedly. "The 2 we think means B!"

George sat up. "You mean the B with the wavy line over it might signify the Black Snake Colony?"

"Yes. Oh, George, this connects the Hale Syndicate with the nature cult here. Now the message reads: "Maurice Hale calling Black Snake Colony meeting – "

"And the 18. How about that?" George asked.

"Not too hard to guess, George. The 18 is the letter R, and *could* stand for Red Gate Farm."

"Nancy, you're a whiz, as I've often told you," her friend declared.

The young sleuth smiled, then said wistfully, "If I could only have had another second to copy the next few numbers, I might have known the exact time."

"What happens now? Will you notify the police?"

At that instant Nancy and George heard soft birdcalls. "No time to phone now," Nancy said.

She grabbed two of the costumes and dashed from the room. George followed with the others. As prearranged, the girls left by the kitchen door to avoid the boarders. Mrs Byrd had been told that the girls might go up the hillside to watch if the nature cult put on a performance.

Nancy and George joined the other girls and they all scurried toward the woods. It was very dark beneath the dense canopy of trees, and Bess gripped Nancy's arm. Joanne was familiar with every path and led the way toward the hillside.

A weird cry broke the stillness. Involuntarily the girls halted and moved closer together.

"What – was – that?" Bess chattered.

"Only some wild animal," Nancy reassured her. "Come on!" she urged. "We must hurry or we'll miss the ritual!"

The girls went through the dark forest as fast as they could. The moon was rising, and ghostly rays of light flitered through gaps in the foliage overhead. A faint breeze stirred the leaves into what seemed like menacing whispers. The girls finally reached the river trail and followed it.

"We must be careful now," Nancy warned in a low voice. "We're drawing near the colony. The cult may have a lookout stationed during the night ceremonies."

"I hadn't thought of that," Joanne murmured.

"I almost wish I hadn't come," Bess whispered nervously. "I had no idea it would be this dark."

"What were you expecting at nine-thirty at night?" George chided in as low a tone as possible.

"It will be lighter when the moon rises higher," Joanne told her. "Still – if you want to turn back –"

"No, I'm going through with this masquerade if the rest of you are!" Bess retorted stalwartly.

Nancy hoped fervently it would remain a masquerade. She was firmly convinced now that the Black Snake group were unscrupulous people working with, or at least friendly with Maurice Hale. Nancy now felt convinced that the mystic rites were nothing but a sham.

Fortunately, for Nancy's purpose, the hillside was covered with large rocks as well as dense shrubs which would provide temporary hiding places. As the girls stole cautiously up the steep path, they could see cult members still congregating.

"We're in plenty of time," she thought.

The girls separated, George and Bess crouching behind a huge rock. Joanne and Nancy took cover behind a heavy growth of shrubs and tall grass.

For nearly ten minutes the girls watched as figures milled about the hillside. Then they heard the sound of cars approaching.

"They must be coming up through the pasture again," Joanne said, listening intently.

An instant later she and Nancy saw the headlights of three automobiles.

"Look!" Joanne tugged at Nancy's sleeve. "More members are coming out of their tents!"

The two girls watched the white-robed figures walking slowly toward the brow of the hill, where the three automobiles had parked.

"I wonder if one of the newcomers is Maurice Hale," Nancy thought.

She and Joanne were too far away to hear what was being said, but they could see distinctly. They watched as a group of men and women, twelve in number, stepped from the cars. Nancy could not distinguish any of their faces.

The new arrivals quickly donned white garments and headgear similar to the outfits Nancy and her friends had made, then joined the other members of the cult.

The ghostly figures soon began dancing about in the moonlight, and Nancy felt that the time was right for her daring attempt to join the group. Before she could tell Joanne, there was a slight stir in the bushes directly behind her.

Involuntarily Nancy jumped, fully expecting to come face to face with one of the cult members. Instead, Bess and George emerged.

"Isn't it about time for us to do something?" they asked, almost simultaneously.

"Yes," Nancy agreed, "we'd better get into our robes as quickly as we can."

The girls were well hidden by the rocks and bushes. They donned their costumes and pulled the headgear over their faces. For the first time, Nancy noticed the scent of Blue Jade on Bess. "I wonder if that was wise," Nancy thought. "If it attracts attention to Bess it might increase her danger, but it's too late now to do anything about it."

As George, overeager, started off, Nancy caught her friend's arm. "Wait!" she warned. "We must slip quietly into the circle one at a time."

"My knees are shaking now," Bess admitted. "I don't know how I'll be able to dance."

"Stay here if you like," Nancy told her. "I think we should leave someone to keep guard, anyway."

"I'll stay," Joanne offered. "I know the way back through the woods better than you girls do."

"Come on!" George pleaded. "If we don't hurry we'll be too late!"

"Good luck!" Joanne whispered as the girls crept away.

Inch by inch, the three girls made their way up the hill. They crouched behind a clump of bushes a stone's throw from where the cult members were dancing. Nancy indicated that she would make the first move. Bess and George nodded.

"The slightest mistake will mean detection!" Nancy thought, her heart pounding.

Waiting for the right moment, she suddenly slipped out among the white-robed figures and instantly began waving her arms and making grotesque motions.

· 16 ·
Startling Commands

Relieved that her entry into the group had not been noticed, Nancy marched along with the other ghostly figures. If only George and Bess were as successful!

Nancy watched her disguised companions and saw that the girls would have no trouble in following the motions, since each person was apparently making them up on the spur of the moment.

"So far, so good," Nancy told herself.

Satisfied now that her own position was temporarily secure, she tried to help her friends. Deliberately moving toward the shrubs behind which George and Bess were hiding, she shielded them from the view of the cult members, all the time continuing her grotesque motions.

George realized what the young sleuth was trying to do and made the most of the opportunity. Choosing her time, she slipped out and joined the group on the hillside.

Bess was more timid. Several times at the critical moment she lost her nerve, but she finally managed to summon enough courage and made the plunge.

"Keep close together," Nancy warned in an

undertone. "If we lose each other, it may be disastrous."

By this time the girls had made up their minds that there was nothing the least bit mystic about the queer rites of the Black Snake Colony. Disguised persons on all sides of them were making crude remarks which assured the girls that the cult members did not take the ceremony seriously.

"This ought to give the country yokels an eyeful!" Nancy heard one man mutter.

"How much longer do we have to do this?" another grumbled. "I'm getting sick of flapping my arms around like a windmill!"

"This cult idea was all foolishness, anyway!" still another said.

"Foolishness, is it?" someone caught him up. Nancy thought she recognized the voice but was not certain. "Let me tell you a girl was prowling around here only a few days ago! I guess the Chief knew his business when he thought up this crazy cult idea."

"Well, enough of this!" a loud voice announced. Nancy decided the man must be one of the leaders. "We may as well go into the cave and get down to business!"

George was just wondering what the girls had better do when Bess clutched Nancy's hand and whispered nervously:

"Do we dare enter?"

"We must," Nancy returned quietly.

The girls stood motionless, watching the white-robed figures march single file toward the entrance to the cave. Finally Nancy signalled, and the three friends followed the group, even though it occurred to them that they might be walking into a trap.

"Keep close behind me," Nancy warned her companions in a whisper.

As they approached the mouth of the opening, Nancy saw a tall figure, robed in white, standing guard. Her heart nearly stopped as she realized that each person was uttering some password.

"We're finished now," she thought.

It was too late to turn back. The three girls could do nothing but hope that in some way they might get past the stalwart guard.

Nancy kept close to the person just ahead of her, and as he muttered the password, she managed to hear it.

"Kamar!"

When Nancy's turn came to pass the guard, she spoke the word clearly. As she had hoped, George and Bess heard, and taking their cue from her, repeated the password. The sentry did not give them a second glance, yet the girls breathed easier when they were safely through the entrance.

The marchers descended into a cold, damp tunnel. Someone was carrying a torch at the head of the procession, but Nancy and her friends, who were near the end of the line, were in semidarkness.

"What do you suppose we're getting into?" George muttered.

Nancy did not reply, but gave her friend a sharp nudge as a warning not to speak. A moment later Bess tripped over some object in the path and would have fallen if Nancy had not caught her by the arm. They walked farther underground, and then, unexpectedly, stepped into a dimly lighted chamber.

The members of the cult seated themselves on the floor, and the girls followed their example. Presently they became aware of the strong scent of Blue Jade perfume. Bess was not the only one wearing it tonight!

"So there *is* a definite connection between this distinctive perfume and the Black Snake Colony!" Nancy thought. "No wonder that man on the train was startled. Perhaps the women use it, and he couldn't identify me but took it for granted I was one of the group. If so, it's just as well Bess has some on."

Nancy suddenly recalled the forged note bearing the Blue Jade scent. "The woman who delivered it to me must be a member of the cult!" she thought excitedly.

After everyone had entered the room, the man who had given the sharp order outside the cave spoke again. He threw off his headgear and glanced over the group appraisingly. Nancy was stunned.

Maurice!

The man she had seen the first time she had stopped at the filling station!

"Is he Maurice Hale?" she asked herself excitedly.

"Everyone here?" he demanded gruffly.

He counted the group, and again Nancy and her friends held their breaths. Apparently some of the members of the colony were missing, for the leader did not notice that three new recruits had been added to his organization.

"We may as well get down to work," the leader announced. "Snead, have you anything to report?"

At the question one of the disguised persons stood up and threw off his mask. Again Nancy was startled. He was none other than the man she had seen in Room 305!

"Here's the good money," he said, handing over an envelope. "Perfect score this time for our main distribution department."

"Very fine. Then nothing's gone wrong at your new office?"

"Not yet, Chief," was the muttered reply, "but yesterday I saw a bird hangin' around the building – looked like a plain-clothes cop to me. I don't want you to think I'm backing out, but if you ask me, I'd say it's about time to blow. This game can't last forever, you know."

"I'll do the thinking for this outfit!" the leader scathingly retorted. "We'll stay here another week and then pick a new spot. What makes you think the cops are wise?"

"Well, they may have got wise to the fact that we're using Yvonne again – "

"That's right!" a shrill, angry female voice interrupted. "Blame me! Every time somebody gets nervous, you bring me into it!"

Nancy could scarcely restrain herself. She had been right about Yvonne! The girl *was* mixed up in the Hale Syndicate racket!

"You deserve blame," Al Snead retorted irritably. "First, you didn't have any more sense than to sell a bottle of that perfume to a perfect stranger —"

"I told you, that girl insisted upon buying it, and I was afraid if I flatly refused, she and her friends would get suspicious. Besides, I don't see what harm it did to sell the perfume to a teenager!"

"No," Snead retorted sarcastically, "you're so simple-minded you wouldn't see it might land us in jail! When Pete was on the train going to River Heights he noticed the scent and thought that the girl was one of the Chief's agents! Lucky for all of us, he saw his mistake before he spilled anything!"

Yvonne sputtered back in defence. "Well, at least I phoned Al at his office right away so he could warn the agents about the stray bottle of Blue Jade. It's not *my* fault Pete happened to be on the same train as those girls."

The leader suddenly became impatient. "Enough of this!" he shouted. "It's not getting us anywhere! Snead, I placed Yvonne in your office and she'll stay there as long as I say. I'm satisfied with the rest of her work. Get me?"

Snead nodded sullenly.

Nancy had been studying the leader intently and by this time was convinced that he was far more clever and intelligent than his subordinates. She figured that Al Snead was right-hand man to the Chief, but resented his superior's favouritism toward Yvonne Wong. The organization was a large one, evidently changing its scene and type of operation from time to time. If only she could slip away and get help from the authorities!

"Another thing," Al Snead continued, addressing Maurice Hale, "we'd better make up a new code. Those girls that have been gettin' too close to our operation just *might* notify the cops."

"All right," the Chief responded. "I'll work one out in a day or two."

He called on another member of the organization for a report. "Two hundred packages passed, sir."

"Good!" the leader exclaimed, rubbing his thin hands. "Now, if you'll follow me to the workroom, I'll give you each your cut, and dole out the stuff for next week."

Nancy and her friends could not have retreated had they wished, and certainly did not want to leave when they seemed so near the truth!

But the situation in which they found themselves was a foreboding one and the very atmosphere of the room was tense and frightening. Boldly they followed the others into an adjoining chamber which was brilliantly lighted with torches.

Though prepared for the unexpected, the girls were taken completely aback at the sight which greeted their eyes!

· 17 ·
Tense Moments

Nancy's first impression on entering was that the chamber appeared to be a cross between a printing shop and a United States mint.

"Counterfeiters!" she thought excitedly.

Hand presses stood about and several engraved plates had been left on a table. Various chemicals and inks were in evidence. Neat stacks of paper money lined one wall and other bills were scattered carelessly on the floor. Never in all her life had Nancy seen so much money!

The room was cluttered with it. Twenty-dollar bills appeared to be everywhere. Money, still damp, was drying on tables. Nancy observed that all the bills seemed to be of the twenty-dollar denomination.

At last she had the answer to the many questions which had been troubling her! This was the secret of the cave! The latest racket of the Hale Syndicate! The nature cult was a hoax, its so-called mysterious rites used only as a screen to hide the work of a clever band of counterfeiters! The Black Snake Colony seemed to her to be a perfect name.

Nancy realized that if she did not try to get away

and bring help now, she and her friends would fail. There was nothing they could do by themselves.

Nancy turned to relay her intentions to Bess and George. A slight tug on their robes was all that was needed to make them understand, but to put the plan into operation was another matter.

The girls attempted to edge toward the chamber entrance by degrees, but Al Snead stood barring the door. For the time being escape was out of the question. They must bide their time.

As long as some members of the organization remained masked, the girls knew they would be comparatively safe. But already several people had stripped off their robes and headpieces. Every minute that the girls' escape was delayed increased the danger of detection.

Since it was impossible to sneak away, Nancy made careful note of her surroundings and tried to identify the faces on her mind. Except for Yvonne, the leader Maurice Hale, Al Snead, and the man she had seen on the train, all were strangers. Six people besides Bess, George, and herself remained masked.

As Nancy surveyed the elaborate equipment in the workroom, she realized that this was an unusually large gang of counterfeiters. The engraved plate which had been copied from an actual United States Government twenty-dollar bill was a work of art. Probably the leader of the gang had at one time been noted as a skilled engraver and had decided to use his talents to unlawful advantage.

Nancy carefully glanced about the room. Maurice Hale was looking over some stacks of counterfeit money while several members of the gang talked quietly. Bess and George automatically followed Nancy's gaze but stood perfectly still next to her near the table.

Nancy, under ordinary circumstances, could not have told the counterfeit money from the real thing – with the picture of Jackson on the face, and the White House on the back. But now that she had been alerted to examine the bills carefully, she noted that the colour and texture of the paper appeared to be at fault.

When Nancy felt sure that she was not being observed, she stealthily picked up one of the bills and tucked it inside her robe as evidence.

"We made a pretty fair week's profit," Maurice Hale said gruffly as he stacked the bills into several large piles. You distributors and passers keep up like this for another month and I'd say we'll all be on Easy Street."

"The racket won't last another month," Al Snead growled. "I tell you, the federal agents are getting wise that the phony stuff's being passed around here."

"Bah!" Hale replied contemptuously. "Let them be suspicious! They wouldn't think of this out-of-the-way place as our headquarters in a thousand years!"

Nancy could not help but smile at his words. "That's what *he* thinks!"

The next voice that spoke startled Nancy. She

recognized it instantly as belonging to Mr Kent –
the would-be buyer of Red Gate Farm!

"Yeah, maybe not," he was saying. "Still, it's too
bad the old lady wouldn't sell her place. Then we'd
really have a setup!"

It flashed through Nancy's mind that her hunch
had been right about Mr Kent being involved with
the hillside cult. No wonder they wanted to obtain
Red Gate Farm; it would have been a better
headquarters for the gang than the cave.

The girl detective strained her ears as the conversation continued. A woman next to Kent said
scornfully, "I only hope your bright idea about that
fake letter we took to the Drew girl, and cutting the
farm telephone wires, doesn't backfire."

So, Nancy told herself, it was Kent, and the
woman who had just spoken, who were the ones
responsible for that part of the mystery. Mr Kent
also was undoubtedly the driver of the car which
had slowed down one evening near the farmhouse.

Meanwhile, the leader went on deftly stacking
the money. Nancy and her friends watched him
with increasing uneasiness. When the various members of the organization were called upon to accept
their share of the counterfeit bills, they would
doubtless remove their masks. How would the girls
escape detection then?

Nancy realized the situation was becoming more
serious. She and her friends must escape before the
actual distribution of the money began. If only Al
Snead would move away from the door!

One thought comforted Nancy. Joanne was on

guard outside the cave. If worst came to worst and escape was cut off, Joanne undoubtedly would become alarmed and hurry back to the farmhouse for help.

"We may have to make a dash for it!" Nancy warned George in a whisper. "If that man moves away from the door, be ready!"

Al Snead did not move, however, and it seemed to the girls that he was watching them. They wondered if their whispering had made him suspicious.

Bess trembled slightly, and moved nearer Nancy. Maurice Hale had finished counting the money, and, glancing over the assembly, announced in a commanding voice:

"Well, those of you who haven't removed your masks had better do it one by one. I want to be sure no one is here who shouldn't be!" He pointed to Bess. "You first!"

Nancy and her friends felt themselves go cold. They were trapped! There was nothing they could do now but make a wild dash for safety.

"Ready!" Nancy muttered under her breath.

Before the girls could put their ideas into action, they were startled by a loud commotion in the tunnel. An instant later the guard, who had been stationed at the entrance of the cave, burst into the chamber. He was half dragging a young girl who fought violently to free herself.

The victim was Joanne!

· 18 ·
Prisoners

Nancy's first impulse was to dash forward and try to help Joanne. But instantly she realized the foolishness of such an act. George half started toward Joanne, but Nancy restrained her.

"Wait!" she whispered tensely.

If the situation had been grave before, it was even more serious now. With Joanne captured there was no one to go for help! The girls must depend entirely on themselves to escape from the cave. No one at the farmhouse knew that they were doing anything more than watching the Black Snake Colony from a safe distance.

"Let me go!" Joanne cried, struggling to free herself.

"Where did she come from?" Maurice Hale demanded unpleasantly.

"I saw her hiding among the bushes," the guard informed him. "She was spying! But she got just a little too curious!"

"Spying, eh?" A harsh expression crossed the leader's face. "Well, we know what to do with snoopers!"

"It's all a mistake," Joanne murmured, on the

verge of tears. "I didn't mean any harm. I'm Mrs Byrd's granddaughter and I was merely curious to know more about the cult."

Even as Joanne spoke, her eyes travelled about the room, noting the stacks of money and the queer printing presses. She tried not to show that she understood their significance, but it was too late. The leader had seen her startled expression.

"So?" he drawled smartly. "This time your curiosity has been the means of getting you into serious trouble. You'll learn, by the time we get through with you, not to meddle in affairs that don't concern you!" He turned quickly to Snead. "Al, see that no one leaves this room!'

"Yes, Chief," the guard answered.

Nancy wondered what he had in mind. Just then Maurice Hale continued in a cold, harsh voice:

"Just to make sure that other spies haven't been pulling a fast one on us, I'll have everyone remove his mask at once. Be mighty quick about it too!"

"No!" Bess whimpered aloud. Then, realizing what she had done, she covered her mouth and sank back against the wall.

All heads turned in her direction. Nancy and her friends had deliberately delayed in removing their masks, but now Nancy knew their effort to gain time was doomed.

With Al Snead still blocking the door, things looked black. Most of the others already had stripped off their headgear.

In addition to Maurice Hale and Al Snead, Nancy immediately recognized Yvonne Wong and

Pete, the man who had spoken to her on the train. Next she spotted Mr Kent, and finally, the woman with the upswept hairdo who had brought her the faked letter.

"That woman's the same one I saw at the service station with the three men," Nancy thought. If she hadn't changed her hair style, I might have recognized her the night she delivered the note."

The other unmasked members were strangers to Nancy. Tensely now she watched as the leader stood before Bess.

"Nothing to be afraid of, dear," he said, and gently lifted off the ghostly head covering. The next instant Maurice Hale practically shrieked, "A spy!"

His face contorted with rage, Maurice snatched the white cloth headpieces from George's face, then Nancy's. Their scheme was exposed to all the members of the counterfeit gang!

For an instant there was stunned silence, then angry cries arose from the Black Snake Colony members.

"They're the ones who bought the Blue Jade perfume from me!" Yvonne Wong shrieked.

Al Snead glared at Nancy. "Yeah. I knew something was wrong when you came into the office wearin' the Blue Jade. I smelled it, but didn't let on."

He then pointed accusingly toward Joanne. "That girl is the one who applied at our city office for a job! When she told me who she was and where she was from I knew she was the last person in the world we'd want to hire!"

"That crazy idea of yours about someone with farm experience," the leader cried. "We didn't need anybody to talk to our agents about cows and chickens – "

"But this place *is* in the country," Al Snead defended himself. "And in our codes we use a lot of that kind of lingo."

"Silence!" Maurice yelled, and turned to Joanne. "So you thought you'd get a job at our office and spy on us! And your meddling friend Nancy Drew was in cahoots with you."

"No, oh no!" Joanne cried out. "It was only by accident. I wanted to find a job and help my grandmother. Nancy was just trying to help me locate the office – "

"Don't expect us to believe a trumped-up story like that," the leader said harshly. "We know all about why you two have been snooping around ever since Al had Pete trail you from Riverside Heights. What's more, we know how to deal with such people!"

Hale turned menacingly to Nancy. "You'll wish you'd taken Pete's advice when he called your pal" – he indicated George – " and warned her that you'd better mind your own business."

"Oh, Maurice, please don't be too harsh with the girls," a timid voice pleaded. "They didn't mean any harm." As she finished, the speaker removed her mask.

Nancy turned quickly to see the woman she had helped in the woods and later had taken to town.

"So she's a counterfeiter!" Nancy told herself incredulously. "I can't believe it!"

"Didn't mean any harm?" Maurice drawled sarcastically. "Oh, no, of course not. They only wanted to land the whole Hale Syndicate in jail! Not that you would care! If I had known what a whiner you are, I'd never have married you! Mind your own business and let me take care of this!"

In spite of the seriousness of her own situation, Nancy felt pity for the woman. Undoubtedly as the wife of such a tyrant as Maurice Hale she had stayed with him against her will. She had hated the life that he had forced her to lead, but evidently she had been powerless to escape from it.

"No wonder the poor woman took a chance and slipped away from time to time," Nancy thought.

Frightened by the harsh words of her husband, Mrs Hale moved back into a far corner of the room. Nancy wished she could help her in some way, but realized that the woman dared not say more.

"What'll we do with these girls?" the leader demanded. "We can't let 'em go. They know too much!"

On all sides angry mutterings arose. Yvonne Wong heartlessly proposed that the girls be tied up and left prisoners in the cave. But Maurice Hale ruled down that suggestion.

"We'll have to get 'em out of here," he said. "They'll be missed and a searching party might visit this joint. How about the shack at the river? It's in such a desolate spot no one would think of looking there until after — "

He did not finish the sentence, but from the sinister expression on his face, Nancy and her friends guessed his meaning. He intended to lock them up in the cabin and leave them without food!

A cry of anguish came from the leader's wife. Rushing forward, she clutched her husband frantically by the arm.

"Oh, Maurice! You couldn't be that cruel!"

Mr Hale flung her away from him with a force that sent the woman reeling against the wall. She uttered a little moan of pain and sank to the floor.

"Oh!" Bess screamed.

Even the cult members were startled.

"Be quiet!" ordered their chief.

The cruel action aroused Nancy. For an instant all eyes were centred on the woman, and Nancy thought she saw her opportunity. Quick as a flash she made a rush for the exit. Bess and George, equally alert, darted after her.

Al Snead, who stood in the opening, was taken completely by surprise. He tried to hold his ground but the girls were too strong for him. He managed to detain Bess and George, but Nancy wriggled from his grasp. She hesitated when she saw her friends had failed.

"Go on, Nancy!" Bess shrieked. "You must escape!"

Nancy darted into the next room, while George and Bess struggled with their captor, trying to block the door and give their friend more time.

"Stop that girl!" Maurice Hale shouted angrily. "If you let her get away, I'll – "

Nancy plunged into the tunnel and was swallowed up by darkness. She ran for her life and for the lives of her friends, realizing this probably was her only chance.

The long white robe hindered her, but there was no time to tear it off. She held it high above her knees. Once she stumbled, but caught herself, and rushed on frantically.

The tunnel seemed to have no end. Behind her, Nancy could hear pounding footsteps and angry shouts. She thought the men must be gaining. If only she could reach the mouth of the cave!

The tunnel wound in and out and several times Nancy brushed against the rough stone wall. The route was so circuitous that she began to think she had taken a wrong turn.

Then, just as she was giving up hope, Nancy spotted a dim light far ahead and knew she must be nearing the mouth of the cave. No one appeared to be left guarding the entrance. Her only chance! In a moment more she had reached the open air.

"Saved!" Nancy breathed.

At that instant a dark figure loomed up from the grass. Nancy felt a heavy hand on her shoulder!

· 19 ·

Destroyed Evidence

"Not so fast there!" The man leered as he clutched Nancy firmly by the arm and whirled her around. "What's the big rush, anyway?"

Nancy, staring into his hard face, saw that he was the man who had been addressed as "Hank," one of the three men she had seen at the filling station. Frantically she struggled to free herself.

"So – " he muttered in satisfaction, "the pretty blonde spy the boys were telling me about. I thought you were warned by the guard to keep away from here! This time, I take it, you're lookin' for something besides a stray cow!"

"Yes, and I'm going to find it!" Nancy said bravely.

"Oh, yeah? You're going to find what? The police?" Hank looked at her costume. "You're a spy. But your little game is up."

Nancy's pulse was racing. How could she get away? She could hear running footsteps coming through the tunnel, and knew her chance of escape would be over in another instant. In desperation she tried to jerk herself free from Hank. But her captor gripped her more securely and laughed as she cried out in pain.

"Let me go!"

Nancy twisted and squirmed, but her efforts only made Hank tighten his grip. By the time the others reached her, she had given up the struggle and stood quietly waiting for the worst to come.

"Good thing you got her, Hank," Maurice Hale called. "The little wildcat! We'll give her a double dose for this smart trick! No girl's going to put anything over on me!"

At the entrance of the cave it was nearly as bright as day, for the moon was high. Maurice Hale glanced nervously about, as though fearing observation by unseen eyes.

"Get back inside!" he sharply ordered his followers. "It's a clear night and some wise bird might see us without our costumes and wonder what's up. We must destroy the evidence as quickly as we can and clear out of this place!"

Even as the leader spoke, Nancy thought she heard a rustling in the nearby bushes. She told herself that it probably was only the wind stirring the leaves. Rescue was out of the question, for no one knew that she and her friends had planned such a dangerous mission. How foolish of them not to have revealed their full plans to someone!

Nancy made no protest as she was dragged back into the cavern. Bravely she tried to meet the eyes of her friends, for she saw that they were even more discouraged than she. Poor Bess was trembling with fright.

"Th-the perfume did it!" she wailed. "I knew this masquerade was far too dangerous for us to try!"

"Cheer up," Nancy whispered encouragingly. "We'll find some way to get out of here!"

Bess only shook her head. She was not to be deceived.

"And to think *I* was the one who couldn't wait for a spooky adventure on the hillside," George moaned regretfully. "I really ought to have my head examined!"

The members of the syndicate were furious. There would be no second opportunity for these intruders to break away. At an order from the leader, Al Snead found several pieces of rope and bound Nancy and her friends hand and foot. He seemed to take particular delight in making Nancy's bonds cruelly tight.

"I guess that'll hold you for a while." He grinned, gloating over the girls' predicament.

"Get to work!" the leader commanded his men impatiently. "Do you think we have the rest of the night? If we don't hurry up and get out of here, the cops are apt to be down on us! Don't know what this girl's done."

All colony members, except Mrs Hale, went to work with a will; the fear of the law obviously had affected them. With a sinking heart, Nancy realized the men planned to destroy all the evidence of their counterfeiting operations.

"The machines that we can't take with us we'll wreck," Maurice Hale ordered. "If we save the plates we can start up again in a new place. Get a move on!"

He stood over the men, driving them furiously. His wife had slumped down in a chair and had buried her face in her hands. She appeared crushed. Only once did she summon her energy to speak.

"Maurice," she murmured brokenly, "why won't you give up this dreadful life – always running from the police? We were happy before you got mixed up with such bad company."

Her husband cut her short with a sarcastic remark. She did not try to speak again, but sat hunched over, looking sorrowfully at the girls. Nancy knew that she wanted to help them, but did not have the courage for further defiance.

The work of destroying the counterfeiting machinery went on, but several times Maurice Hale glanced impatiently at his watch.

"No use waiting until we're through here," he observed after a time. "Let's get the prisoners out of here pronto. The sooner we're rid of them, the safer I'll feel. Al, you start on ahead with one of the automobiles. You know the way to the shack, don't you?"

"Sure," Al Snead agreed promptly.

"Then take Hank along to keep guard and get going!"

Nancy and her chums were jerked to their feet. The cords around their ankles were removed to permit them to walk, but their arms were kept tied securely behind them.

"Move along!" Al Snead ordered Nancy, giving her a hard shove forward.

The girls stumbled along through the dark passageway from the inner room to the mouth of the cave. Men and women followed them with angry, menacing threats.

Al and Hank pushed the girls to make them hurry. Nancy and her friends exchanged hopeless glances from time to time. George held her head up contemptuously, but Joanne was white as a sheet and Bess was on the verge of tears.

"Guess this'll teach you girls to mix with the Black Snake Colony!" a raucous voice said as the group made its way toward the exit.

Nancy held back a retort, but her icy look told the man she did not appreciate the remark. Their walk seemed interminable. Finally, however, moonlight could be seen. In a moment they were approaching the mouth of the cave.

Nancy took a few halting steps and then paused as if she had turned to stone. Her eyes were riveted upon the entrance. There stood Mr Abbott's son, Karl Jr!

"Oh, Karl!" Nancy cried out. "These men are counterfeiters! Don't let them capture you too! Run!"

· 20 ·
A Final Hunch

Karl Abbott did not run. Instead, he signalled with his hand. At once seven armed men sprang from the darkness of nearby bushes.

"Secret Service agents," Karl explained quickly to the girls.

"Stand where you are! Don't anyone move!" ordered one of the federal men.

So unexpected was their arrival that the counterfeiters were stunned. For an instant no one moved. Then, with a cry of rage, Maurice Hale darted into the cavern. He had taken only a few steps when one of the other agents grabbed him firmly by one arm.

"None of that! We have you right this time, Hale. You won't try any funny stuff with Uncle Sam again!"

Some of the counterfeiters who had not yet come from the cavern had turned back.

"They'll get away through the other exit!" Nancy cried out.

Karl smiled. "We have that covered too."

He now introduced the four girls to Secret Service Agent Horton who was in charge of the group.

The federal man gave Nancy Drew a quick word of praise for revealing the headquarters of the counterfeiting ring.

"Outwitted – by that snooping kid!" Maurice Hale screamed.

The thought seemed to unnerve the man completely. He did not protest when handcuffs were put on his wrists. Other members of the syndicate submitted to the agents without resistance, although Yvonne Wong vehemently protested her innocence.

"I didn't know what it was all about until tonight," she cried angrily. "It isn't fair to arrest me! I've worked for Mr Snead only a few days – "

"You'll have to think up a better story than that!" she was told bluntly. "Your name has been mixed up in underhanded deals before, but this is the first time we've been able to get any evidence against you."

While the prisoners were being rounded up, Karl Abbott rushed over to the girls and quickly freed their hands.

"Are you all right?" he asked anxiously.

"Yes," Nancy told him, "but if you hadn't arrived just when you did, it might have been a different story!"

She was on the verge of asking what had brought him to the cave at the psychological moment when she saw that two federal agents were placing handcuffs on the wrists of Maurice Hale's wife. Breaking away from her friends, Nancy darted to the other side of the room.

"Oh, don't arrest Mrs Hale," she pleaded. "She isn't like the rest. She tried to save us, but they wouldn't listen to her."

"Sorry," Horton returned, "but we'll have to take her along. If you want to intercede for her later, we may be able to have her sentence lightened."

After the prisoners had been herded out of the cave to waiting government automobiles and the printing plates used in the making of the counterfeit bills had been collected, Nancy felt explanations were in order from Karl.

"How did you know we had come here?" Nancy asked him.

"From Mrs Byrd. She was greatly worried. When I came to see Father tonight she told me that after you'd gone she found evidence of your costume making. She confided in me you might have done just what you did. She asked me to try and stop you."

"Yes. Go on," Nancy urged.

"Well, I've been suspicious of this hillside ceremony stuff, and after talking further with Mrs Byrd, I decided to get in touch with the Secret Service men she said you had told her about. They couldn't come, but the chief agent in this area sent some of his other men."

"How marvellous of you to have put two and two together!" Bess exclaimed.

"By the time we all got here," Karl went on, "no one was around. I sneaked inside just as all of you were coming out. Mr Horton thought you girls would not be harmed if you walked outside before the gang was captured."

"Thanks for that," said George. "I've had enough!"

Just then Secret Service Agent Horton came over to Nancy's group and extended his hand to her. "Miss Drew," he said earnestly, "I want to thank you for your work which has resulted in the solution of one of the most baffling cases of counterfeiting the United States Government has ever had. How did you do it?"

Nancy blushed at the praise. "It was sort of a chain reaction, I guess," the young sleuth replied, and told of the various circumstances that had led to tonight's adventure.

When she finished, the agent shook his head in amazement. "You cracked a code this gang had thought was unbreakable. My congratulations."

It was late when the four girls, escorted by Karl Abbott, left the cave. As they neared the farmhouse, Joanne observed that the lights were on. "I hope Gram hasn't been too worried."

Before the girls reached the porch, Mrs Byrd came hurrying toward them. She clung tightly to Joanne for an instant.

"I'm so glad you're back," she murmured in relief. "And you girls are all right. I was terribly afraid those members of the Black Snake Colony —"

She was interrupted by Mrs Salisbury's voice from the dark porch. "You had us so worried we couldn't go to bed. The idea of girls running around the country at this hour! That nature cult is all foolishness, anyway!"

"Absolutely!" Mr Abbott agreed. "The less you meddle with their affairs, the wiser you'll be!"

"You're wrong this time, Father," Karl Jr announced. "If the girls hadn't meddled, those counterfeiters would have operated indefinitely."

"Counterfeiters!" the two boarders and Mrs Byrd exclaimed together.

They were tense as Karl Jr related everything that had happened. In fact, it was not until the next day that Mrs Salisbury recovered from the shock sufficiently to boast:

"Well, I always said those girls were up and coming!"

Mr Abbott was very proud of the part his son had played in the case, and said so several times.

Mrs Byrd had nothing except praise for Nancy and her friends. "And who would think," she said incredulously, "that Bess's innocent purchase of a bottle of perfume would lead you girls to a mystery right here at Red Gate Farm!"

However, the removal of the Black Snake Colony from her property left her a serious financial problem. "I'm glad they're gone," she said, "but I'll miss the money. I can't hope to rent the land again. It isn't fertile enough for farming. All this talk about counterfeiters is apt to give Red Gate a bad name, too. I'll probably lose those other boarders who were coming!"

"Publicity is a queer thing," Nancy said thoughtfully. "Sometimes one can work it to one's advantage. That's what we'll do now."

"How?" Joanne asked.

"We'll advertise that counterfeiters' cavern to sightseers and make enough money to lift a dozen mortgages!"

The others were enthusiastic. During the next week the girls, with Karl Jr's assistance, placed in the cave for public display an imitation setup of the counterfeiting operation. There were several old printing presses, and some dummy figures arranged before them as if "at work." Scattered about the cave floor were stacks of homemade "money" – to represent counterfeit bills.

The following week Mr Drew came to Red Gate Farm. A few miles away he halted his automobile at the side of the road, and with an amused smile studied a large billboard which read:

Follow the arrow to Red Gate Farm! See the mysterious cavern used by counterfeiters! Admission fifty cents.

As Carson Drew continued slowly in his car, he presently came to another sign, bolder than the first:

Regain health at Red Gate Farm. Boarders by Day or Week.

The traffic was unusually heavy, and the lawyer soon realized that all of the cars were headed for the farm. The place was crowded. He parked as near the house as he could and walked up the path. The grounds were well kept and equipped with swings and huge umbrellas. A number of persons, evidently boarders, were enjoying the garden.

Before Carson Drew had reached the front door, it was flung open, and Nancy rushed to meet him. "Dad!" she cried joyfully. "Isn't this wonderful?"

"You've done a magnificent job, Nancy."

After a hearty dinner Nancy and her friends took Mr Drew to the hillside cave. Reuben Ames, looking most unlike himself in a new suit which was a trifle too tight, was in his glory as he conducted groups of visitors through the cavern.

"I've collected thirty dollars already today," he hailed Nancy as she came up with her friends. "This beats plowin' corn."

Bess grinned. "Didn't I always say that adventure follows Nancy Drew around?"

And Bess was right, for another exciting adventure awaited her courageous friend, who very soon was to become involved in *The Secret of the Wooden Lady*.

Mr Drew laughed. "Nancy," he said, "as I think of your adventure at Red Gate Farm I can't decide whether you're better as a detective or as a promoter!"